Beautiful Ugly

Shelia Writes Books

Perfect Stories About Imperfect People Like You...and Me!

"Perfect Stories About Imperfect People Like You...and Me"

SCANLIFE

[Scan barcode w/mobile device for more information]

Beautiful Ugly

Shelia Writes Books
Perfect Stories About Imperfect People Like You...and Me!

"Perfect Stories About Imperfect People
Like You...and Me"

National Bestselling Author
SHELIA E. BELL

To Ugly

Everyone in the apartment complex I lived in knew who Ugly was. Ugly was the resident tomcat. Ugly loved three things in this world: fighting, eating garbage, and shall we say, love. The combination of these things combined with a life spent outside had their effect on Ugly.

To start with, he had only one eye, and where the other should have been was a gaping hole. He was also missing his ear on the same side, his left foot appeared to have been badly broken at one time, and had healed at an unnatural angle, making him look like he was always turning the corner. His tail has long since been lost, leaving only the smallest stub, which he would constantly jerk and twitch. Ugly would have been a dark gray tabby striped-type, except for the sores covering his head, neck, even his shoulders with thick, yellowing scabs. Every time someone saw Ugly there was the same reaction: "That's one ugly cat!"

All the children were warned not to touch him, the adults threw rocks at him, hosed him down, and squirted him when he tried to come into their homes or shut his paws in the door when he would not leave. Ugly always had the same reaction. If you turned the hose on him, he would stand there, getting soaked until you gave up and quit. If you threw things at him, he would curl his lanky body around your feet in forgiveness. Whenever he spied children, he would come running meowing frantically and bump his head against their hands, begging for their love. If you ever picked him up he would immediately begin suckling on your shirt, ears, whatever he could find.

One day Ugly shared his love with the neighbor's huskies. They did not respond kindly, and Ugly was badly mauled. From my apartment, I could hear his screams, and I tried to rush to his aid. By the time I got to where he was laying, it was apparent Ugly's sad life was almost at an end.

Ugly lay in a wet circle, his back legs and lower back twisted grossly out of shape, a gaping tear in the white strip of fur that ran down his front. As I picked him up and tried to carry him home I could hear him wheezing and gasping and could feel him struggling. I must be hurting him terribly I thought. Then I felt a familiar tugging, sucking sensation on my ear. Ugly, in so much pain, suffering, and obviously dying, was trying to suckle my ear. I pulled him closer to me, and he bumped the palm of my hand with his head, then he turned his one golden eye toward me, and I could hear the distinct sound of purring.

Even in the greatest pain, that ugly battled-scarred cat was asking only for a little affection, perhaps some compassion. At that moment I thought Ugly was the most beautiful, loving creature I had ever seen. Never once did he try to bite or scratch me, or even try to get away from me, or struggle in any way. Ugly just looked up at me completely trusting in me to relieve his pain. Ugly died in my arms before I could get inside, but I sat and held him for a long time afterward, thinking about how one scarred, deformed little stray could so alter my opinion about what it means to have true pureness of spirit, to love so totally and truly.

Ugly taught me more about giving and compassion than a thousand books, lectures, or talk show specials ever could, and for that I will always be thankful. He had been scarred on the outside, but I was scarred on the inside, and it was time for me to move on and learn to love truly and deeply. To give my total to those I cared for.

All of us would want to be richer, more successful, well-liked, or beautiful, but me, I will always try to be "Ugly".... *Unknown*

To All the Fearfully and Wonderfully Made People of the World, finally, my brethren, whatsoever things are true, whatsoever things are honest, whatsoever things are just, whatsoever things are pure, whatsoever things are lovely, whatsoever things are of good report; if there be any virtue, and if there be any praise, think on these things.
Philippians 4:8 (The Bible King James Version)

1

"The world is a beautiful place. It's just the people in it that make it ugly." Rick Thompson

"It coulda been me, it shoulda been me, it woulda been me..."
Envy was deep in thought. *Why is it that most obese people can hum? I mean they just don't sing, they sang. Is it something with the make-up of their vocal cords or what?* Envy listened from the middle row of the church pew at her 350-plus-pound friend, Layla, her voice so strong it echoed off the wall of the sanctuary like she was singing from a mountaintop. She could easily compete against Yolanda Adams.

Even from the middle pew, Envy could see beads of sweat glistening and dripping down Layla's face. The church seemed on fire, moved by the Holy Spirit spreading through the choir stand.

Kacie sat next to Envy on the royal purple pews. Leaning over and whispering in a harsh voice, she chastised her children, Kali, Kendra, Kenny, Kassandra, and Keith, while holding onto nine-month-old baby Keshena. "Didn't you hear me? I said sit y'all tails down and be still. I told y'all about acting a fool in church. Now, stop it or you know what's good for you."

Kacie turned toward Envy and mumbled, "I don't know why they can't have Children's Church every Sunday."

The five children barely acknowledged their mother's threats until she hauled off and slapped four-year-old Kali and five-year-old Keith on their legs. Before tears could gush from their faces, she pointed one long polished fingernail at them.

"You better not let a single, solitary tear," she demanded of the two kids. Two-year-old Kendra, seven-year-old Kassandra, and ten-year-old Kenny's eyes widened in fear like they were hoping they wouldn't be next.

When Keshena started crying, Envy reached over and quickly removed her from Kacie's arms. No sense in all of Kacie's kids keeping up a ruckus. Envy searched in the baby's diaper pouch until she found her juice bottle and Keshena immediately grabbed it out of Envy's hand, placed it in her mouth, and leaned back in the comfort of Envy's arms.

"It was mercy and grace," Layla belted. With upraised arms, and bowed head, Layla started jumping up and down in the choir stand. Envy saw two teenage boys on the pew in front of her snickering when Layla broke out in a Holy Ghost dance. Envy hated to admit it, but it was sort of funny to see Layla in a purple robe, jumping up and down. She put her in the mind of the purple dinosaur she'd seen Kacie's kids watching on television from time to time. Just as quick as the thought invaded her mind, did she see the inevitable unfold before her nut-brown eyes, enhanced by the designer eyeglasses she wore. Nervously, Envy pushed her frames up on her nose.

Suddenly, Layla's humongous legs pointed toward the ceiling at the same time that her backside landed on the purple carpet. Gasps and aahs, and more than a few giggles filled the air while deacons and ushers rushed to Layla's side.

Envy's hand flew up against her mouth, while Kacie's kids pointed and laughed at their 'Play Aunt Layla' sprawled on the floor at the front of the choir stand for everyone to get a first-class view.

Kacie popped each of her kids one by one and warned them to shut up. It took several minutes for the church

2

staff to get Layla up on her feet. While they led a limping, disheveled Layla to the choir room, Envy stood and shuffled quickly past Kacie and her kids.

Rushing to the choir room, Envy halted for only seconds and then burst inside to find Layla crying, probably more from shame and embarrassment than anything else.

"Layla, girl, are you all right?" Envy asked and knelt beside Layla. She pushed back several locks of the twists that partially shielded Layla's blood-red face.

"Yeah, I'm okay," Layla whispered.

"Are you sure? Why don't you let me take you to the doctor to the emergency room to get checked out?" Envy offered.

"No, I said I'm fine." Layla snarled.

"Sista Layla, if you need anything, let me know," one of the ushers told her.

"Thanks, Sista Jones, I'm fine. Y'all can go on back in the sanctuary."

"Okay, honey. Come on, y'all," Sista Jones ordered the rest of the ushers who were still gathered in the choir room. "We need to get back to our posts before Pastor Betts starts his message," she told them.

The ushers left and Layla and Envy were alone.

"I can't believe I did that," Layla cried. "My fat tail fell. I know I musta looked like an elephant. I know folks were laughing. They're probably out there still laughing and talking about me." Layla wiped tears from her eyes.

"I told you about downing yourself, Layla. People fall every day. What makes you think it shouldn't happen to you? Think about Kacie. You don't hear her feeling sorry for herself and she's fallen way more times than you ever have. And kids used to make fun of me because I'm dark-skinned. What I'm saying is that calling yourself names is not going to make things better. How many times have I told you that talking about yourself only makes you feel worse? So what if you're a little overweight? If you're tired of it, then do something about it," Envy lashed out.

"I am not going to get into this with you here in the church. You know I'm more than a little overweight, so don't try to pretend that I'm not. I already feel stupid enough for being so careless. And just 'cause you are a size six doesn't make me feel better, and whether you're dark or light has nothing to do with the way people treat you." Layla wiped the last tear from her round full figured face. "It's not as easy to lose all of this." Layla pointed at herself with her hands. "It's hard; downright impossible for me."

Layla stood and moved toward the door. Peeping to see who was in the hallway, she walked out when she didn't see anyone. Envy followed. Layla was not about to go back into the choir stand. Instead, she went into the sanctuary and took a seat next to the last pew, and listened to Pastor Betts's message.

"Go back up there with Kacie. You know she needs help with all of them children," Layla said.

Envy agreed and tip-toed back to her seat.

"Is she all right?" Kacie whispered when Envy sat down.

"Yeah, her ego is bruised more than anything," Envy said and focused her attention on Pastor Betts.

When services ended, Kacie rushed the children along by pushing them one after another into the crowded aisle of people. Envy held Keshena until they all made it to the Fellowship Hall located in the back of the church where muffins, juice, and coffee were prepared for whoever wanted a light snack.

Kacie was glad the church provided snacks every Sunday. That way she wouldn't have to worry about rushing home to cook. She wanted to lie down, relax and

4

chat on the phone, which was more like a hobby for Kacie.

"Sista Layla, are you all right?" Several church members asked while Layla stuffed herself with muffins.

She assured them that she was fine.

"You know you did your thing this morning, girl," said another church member.

"Thank you. That's one of my favorite songs," replied, a still shaken Layla.

Envy stood next to Layla, holding Keshena. She fed the baby a finger full of a blueberry muffin.

Layla pushed the last portion of her third muffin into her mouth, washing it down with a box of juicy juice. Scanning the fellowship hall, Layla spied Kacie all up in some man's face, skinning and grinning while her children ran around in and out of the crowd, slinging chunks of muffins all over the place and splattering juice.

"When is she ever going to learn?" asked Layla.

"No time soon, believe me. But I'm not going to stand here and hold Keshena while she pushes up on some man. My arm already feels like I've been holding a piece of lead." Envy made her way over to Kacie. Without uttering a word, she placed Keshena in Kacie's arms. Right away Keshena started crying. "Layla and I are about to leave. I guess we'll check you later."

Appearing somewhat embarrassed by Envy's gesture, and her baby's crying, she flipped Envy off. "No problem. I'll talk to y'all later," then turned and continued flirting while Envy and Layla walked away.

Layla and Envy continued their conversation about Kacie while Layla squeezed inside Envy's champagne Saturn VUE. "I don't understand Kacie. The only real reason she comes to church is to look for a man, anybody's man at that. She ought to have enough. She ought to just stay home," said Layla.

5

Envy readily agreed. "I know that's right. She's thirty years old and already has six children and five or six baby daddies. She needs to be anointed with a well full of blessed oil." Envy and Layla laughed as Envy started the car and maneuvered between the other cars leaving from the parking lot. "You need to stop anywhere before I take you home?" asked Envy.

"Yeah, I want to stop by Chicken Shack. I want to get a three-piece meal. I want to go home, eat, and then soak in a hot tub of water before I get stiff from that fall. Plus, it's supposed to storm later this afternoon, so I don't plan on getting back out."

"It's getting cloudy already," Envy remarked as she drove in the direction of Chicken Shack.

Envy and Layla started talking about the morning worship service, and how much they loved Pastor Betts's preaching. When they made it to Chicken Shack, it didn't take long for the cook to prepare Layla's order.

Less than half an hour after leaving the church, Envy drove into the main entrance of the newly renovated Uptown Housing Development. She made several turns until she arrived in front of Layla's apartment.

"I guess I'll talk to you later. I might go over to my sister's house and chill for a while," said Envy.

"I don't know why you want to do that. You're the one who's always talking about how she's always riding you about the fact that your mother lives with her and her husband."

"I know that's right," Envy said like she suddenly remembered how much Nikkei complained. "But why shouldn't Mother live with them? Nikkei has plenty of room. She acts like Mother's dementia is easy for me, but it's not."

"I know that. And your mother is so young to have dementia. I'm thankful that my parents are in good

6

health," Layla told Envy. "I know you want to see your mother, but seeing her today means dealing with Nikkei. Think about it." Layla looked at Envy in silence.

"I will," answered Envy.

Layla adjusted her short, obese body by moving one way and then the other. Getting out of Envy's car was always easier than getting in. After a few seconds, she stood erect, pulled her blue dress out of her butt with one hand, and used the other hand to grab her chicken dinner.

"Bye," said Layla as she turned and walked toward her apartment.

"See ya." Envy waited until Layla was at her front door before she sped away.

After replaying Layla's comments about Nikkei, Envy changed her mind about going to see her mother as soon as she left out of the gate of Layla's apartment. She turned up her radio and sang along with the tune playing.

Envy parked and turned off the ignition when she pulled up in front of her two-bedroom duplex. She sat quietly with her hands gripping the vinyl steering wheel cover and her head bent over resting on them, thinking about how glad she was that she had changed her mind about going over to Nikkei's.

She inhaled deeply and exhaled slowly, hoping that the frustration mounting inside her would not overflow this time. No such luck. She questioned God like she'd done many times before.

"I know I've asked you this before, Lord, but why did my mother name me Envy? What was going through her mind? Was she demented then?"

Envy balled her hands into fists and pounded the sides of them against the steering wheel until they turned cherry red.

"I can't get up for going down. I can't take a step forward without taking ten steps backward. I look at other

7

people, including my sister, and I just don't understand. She has a beautiful home, a great job," with emphasis she added, "and a husband with a good job who simply adores her. But look at me. Here I am still struggling, groveling, wishing, and hoping that things were right in my life. So what if I make good money? Where has it gotten me? I have no man, no real life. So tell me, what's the difference between me and Nikkei?"

Envy's anger toward God mounted with each word that spewed from her mouth.

"I don't understand why you don't allow me to have one good opportunity, a real chance at having good things happen in my life. Everything that's good flies right past me and into somebody else's lap. Even Kacie has it better than me, and she has six children tugging at her twenty-four-seven. She may work a little part-time job, but she still seems to live better than me and I don't have not one little crumb snatcher. I guess I should be fake, like Kacie, before you show me some love. I don't know what you want, God. And Layla? Well, Layla is Layla. She loves you, I do know that. But you don't act like you want to give her a break either. Seems like she doesn't realize the game you're playing with her. What is it with you, God?"

Envy suddenly ended her conversation with God just as quickly as she'd started it. She opened the car door, got out, and slammed it behind her.

She raised her hands in surrender and bolted off. "I don't know why I even bother talking to you," she hollered at the sky before rushing up the walkway leading to her front door just as the first big drops of rain began to fall –upon her head.

***

The three women met and became fast friends while attending vo-tech. Not one of them, if asked, could explain what drew the three of them together, but whatever it was, they had remained friends for eleven years.

Layla was about seventy pounds lighter back then and just like now, she was heavily involved in church.

Kacie was pregnant with her first child when they met, and Envy lived at home with her mother and worked part-time at FedEx while attending vo-tech.

Over the years, their circumstances in life changed but their friendship remained sturdy. Envy decided to attend the University of Memphis, and after three years she received a Bachelor's degree in Business Administration. She was a manager at a large company with an extra nice salary and annual bonuses attached.

Layla completed her cosmetology courses but never managed to pass the board exams required to become licensed. So whenever she got in a serious tight, she'd fix hair in her apartment.

One by one, each of them faced the game life plays on each person who lives it. The alternative to living was dying, and neither of them wanted to go down that pathway. There was too much zest in living for them, too many things to see, places to go, and an endless list of mistakes yet to be made. So, through it all, the three of them clung to each other without judging each other's actions and decisions.

2

"Without a rich heart, wealth is an ugly beggar."
Ralph Waldo Emerson

Pellet-sized raindrops crashed against the windows of Kacie's house. Lightning catapulted across the sky and sounds of thunder roared like the devil walking around seeking whom he might devour.

"Kassandra, I'm scared."

"Kali, shut up will you, before you wake up Kendra and Keshena, then Momma's gonna come in here and tear all our tails up. Don't you remember what Mrs. Caples told us last Sunday? She said to keep quiet and be still when it storms 'cause God is doing His work." She looked at the ceiling from the top bunk bed.

Kali muttered in a state of utter fear. "But I can't help it. It's thundering and lightning. The wind sounds like a big bad wolf."

"Why don't I get in bed with you? Then will you go to sleep?"

"Uh, huh," Kali said.

Kassandra climbed down the bunk bed ladder and huddled next to her frightened sister. "When we wake up, the storm will be over."

"But I'm hungry."

"Make up your mind, Kali. Are you hungry or are you scared?" Kassandra was losing her patience with her little sister.

"I'm hungry…and I'm scared."

Kassandra threw off her covers, looked over at the toddler bed where Kendra lay, then looked at Keshena in her crib. Satisfied that they were both sound asleep, she got out of Kali's bed and went into the dark kitchen, with Kali jumping up, following closely behind, holding on tightly to the edge of her big sister's nightshirt. Shadows of trees outside lined the walls of the house and bolts of lightning striking their target made both of them jump.

Kassandra quickly turned around and raised a finger to her lips. "Shhh," she warned Kali.

"You don't want Momma to hear us do you?"

Kali shook her head from side to side. Trembling, she stayed on the heels of her sister. Kassandra heard her mother's voice. She was in her bedroom, on the phone, like nothing was going on outside. Entering the kitchen, Kassandra didn't bother turning on the light. She quietly opened the cabinet and felt around for a package of saltines and a jar of peanut butter and then moved toward the refrigerator. Opening it, she grabbed an already made bottle of milk for Keshena just in case the storm woke her up during the night, then Kassandra wouldn't have to get back up to go get her a bottle. Finding everything, Kassandra returned to the bedroom she shared with her three sisters.

The two girls sat on the floor and used the saltines to dig hunks of peanut butter out of the jar until their bellies were satisfied. Kassandra made sure to clean up everything. She hid the jar of peanut butter and crackers underneath the bottom bunk bed. She'd make sure first thing tomorrow morning to put it back in its rightful place before their mother found out they had been eating in their rooms. After that, sleep came quickly for the two sisters while the storm raged fiercely outside.

It was obvious that Kacie didn't hear Kassandra and Kali shuffling around in the kitchen because she continued talking on the phone.

"Of course, I enjoyed church today. The best part was seeing you there," she flirted.

Rain pelted heavily against her rooftop and windowpane, but Kacie wasn't bothered in the least bit. There was a storm brewing within her as she used her womanly wiles to capture the man named Deacon she'd met at church a couple of Sundays ago.

"I don't know how you do it."

"What are you talking about? Do what?" Kacie lay back on her full-size bed and awkwardly crossed both legs.

"Six children and you're still finer than Halle Berry. You're an amazing woman."

"Oh, yeah. I thought I was much finer, but thanks for the compliment."

Kacie smiled when she heard Deacon chuckling on the other end of the phone. "When are you going to let me become a part of your life? All of this talking at church and on the phone is good but I want to spend some real time with you."

"We'll see. But I will promise you this?"

"What?" Excitement could be heard in Deacon's voice.

"It'll be worth the wait. That you can bank on, Mr. Deacon Riggs."

While Kacie turned on the charm with Deacon, Layla sat in her oversized chair in her apartment like she was oblivious to the storm raging outside her window. Her focus was strictly on watching the classic movie Sparkle on TV One while munching away on her last piece of fried chicken. "If I could just lose some weight, maybe I could be on television singing. That would be a miracle." she berated herself followed by sucking the last piece of meat off the chicken bone.

Layla set the empty plate of bones on the end table, then quickly replaced the plate with a container of peach cobbler she had sitting on the table too. Her telephone rang and she struggled to lean over to get it, huffing and puffing with each movement.

"Hello."

"What's going on, baby?"

"Nothing; just watching TV."

"But it's storming outside. That makes things romantic, don't you think?" the light voice asked on the other end.

"Romantic? I don't know if I agree with that, Mike."

"Let me come over there and show you what I mean?"

The tone of Layla's voice changed to one of agitation. "You must be crazy. How many times have I told you that I am not somebody to just lay up with?" She played with her black neck-length dreads. "I've tried that and it's gotten me nowhere, Mike, especially with you."

Layla had been messing around with Mike on and off for the past two years. He lived with his mother in one of the units behind her apartment. She used to pray that she and Mike could have a serious relationship, but things hadn't turned out exactly like she'd hoped.

Mike was the kind of man who wanted to lay up with whoever was convenient for him at the time. She sometimes felt like a tramp after sleeping with him, especially when he asked for money minutes after they finished messing around. Most of the time she gave it to him, somehow feeling as though it was the least she could do for someone who found her attractive enough to sleep with her. But enough was enough. The girlfriend Mike had now was practically living with him and his momma.

One night, after following him, Mike's girlfriend caught him at Layla's house. When she laid eyes on Layla, she laughed so hard that she started to cry and called Layla every name but a child of God. That was the last straw for Layla. She told herself that never again would she allow anyone to humiliate and use her again.

"Mike, why don't you lay up with your girlfriend? You think I'm going to set myself up again for her to come knocking at my door and cussing me out? I don't think so," rebutted Layla.

"Be like that then. Look, let me hold a few dollars. I need to get me a pack of cigs."

"I do not have a few dollars. Not today and no other day," she retorted. "Now I said, leave me alone and I tell you what. Don't call here anymore."

"Forget your butt then. You ought to be glad I even want to be with you in the first place. It ain't like guys beating down your door to get in. Maybe to get out." He laughed after each of his insults. "Anyway, who needs your fat, stanky tail."

Layla held the phone in utter shock and disbelief for a few seconds before hollering into the receiver, "Forget you, Mike. I don't need you. I got who I need, and that's God," She said then hung up the phone.

Layla didn't know who she was trying to fool. Mike's words stung her like a swarm of killer bees. Whoever said sticks and stones may break my bones but words will never hurt me, was nothing but a liar. Layla pulled herself up from the chair and carried her tears to the bathroom. Maybe a long, hot shower would help to wash away her tears and her fears of being lonely and all alone for the rest of her life.

3

"What has a man's face to do with his character? Can a man of good character help having a disagreeable face?"
Ann Radcliffe

Mid-Monday Kacie turned over in the bed and searched groggily for the remote. She felt Keshena lying next to her and knew she was asleep, which meant that the other kids had left for school and daycare. They knew the rules – put Keshena in their mother's bed before they left for school. Kacie was glad she didn't have to get up early every morning and get her children ready. She taught them how to get dressed and how to use the microwave as soon as they were old enough to push the button. No time for whining, spoiled children. She had too many for that.

Kacie rubbed her fingers through her honey-blonde micro braids. She climbed out of the bed clad in her panties and bra.

Glancing at the cupid-faced baby, Kacie eased up from the bed hoping she wouldn't wake her. She didn't want to start her day off with a whining child. Her extra measure of caution worked because Keshena didn't move a hair.

With her signature sunken knees limp, Kacie hurried to the bathroom to take a wash up and pee. Afterward, she ran into the kitchen, grabbed a juice bottle for Keshena, and a couple of blueberry muffins for herself.

The phone rang just as Kacie stepped into the bright, airy mint julep kitchen. Cereal bowls with splotches of spilled milk and cereal scattered on the breakfast table. Dishes from last night's dinner were still in the sink.

"Hello, what's up?" asked Kacie.

15

"I was hoping you'd tell me. You're the one who has the winning hand." Deacon's smooth words dripped from his mouth like honey from a honeycomb.

If he could have seen through the phone, Deacon would see the blush that covered Kacie's face. "Is that right? Well, since you put it that way, then I'm going to see what kind of hand I really do have. Why don't you come and keep me company around noon," Kacie said to Deacon.

"That sounds tempting, and I wish I could. But baby, you know I'm at work. But what if I come by your place later on when your kids are having visions of sugarplums dancing around in their heads?" Deacon chuckled lightly.

"I don't know if I can wait that long. I was hoping I could see you before tonight. I tell you what. Why don't you come over here for dinner, say around six-thirty? We can eat with the kids and then I'll make them take their baths and go to bed. We'll have the rest of the evening to spend devouring our dessert," Kacie teased over the phone.

"Why are you working on my emotions like this, girl? You know you got me going around in circles. I'm already spending more time on the phone with you than ever. And I don't want to get attached to your kids and then you up and dump me, you know."

"What are you talking about, Deacon? Why, I would never think about doing any such thing. You're too nice of a man. One that me, and my kids, could get used to," Kacie responded, and hoped she wouldn't run him off by including her kids in the equation.

Deacon already seemed like the man of her dreams. He appeared to be kind, church-going, and polite. He was the kind of man she hoped she had in each of her baby daddies, but each time she was proven wrong.

"What I'm talking about is getting attached to you. I like you, Kacie. I don't care whether you have six kids, and I don't care about your handicap either. You're someone who can be special in my life. I'm tired of all these women with their tricks. They're always out to get over on a man. I want a fine, Christian girl like you in my life. That's what I need." Deacon poured it on like sorghum syrup, slow and easy. Every word found residence in Kacie's heart.

Keshena's shrill cry from the bedroom quickened their conversation. "Look, I can't stand here and listen to any more of this. Just be here tonight, say around eight o'clock since you sound like you don't want to eat dinner with us. We'll talk about things then."

"Don't be like that. I don't mind having dinner with you, but I might not get away from the office that early. If I can get away at a reasonable time, then I'll be over. If not, then don't worry your pretty little head about it because I'll make it up to you."

"Still try to come. I do want to see you, Deacon."

"Me too. But for now, I have to go. I'll call you later. Have a good day, sweetheart."

"Yeah, you too. Bye now." Kacie hung up the phone and swore under her breath as she heard Keshena's cries become more demanding. She opened a packet of peaches and cream oatmeal and hurriedly prepared it for Keshena. She didn't want to miss any of the Young and the Restless so she got everything together just in time to hear the familiar soap opera music starting to play.

Sitting in the bed and leaning against her pillow, she spoon-fed Keshena the oatmeal and nibbled on a muffin with her eyes glued to the television screen. She watched the soap opera couple share a passionate kiss while she thought about Deacon and the growing possibility that she'd found the one.

***

Early afternoon and another few dollars, Envy traveled the usual route she did almost every day after work. One of the added luxuries of living in midtown was the proximity to downtown and her job. Her exempt managerial status often afforded her the perk of flexible work hours. After a weekend of being cooped up in the house, she was ready to make something exciting happen. So what if it was Monday? No Monday blues for her. She made every turn with ease in her older but trustworthy Saturn. She could afford a spanking brand new car off the showroom floor if she so chose. But she opted for a nice sizeable savings account and investment fund rather than frivolous spending.

The parking lot at Precious Cargo was near its capacity and it was barely five o'clock. Envy's sleek leg exited the car like she was a movie star stepping out of a stretch limo. Clad in a pair of classic black pumps that matched her one-piece black dress with buttercream buttons, Envy got out of the car and closed the door. Her mouth seemed to become drier with each step that brought her closer to the entrance.

Once inside, she went in the direction of her favorite hangout area – the bar. Without asking, Tyreek the bartender, when he spotted her in her usual seat, prepared her favorite, vodka with a spot of cranberry juice and one cube of ice.

"Hi there, gorgeous," Tyreek flirted and placed the drink in front of her. "Long day already?" he inquired with raised eyebrows and a daring smile.

"More like a boring weekend and a long day." She took a sip of her drink. "Ahh, this is good." She immediately took another sip, this time a deeper one.

"I know what you like," he whispered.

"Yes, you sure do which means you know that I can't stop at one of these babies, either." She swallowed the rest of the vodka, and Tyreek presented her with another one stronger than the first.

"What plans do you have for later?" he asked at the same time he raised his index finger to tell the next customer to hold on just a moment.

"I sure don't plan to spend another night at home bored out of my wits. What's on your mind?" Envy asked as if she didn't already know.

"You. I'll be outta here…"

"I know your schedule, Tyreek, so cut the formalities. Fix me another drink and be at my place by ten," she said in an almost commanding tone.

Envy walked around the club and talked with some of the regulars. An hour or so later, she left Precious Cargo just as quickly as she'd entered.

Sitting in her car outside of the club, Envy waited for some of the effects of the vodka to wear off before she started driving. With her head laid against the headrest, she closed her eyes and thought about being with Tyreek tonight.

Ring, ring, ring.

The phone startled her from her daydream, and she cranked the car and pulled out into the flowing traffic to head home.

"Hey, what's up?" she asked. To anyone passing, it probably looked like Envy was inside the car talking to herself because her Bluetooth was hidden underneath her auburn weave tresses.

"Where are you?"

"I made a couple of stops after work. I'm on my way home now. Why?"

"I wanted to know if you could stop by here and take me to the store, but forget it since you're almost at home.

Envy focused on Layla's eating habits. Going to the store meant Layla didn't lack food in the fridge, but she'd more than likely eaten all of her junk food and was craving more.

"Is it something you have to have this evening? I'm exhausted, *tipsy, and horny* but she kept the last two feelings to herself.

"No, it's not crucial. I just needed to pick up a couple of items, is all."

Envy knew Layla all too well. She heard the sound of disappointment in her voice, but going without a box of cookies and a couple of king-size chocolate bars certainly was not going to kill her, Envy concluded.

"Look, I'll come by there tomorrow and take you unless you get someone else to run you to the store."

The only time Layla seemed to have no problem getting to the store was the first of the month when her check and EBT card were full. Then her so-called friend, Mike, made sure he found a way to take her wherever she wanted to go. Envy couldn't be sure if Mike was a broken-down wanna-be gigolo, but every time Envy happened upon him, he was always between jobs.

"If you're asking where Mike is on the sly, he went to North Memphis, to his brother's place. He was hired at one of the manufacturing plants out there so he'll be staying out there during the week," Layla explained in a less-than-friendly tone.

"I didn't say anything about Mike, but since you brought him up, I'm glad his tail has a job – again. Hopefully, he'll keep this one for more than six weeks. I don't know why you deal with that bum anyway. The man has no scruples, and practically lives with a woman he swears is just a friend. But you and I know better than that. Then he never seems to come tipping around your place until the first of the month." There, Envy had said what was on her mind. The liquor made it easy for the words to drip from her tongue.

"Look, I'm sick of you judging me, and Mike too for that matter. I've told you more than once that we're friends. So whatever you're trying to make us out to be is a downright lie, Envy."

Layla took an extra deep breath like she'd just run a marathon. Knowing that Mike used her like an addict uses drugs; every chance he got, but no way was she ready to admit that to Envy or anyone else.

"Whatever, Layla. I don't have time to get into this with you tonight. You're a grown woman. Do whatever makes your boat float. Anyway, I've gotta go. I just walked in the house and I'm going to take a shower and hit the sack," Envy said without another moment's thought of the disagreement between her and Layla. "I'll come through there around lunchtime tomorrow and take you to the store. But call me if your mother or someone else comes to take you, okay?"

"Okay. I'll see you tomorrow." Layla sounded like she was glad that the conversation about her relationship with Mike was over.

***

Envy pulled into her driveway. The door to her next-door neighbor's apartment opened just as the click-clack of Envy's silver pumps against the concrete steps reached her door.

"Mrs. Rawlings. Dang, it happens every time," Envy said underneath her liquored breath. "Good evening, Mrs. Rawlings." Envy mustered a half smile.

"Hello, young lady." Mrs. Rawlings stepped outside. She held her front door open with one hand and rested the other hand on her hip. "You just coming from work, I guess."

"Yes, ma'am. I'm tired too. I had a busy day, at least more than usual."

Her uneven brows pushed the wrinkles on her forehead up closer to her scathe hairline. "I won't hold you. I just wanted to speak to you. You had a pretty quiet weekend over there." Her eyes shifted to Envy's side of the duplex.

What does she mean by that? Spying again? Uh, the nerve of this woman. "Yes, it was rather quiet." Envy spoke between clenched teeth, holding her composure so as not to sound disrespectful to the old woman. Mrs. Rawlings was a nice woman but just a little too nosy for Envy's taste. Mrs. Rawlings watched her like a momma bear.

"Do you need anything?" Envy turned the key in the door and opened it. Glancing back over her shoulder, she waited for Mrs. Rawlings' response.

Fischer raced to the door, jumping up and down, turning round and round like the devil whipping his wife.

"Down, Fischer." Envy patted her golden Labrador on his head.

Fischer used his cold, brown, snoozer to open the door wider. Fischer pounded past her onto the porch and raced to Mrs. Rawlings' side.

Mrs. Rawlings patted Fischer's head. He sat next to the woman, content.

"No, I'm fine. I don't need a thing. God is right here with me. As long as I got Him, I don't worry about a thing." She looked at Fischer. Out of the clear blue sky, the old woman said something that made Envy stop dead in her tracks.

"Envy, you're more than who you act like you are. Mark my words. G'nite, child, and lock up. God didn't raise you to be a fool." Mrs. Rawlings went back inside, leaving Envy standing in her doorway.

The words were confusing to Envy. "What does she mean by, I'm more than who I act like I am? Just who does she think she is anyway?" Pushing her rectangular-rimmed glasses up on the bridge of her nose, she slammed the door behind her.

Soaking in the hot, soothing water, Envy reflected on her life. She was proud of her managerial position at Nuvatek, her nice salary and bonuses, and the fact that finances, weight, and constant *baby daddy* drama were not part of her life like it was for Layla and Kacie. She had men at her beck and call. She was free to do her.

Nestling her head back on her satin bath pillow, Envy heard her mother's words replaying. *I named you Envy because I was the envy of my neighborhood and my school. I was pretty, with long, good hair, a fine figure, and skin as smooth and dark as a chocolate bar. Anything I put on was a fashion statement. Girls couldn't stand me because they said I was conceited. I was. It didn't stop when I got knocked up with you either. And then you, thank God, were born even more beautiful than me, your mother. I couldn't have chosen a better name than Envy. Until when you were about eight years old, you started acting like you were somehow better than me, your mother who brought you into this world. Folks started filling your head with a bunch of garbage. Always talking about you looked like an angel and that you could be a model or a child star. That's why when you got to be a teenager, I had to bring you down a couple of notches. I had to remind you that if it wasn't for your looks, you wouldn't be nothing.*

The phone lying on top of the closed toilet seat quipped Envy from her deep thoughts.

"Hey, pretty lady. You ready for me to relieve some of your tension? I can be there in…say…twenty minutes."

The offer sounded enticing. "Not tonight, Cedric. I've made other plans." She stepped out of the bathtub and grabbed the tangerine bath towel from off of the towel warmer.

"Aw, come on, Envy. Can't I change your mind," he said in a pleading but sexy manner.

Hesitating, Envy considered calling Tyreek to tell him something had come up, but the thought quickly vanished as she remembered that she was the shot caller, not Cedric or any of the numerous other men she bedded regularly.

"You know it doesn't work like that, Cedric. Check with me later in the week and maybe we can hook up. Gotta go." She ended the call before Cedric could so much as part his lips with an answer.

Envy finished preparing herself for her first visitor of the week. She put on revealing lingerie and afterward, she made herself another drink. The doorbell rang and Fischer barked.

"Quiet, boy. It's all right." Fischer followed her to the door and sat next to her like he was eager to see who was on the other side.

Tyreek stepped in and leaned over and kissed Envy on the cheek while Fischer's tag wagged back and forth. "Hi, baby."

"Hi. Come on in, Tyreek." She hurried him inside the door just in case her nosy neighbor was over there playing I Spy through her curtains.

Tyreek patted Fischer on his head. "You want a drink?" Envy asked him and walked toward the kitchen. Tyreek grabbed her by the elbow.

"I don't want anything. I just want you," he answered and tried to kiss her passionately. She pulled away and changed directions and headed for her bedroom

"I've missed you," Tyreek whispered hungrily in Envy's ear. He lightly bit on her ear lobe and continued with kisses that trailed along her neck, throat, and eyes.

Envy turned her head rapidly when he went for her lips.

"Stop it! You know how I feel about kissing." Her voice was stern. Kissing was not her forte. Kissing meant commitment, love, and a special closeness, something she refused to feel for any of the almost hundred men she'd slept with since she lost her virginity at age fifteen.

Tyreek answered with a groan. He continued to kiss her soft, sweet-smelling body while he encased himself in protection. Reaching his final destination, Envy gave in to his demands. With each movement, Tyreek sought to please Envy. Her sculptured nails embedded in his back and upper shoulders assured him he'd accomplished what he'd set out to do. Their final embrace and moment of ultimate pleasure was evident in the tiny droplets of sweat that fell from his forehead and landed between her voluptuous mounds of flesh.

Envy tightened her grip on Tyreek and the frustration that had been penned up all weekend was released.

Tyreek collapsed on the other side of her queen-sized bed and immediately closed his eyes to sleep.

Envy lay quietly on the other side of the bed until Tyreek turned toward her, grabbed her around the waist, and kissed the back of her hair. Envy moved away from his endearing touch and climbed out of the bed.

"I'm going to take a shower," she said without emotion. "Lock the door behind you."

Envy welcomed the soothing jet streams of water enveloping every curve of her body. Underneath the shower, she felt rejuvenated as the water pelted her over and over again. She halted momentarily when she heard

Tyreek on the other side of the door getting dressed so he could leave. He knew the routine.

She was relieved when she heard her front door close behind his familiar steps and the sound of Fischer's bark confirming their visitor had indeed departed the scene.

Putting on a melon thigh-length teddy, Envy went to the living room to make sure Tyreek had locked the door. He had. Fischer trailed happily behind her like he was glad the two of them were finally alone. She stopped at the hall linen closet, pulled out a clean lavender sheet set, and proceeded to remake her bed.

After inhaling the fragrant scent of the fresh sheets, she knelt next to the bed and prayed her nightly prayers. There used to be a time when she was much younger that she would pray and ask God to forgive her for being so promiscuous. She didn't know why she was the way that she was, but she'd come to terms with it. *No need to ask for forgiveness when I'm just going to do it all over again*, she surmised a long time ago. She opted instead for asking God the usual; to bless her friends, her loved ones, the sick, the lonely, and the homeless.

When she got up off of her knees, she climbed into the bed, underneath the cozy comforter, and started reading a novel she started the day before. Sleep came quickly, but not without its consequences.

In the midnight hour, Envy bolted upright in her platform bed like an electric current had ripped through her. Sweat formed quickly along her brow and her breath was quick. She stared around the darkened bedroom where she had fallen asleep while reading.

The nightmare was familiar. It aroused a fear so incomprehensible nothing could make it go away. If only she had some control over it. Why couldn't she somehow forget the pain of the past? Tears flooded into the palms of her hands.

Shelia E. Bell

Fischer plopped at the side of the bed and rested his head next to Envy's thigh, but Envy's bowed head grew heavy with the weight of her present, sinful acts. But all of her sins piled together couldn't banish her mind of the one, contemptible sin she had committed. The one only she and God knew about.

4

"A person is only beautiful, when their own beauty, is reflecting on to others." Tara Grady

After a solid week of rain and thunderstorms, the sky had cleared and the sun peeped from behind the piercing blue fall clouds.

Tenderly, Deacon kissed his wife on her cheek, playfully patted her on the butt, and then departed his ranch-style home. Twenty-three years of marriage. His wife attended her home church, like always. When he and his wife initially met, he was a member of Broadway Church. They were innocent, happy-go-lucky teens that quickly fell in love one summer while attending a Bridge Builders retreat. They married when they were barely out of their teens. There was never a disagreement between the two of them about remaining active members at their respective churches. The decision worked out well for Deacon. Less conflict. More freedom. Naïve and captivating wife. No kids. Chick on the side. Another chick on the side. And now a new chick on the side.

En route to an overnight business meeting in Murfreesboro, Deacon thought about Kacie. Cerebral palsy, bae-bae kids and all; the girl was still hot. He couldn't seem to keep his mind off of her. She would be easy to maintain. The main reason—too many kids to be able to get out and about a lot.

Deacon never desired children of his own and Kacie's kids running around every Sunday after church, reminded him several times over that he'd made the right decision when he had a vasectomy less than a year after he and his wife married.

In a peculiar way, Kacie reminded Deacon of his wife—needy, lonely, and with a bit of low self-esteem.

He saw it all in Kacie like he'd seen it in his wife. All the years they'd been married and she was still the same.

Since meeting Kacie three months ago at church, he'd been spending every extra, deceitful second he could talking to her on the phone or after church, getting to know as much as he could about Sister Kacie Mayweather.

Pressing the number seven key on his phone, Deacon listened through his Bluetooth for the phone to ring. It was time for him to take their phone conversations to the next level.

"Hello," answered Kacie.

"Hey, girl. Whatcha doing?"

"Waiting on you to call."

Deacon believed her. He seemed to read her like a bestselling novel. He could hear genuineness in her voice through the cell phone.

"I'm on my way out of town to meet a potential client. I'll be back early tomorrow afternoon. I want to see ya. Alone. Just you and me. Think you can make that happen?"

"I think that can be arranged," Kacie answered, but tried to hold back the excitement in her voice."

"That's my girl. Let me know how much a babysitter costs and I'll take care of the tab. I don't want you to worry about a thing when you're with me. I owe you some alone time since I haven't been able to get away to see you."

"Sounds good. You're so good to me, Deacon."

"I try, Kacie. You deserve it. I want you to take the kids to the babysitter tomorrow and when I get there, which should be around eight o'clock, we'll go out to dinner. I might even take you dancing." He paused, waiting on her comeback. He didn't know yet if she could dance or not. The bend in her knees might make it difficult. He felt empathy for her, but only for a moment.

"Sounds good. I haven't been out without the kids in a long time. Unless you call going through the drive-thru at Mickey D's," Kacie laughed over the phone. "As for dancing, I don't try to keep up with the latest dances anymore. My kids keep me moving enough. I don't think I can see myself doing the Soulja Boy or Cupid Shuffle," Kacie chuckled loudly.

"Well, we'll see if we can make our own dance moves tomorrow."

"Momma." Deacon heard one of Kacie's children calling her in the background. Then another one sounded like she, or he was right inside his Bluetooth.

"Momma, Keith hit me," the voice cried out.

"No, I didn't," another voice countered.

"Yes, you did."

"Stop it, y'all." Kacie's voice rang loudly into Deacon's ear. "Stop it right now. Don't let me have to get up and beat the fire out of y'all."

"Look, you better see about your kids. I'll try to call you when I make it to my hotel in a few hours."

Kacie's shrill and angry tone quickly reverted to one of calmness. "I wasn't through talking," she said pleadingly.

"I know, but you need to take care of your children's needs. As for me, I need to concentrate on this highway."

"O...kay. I guess you're right. Drive safely and call me back. I don't care what time it is. I want to know you made it there safely."

"Sure. Talk to ya later, sweetness." He pressed the end button on his cell phone until he heard the dial tone.

***

Shelia E. Bell

Friday afternoon, Kacie packed the kids' backpacks, stopped at the grocery store, and then drove her kids over to Layla's house. She was delighted Layla had agreed to babysit. As soon as she pulled up to Layla's apartment, the kids hopped out one by one.

Kenny carried Keshena in one arm and a bag of groceries in the other. Kali raced past him and knocked on Layla's door.

"Hello, everybody," Layla said with a smile plastered on her face as if she was really glad to see the kids. "Come on," she barely had time to say because the kids scurried right past her.

"Thanks, Layla. I don't know what I would do without you, girl." Layla remarked as she entered the apartment.

"You know you're welcome. Your kids keep me company. When they're around there's not a dull moment that passes." Layla chuckled and her breasts jiggled like a bowl of Jello.

Kacie reached inside her jean pocket and pulled out some money. "Here's your money." Kacie counted the money and gave it to Layla. She decided to pay Layla now instead of waiting on paying her after she picked up the kids.

"I thought you said your date was going to pay me?"

"He is paying you but I feel better paying you now. I'll keep the money when he gives it to me tonight. That way you don't have to wait on your money, just in case you have to buy something. I'm going to put this sack of groceries in the kitchen." She picked up the sack of groceries that Kenny had left in the living room. "There are plenty of snacks, juice, and food for them and I packed some for you too. I know how much you love microwave popcorn and there're some chocolate candy bars in there too."

31

"Kacie, you didn't have to bring all of this stuff, especially for me. I told you about that."

"Look, I don't want to hear it. I don't expect anybody to keep my kids and feed them too. You'll be broke for sure." Kacie laughed and walked toward Layla's galley-style kitchen with Layla and two of the kids trailing behind her. Kenny held Keshena in his arms while Keshena pulled on her sippy cup of juice.

"Keshena's things are packed in her diaper pouch." Kacie carefully pointed out everything to Layla. "I'll put away the stuff that needs to go in the refrigerator." She turned toward her children, some planted in front of Layla's television. "Keith and Kassandra, y'all get from in front of that television and come help Miss Layla. Kenny, Kali, and Kendra come in here and help too. You hear me?"

"Yes, ma'am."

"There's no need to do that, Kacie. I got this. You go on and have a good time. I know you can use a break every now and then."

Kacie sighed heavily and shifted her weight from one side to the other. "You sho' got that right. I love my kids, but I'm not going to lie to you, they can be a handful, especially since I'm trying to work a part-time job and have some kind of social life. You don't know just how much I appreciate you for doing this."

Layla waved her hand. "Go on. I'm glad to help out and make a few dollars too. And, it's good to know someone has a social life. I sure don't." Layla patted Kacie on the side of her shoulder.

"Kids, y'all better be good. If Auntee Layla tells me any of y'all acted up, you know what you're going to get when you get home."

The oldest boy appeared to speak for them all. "Yes, ma'am." The other kids looked knowingly at their mother.

"I'll be here to get them tomorrow by noon, if that's okay with you, Layla?"

"Noon is fine. I'm sure we'll find something to do until you get here. Now go. Have a good time. Oh, and remember, whenever you need me, just call since you're working now too."

"You're an angel. Now let me get out of here. I need to get back home and start getting ready." Kacie turned away from Layla and walked out of the kitchen, almost losing her balance while trying to avoid the circle of children gathered around her feet.

"Will y'all stop crowding up on me? I told y'all about that. You can make me fall when you're all up on me like that. I'll see y'all tomorrow now." The kids moved, giving their mother the room she needed to maneuver safely.

"Bye, Momma," they said one by one. Baby Keshena's chubby fingers curled in and out while she continued to hold her nearly empty sippy cup with the other one.

"Bye, y'all. Thanks again, Layla."

"Sure, see ya tomorrow."

Kacie hurried home. Deacon would be at her house at seven o'clock. Stepping inside, she stopped at the sound of her cell phone ringing in her clutch purse. "Not the kids already. Hello," answered Kacie. It was Envy on the phone. "Hey, Envy. I thought you were one of the kids calling."

"Where are they?" asked Envy.

"Layla has them. I have a date this evening."

"With who? No, no, let me guess. Is it the man from church? Derrick or Deacon, whatever his name is?" Envy's voice rang with excitement and curiosity.

"Yes, his name is Deacon. Anyway, this will be our first real, what I call 'out of the house' date. He's going to pay Layla for babysitting and everything, girl." Kacie's face lit up like a burst of sun. She maneuvered through her house, chattering away. "I've got to look like a diva tonight, Envy."

"What are you wearing?"

Kacie went to her closet like Envy could see her through the phone. From its hanger, she removed an onyx and silver translucent dress with cap sleeves, a natural waist, and a high back. The dress reached just above the knee. Describing the dress to Envy sent wave after wave of excitement gushing through Kacie on the inside. The thought that she was going to spend the evening with Deacon, the man of her dreams, filled her with anticipation. "I have a waist-length wrap to wear with it since it's a little cool tonight.

"Sounds like you are going to set that man ablaze tonight." Envy giggled into the phone.

"If I don't, it won't be because of lack of trying," Kacie remarked flippantly. "Anyway, I need to start getting ready." Kacie glanced at the bedroom clock. "It's already five-thirty and he's supposed to be here at seven."

"Do you need me to come help you with your makeup? I don't have anything planned tonight, so it won't be a problem for me to run over there."

"Nope, don't worry about it. I can manage. But thanks. You're an angel," Kacie responded graciously. "I gotta go. We'll talk tomorrow."

Kacie hung up the phone and then stepped into her dress. She positioned herself in front of the floor-length mirror on the back of her closet door. "Dang, I look pretty good, if I must say so myself." She slipped on a pair of pumps. Cerebral palsy already caused her to walk on her toes so wearing too high of a heel might cause her condition to be more pronounced and threaten her stability.

Deacon arrived at seven-fifteen. Kacie felt jitterbugs in her stomach when the doorbell chimed. When she opened the door, a glowing smile enveloped Kacie's face at the sight of Deacon.

Deacon reared back. "Wow, don't you look like, well gorgeous." He complimented her at the same time he stepped forward and bent to kiss her full on her polished lips.

They stood at the entrance of the door making out for a couple of minutes before Deacon eased away and walked inside the house. He looked around as if expecting to see Kacie's kids. None were in sight. "You got the kids to the sitter, huh?"

"Of course. I told you I would."

"Yeah, I know, but I wanted to be sure before I did this." He studied her sexy frame until he captured her coffee eyes with his.

Before Kacie could react, Deacon reached for her waist and pulled her in his arms again, kissing her with passion as he ran his hands up, down, and across her hips and butt. She was pressed against him so tight that he felt like she was part of him. The night had barely started and here he was, getting exactly what he'd hoped for and he hadn't taken her out the door yet.

The intimate evening Deacon spent with Kacie was more than he had hoped for. He liked Kacie but by the same token, he had to be extra cautious about the two of them being seen out in public. Kacie didn't know there was a *Mrs. Riggs* waiting for him at home. He had to make sure he kept it that way. No woman was going to make him mess up what he had at home.

The couple snuggled and kissed on the sofa for at least a half hour until Kacie pulled out of his arms.

"I'm hungry. What about dinner?" she said and toyed with his ear.

"I'm hungry too, but not for dinner," Deacon answered in a hoarse voice. He used one hand to pull Kacie close to him again and began nibbling on her neck and caressing her hair.

She eased away again. "Come on, Deacon she said in a pleading voice. Let's go grab something to eat. Then we can come back here and have dessert," she crooned lowly.

Deacon stood, grabbed Kacie by the hand, and helped her to her feet. "How does The Carabbas sound? I heard they serve a mean shrimp and scallops," suggested Deacon.

"I like that. Carabbas it is."

Deacon carried her to Carabbas in Collierville, far enough away that they would hardly run into anyone they knew. Kacie was impressed. None of her children's fathers had ever taken her to such a nice place. Kacie seemed to savor every bite of the chicken marsala, a grilled chicken breast topped with mushrooms, prosciutto, and Lombardo Marsala wine sauce, while Deacon chose chicken and spinach cannelloni.

"Deacon, I'm having a wonderful time tonight. I feel…I feel so special," Kacie told him.

"That's because you are special and you deserve nice things. I can't imagine that you aren't married. What happened, if you don't mind my asking?" Deacon took a sip from his glass of red wine.

Kacie swallowed hard. It took a few seconds before she answered. "Bad choices. Without going into detail, that's what it amounts to. It's why I'm trying to get my life in order. I need to make sure my kids don't make the same mistakes I've made in my life." Kacie lowered her head like she was in shame.

"Hey, hold your head up," Deacon told her and reached across the table to raise her chin with the tips of his fingers. "Look, you're a nice lady. You said you're trying to make a change in your life. That says a lot about the kind of woman you are." Kacie's eyes locked with Deacon's golden brown eyes. "Nothing beats a try and I say you're doing a great job." Deacon used one hand to rub his low-cut afro back with his hand. "I have a lot of respect for you, Kacie. I really do."

Kacie blushed. "Thank you." Deacon threw his napkin down on the table and turned slightly to call their waiter for the check.

"I say it's time to get out of this place."

"Me too, as long as we don't go dancing. I'm stuffed. I don't think I can stand on a dance floor right now." Kacie dapped her mouth with her napkin. When the waiter approached Deacon placed his American Express card inside the check holder.

"I agree that we skip the dancing too," Deacon added, "and go back to your place for that dessert you promised me." He looked at her with seductive eyes. The waiter returned with Deacon's card and receipt; the couple left and went to Kacie's house.

On the drive home, Deacon could barely keep his hands off of Kacie. The fragrance of her perfume, the way she laughed, her luscious legs, everything about her turned him on. He massaged her leg closest to him up and down. Each time he touched her, he moved up higher beneath her dress without a protest from Kacie.

Kacie and Deacon didn't waste time. She locked the door and right away Deacon drew her into his arms.

Kacie held onto him like she was holding on for dear life. The passion ignited between them like a blaze on a bonfire – growing higher and higher with intensity.

Kacie lead him into the bedroom and they yielded completely to each other over and over until the two of them collapsed into each other's arms and fell asleep.

Hours later, Deacon opened his eyes. He peered around the dark room until he realized where he was. He sat up in the bed slightly and stretched his arms out and yawned. He peered over Kacie's shoulder and picked up his cell phone from off the bedside table. He eased his bear-sized body away from Kacie's and slowly slid out of the bed. Kacie stirred slightly about in the bed but didn't wake up. Deacon picked up his clothes that were strewn all over Kacie's bedroom floor and went into the bathroom to take a quick shower. He had to get the smell of adultery off of him before heading in the direction of the place he called home. Not that his wife would suspect a thing. She never had before. He was always careful like that.

Kacie sat up groggily in the bed and saw Deacon buttoning his shirt. "What time is it? Where are you going?" she asked while she rubbed her sleep-filled eyes.

"Baby, it's three in the morning. I need to make it to my side of town. You've worn me out. If I stay here all night, I won't be able to leave you, girl." His smile flashed and the look she flashed back told him that he'd captured her heart.

Walking over to where she was, Deacon leaned down and kissed Kacie's thick lips. She used her left hand to ease her leg out of the bed. Without any help, she placed her right leg on the side too.

"Don't get up," he said and gestured a halt sign with his hand. "I'll find my way out." Deacon kissed her again. "Lay back down and go back to sleep, my hot, sweet, sexy angel."

"But, Deacon, I don't want you to go and leave me here all alone," Kacie pleaded.

"I know, honey. But you know I just got back into town. I need to go check up on things at my crib. And you don't want Layla thinking you left the kids on her, do you? If that happens, she'll be mad at you and we won't have a babysitter anymore. You want that to happen?"

Kacie looked at the clock. She shook her head from side to side and pouted. "Like I said, it's near three o'clock, Deacon. I don't understand why you have to leave at this time of the morning. I told Layla I wasn't going to pick up the kids until noon." Her voice began to escalate.

Deacon looked at her with his hypnotic eyes and smiled. "Now whose fault is it that we made love until we both passed out? You put that whip appeal on me and it was over." He pinched her cheek. "You ought not be so good to me."

A slight smile formed on Kacie's face and she bowed her head down and blushed.

"If I try, and I said try, to come back later, I'll take you for brunch before you go to pick up your kids. Will that make you feel better?"

Kacie's head popped up. Like a jack in the box, she jumped up and plopped a kiss on Deacon. "I'd like that." She chuckled.

"Okay, so there. It's settled. Now be a good girl and go back to sleep. I'll call you when I'm on my way back over here. Okay?"

"Ok." She waited until she heard Deacon close the kitchen door. With a smile on her face, she lay back in the bed and reveled in the night she'd spent with the answer to her prayers – Mr. Deacon Riggs.

While Kacie had spent the night making out with Deacon, Layla spent the night babysitting and Envy spent most of her evening with her head in a novel.

After reading several chapters, Envy started craving something salty. She laid the book aside and went to the kitchen pantry in search of a snack. Finding a package of potato chips and a bottle of fitness water, she returned to the den to finish reading. Her mind transferred thoughts from the novel to Kacie and Deacon. *I hope this one turns out to be right for her. These men are so unpredictable that it's hard to tell if they're real or not. God, you know Kacie has had more than her share of bad relationships. If you have an ounce of empathy, let this man do right by her.* Envy returned to reading, and munching her snacks. The phone rang seconds later.

Staring at the caller ID, Envy was hesitant to answer. On second thought, suppose there was something wrong. There had to be for the woman to be calling her this time of the night. After the phone rang three times, Envy relented and answered it.

"Hello, Mrs. Rawlings. How can I help you?" Envy asked drily. "What are you doing up at this time of night?"

"I'm not on a time clock. I sleep when I want to sleep, day or night. I saw a man walking away from your porch last night. It was late too, real late. Is everything okay over there?"

"Yes, ma'am, everything's fine. It was a friend." Forming her lips like a blowfish, Envy sighed into the receiver. "Mrs. Rawlings, there's no need to worry about me. I can handle myself."

Mrs. Rawlings responded like she didn't hear Envy's comments. "Late at night is too late for friends to be coming in and out of your house. 'Specially men. You don't know what can happen. Folks are crazy these days.

And respectable girls don't allow men to come visit at all times of the night. You hear me?" Chastisement dripped from her lips, through the phone receiver and landed on Envy's ear. "You're a child of God. Your body is 'spose to be a temple. How is a man going to look at you as a temple if you're allowing him to act like your house is a den of thieves?"

Inhaling and taking some seconds before answering, so as not to come off disrespectful of her elders, Envy remarked in a curt-like tone. "Advice taken, Mrs. Rawlings. Now, if you don't mind, I need to go. I'm tired, it's late, and I have a long day tomorrow."

"Okay, but I'm telling you, don't let what I'm saying fall on deaf ears. G'nite and God bless you, child." The buzzing sound in Envy's ear let her know that her meddlesome neighbor had hung up the phone.

Envy reached for her novel and her chips again only to recognize that her desire to complete the last two chapters had disappeared.

"Why can't she stay out of my business?" Envy eyed Fischer like she was expecting him to answer.

Fischer's neck crooked to the side and his ears popped up.

Envy slung the book to the other side of the room. "Uhhh," she seethed. She jerked her head up toward the ceiling. "Thanks a lot," she said angrily. She jerked back the throw and let it fall to the floor too. "Leave me alone. Just leave me alone, won't you," she said again out loud.

This time sleep evaded Envy and thoughts of Mrs. Rawlings and her holier-than-thou preaching infuriated Envy to the point that she tossed and turned most of the night. When she caught a glimpse of light peering through her plantation shades, she welcomed the daylight. Somehow, the daylight helped to keep her mind away from the demon thoughts that tormented her.

5

"Beauty lies in the specific looks of a person, rather than the object, because different people feel beauty in different things." Vally

The following Saturday morning, the skies were clear and the weather was a perfect 64 degrees. Envy took a bath and hoped that her sleepless night wouldn't catch up with her today. There was far too much for her to do. Saturday was her only free day, and already a busy day for her with errands to run, cleaning house, and today she was determined to visit her mother. She thought that she'd visit her mother first and then afterward she would take care of her errands.

Envy drove along Holmes Road until she arrived in the county where Nikkei lived. It was at least a thirty to forty-minute drive from where Envy lived. She pulled up in Nikkei's driveway, exhaled, and prepared herself to meet the horrors of her baby sister. Envy rang the doorbell and Nikkei answered promptly. Without so much as a hello or good morning, Nikkei started her usual banter with Kacie.

"I don't know what kind of daughter you call yourself. You haven't been over here to check on Momma in weeks, and I can just about count the times you've called."

Envy waved her off with her hand and walked inside the house. She took it upon herself to walk through the house until she found her mother in the family room. "I'm sick of you, Nikkei. You don't run me and you don't tell me when to come and when to go. By the looks of it, Momma is doing just fine, so what's all the hassle?"

Envy flung her hands in the air, flipped around, and placed her backside to her sister. Storming off, she

walked over to the recliner where her mother sat in front
of the picture window. "Momma, how are you doing?"

Her mother slowly turned around and looked at her
daughter. "Hi, sweetheart. Your momma's just fine," she
spoke in a low, weakened voice. "What are you doing
back over here so quick? I just saw you yesterday." Her
mind was confused about the passage of time.

"I came to check on you, Momma."

"You're such a good daughter, Envy. Where's that
husband of yours?" she asked in a cloud of confusion.

"Mother, I'm not married, remember? Nikkei is the
one with the wonderful husband and the oh-so-perfect
family." Envy turned her head and met her sister's
sizzling gaze before Nikkei did a superhero turn and
stormed out of her sister's sight.

"Oh, that's right. I'm so glad to see you, precious.
You're still as pretty as can be. I know everybody is
jealous of you. They're jealous just like they used to be of
me. That's why I named you Envy. My sweet, sweet,
beautiful Envy." Her mother's mouth turned upwards
until a smile formed on her face. She reached up and
pulled Envy closer to her. "Even your sister is envious
'cause you're so beautiful," the woman whispered real
low in Envy's ear.

Envy smiled in return and hugged her mother.
Sometimes Envy's mother could be so sweet and other
times when Envy visited, her mother was mean as the
devil's sister.

Nikkei wore a smirk on her face as she listened and
watched. Envy turned again and rolled her eyes at her
sister.

"Envy, honey. Where is Charles? Is he home yet?"
Envy's mother leaned forward and looked past her
daughter out into the open living room. Her eyes scanned
the perimeter of the living area, searching for Charles.

"Momma, Daddy doesn't live here. He's been gone for years. Remember?"

"Heavens, no. Charles isn't gone. Gone where?" her mother screamed.

Nikkei came bolting back into the living room. "What did you say to make her upset?" Nikkei shoved her sister aside and her voice rang out in full rage at Envy.

"Where is my husband? Where is Charles?" Their mother grabbed hold of Nikkei's wrist and held on for dear life, almost causing Nikkei to fall to her knees.

"Mother, calm down. Daddy will be back soon." Nikkei lightly rubbed the top of her mother's thinning, graying head of hair. She hugged her against her waist until their mother's tears settled. Looking over to the side, she spotted tears in Envy's eyes too. "No need for you to cry. You've always been the one to wreak havoc in this family. Why don't you go? I'm going to take Mother to her room and give her some medicine that will help calm her down and let her rest."

"Momma," Envy moved in front of her sister. "I'll be back soon, you hear me? I love you, Ma." She kissed her mother on the forehead and wiped away a tear that was about to fall from her mother's vacant eyes. Envy turned around and walked away.

Nikkei's husband and kids walked into the house just as Envy was getting ready to leave.

"Hi, Envy. You leaving already?" Nikkei's husband, T'juan, asked.

"Yeah, I'm leaving. Nikkei is about to put Momma to bed." Envy looked down and acknowledged her niece and nephew. "Hello, you two."

"Hi, Auntie." The little girl and boy hugged Envy one after another. "Can't you stay?" One of them asked.

"I wish I could, but Auntie has somewhere else to be. Next time I'll stay longer." Envy reached inside her purse and pulled out two five-dollar bills. "Here's a little something for each of you. Buy yourself something from the candy lady."

"Thanks, Auntie." They grabbed the money and ran past Envy and into the house.

"Looks like you and my wife had another round, huh?"

"How could you tell?"

"Because your eyeglasses are about to fall off your face, tears are in your eyes and your cheeks are red as strawberries. I have to say that's a sign." He smiled slightly.

"Something like that," Envy remarked. "She has a way of working my last nerve. Anyway, I'm outta here."

"She doesn't mean any harm, Envy. It's hard for her to see her mother's health deteriorating right in front of her face." He patted Envy's shoulder and then hugged her. "Believe me."

"Sure. Look, I've got to get going, T'juan. I'll see you the next time." Envy waltzed past her brother-in-law and out to her car.

Envy got inside her car and drove away toward the open-air mall in Southaven. She hit the speed dial button on her phone and called Layla. She somehow found it easier to talk to Layla than Kacie. Maybe it was because Kacie had so much daddy drama and was always into herself. Layla's phone rang several times but there was no answer. Layla's voice mall popped on.

"Layla, call me," Envy said without leaving her name. "Where could she be? She can't drive."

***

"Who could this be? Did Kacie forget some of the children's things? Layla spoke out loud while looking around at the same time she headed to the front door from her bedroom. It sure bet not be Mike, 'cause I'm not letting him in." The phone started ringing but Layla didn't bother going back to her bedroom to answer it. She could always call whoever it was back.

Layla went to the door, pulled the crescent curtain slightly back, and viewed the stranger on the other side. Like she was in slow motion, Layla perused the handsome man in the postal uniform. He had a package the size of a shoe box in his hand and several pieces of mail piled on top. His bearded face was finely sculptured like he'd just left the barbershop. The uniform pants showed off a pair of bodybuilder-shaped legs with bulging muscles. Biceps and triceps tried to escape from underneath his shirt. It was the beginning of fall but Layla didn't question his attire; she indulged in it.

"Uh, yes, may I help you?" Layla refused to open the door. He must have the wrong apartment because she wasn't expecting a package.

"Yes, ma'am. I have a package for Layla Hobbs," he said through the closed door.

The postman's voice was strong and rang with an air of calming confidence. Layla's stare stopped at the postman's set of thin lips and from behind them a set of straight even teeth topped off a perfect specimen of a man.

Layla opened the door slowly. "I'm…I'm Layla Hobbs."

He appeared to look at Layla until she began to twitch uncomfortably. Until he smiled. "Mrs. Hobbs, I need you to sign here." He passed an electronic device to her with an electronic pen attached.

Moving like she was in a state of distress, Layla signed for the package.

"Here you go." He offered the package to her.

"Thank you."

"You're welcome." His smile deepened. "Have a great day."

"You do the same." Layla turned, nervously closed the door, and then eased the curtain back one more time to catch another glimpse of the attractive-looking postman. "Mercy, mercy, me," Layla hummed. The doorbell chimed again just as she was about to open the package.

Layla hurried back to the door and pulled the curtain back. Her heart raced wildly when she saw it was him again. "What could he want?"

"Sorry to disturb you again, Mrs. Hobbs."

"Miss. Miss Hobbs," Layla corrected him.

"I forgot that there were two packages for you instead of one. Sorry about that."

"Oh, that's okay. You didn't disturb me. Thanks for bringing it back."

"My pleasure." He turned and walked away for the second time.

Layla wasn't sure, but she thought she heard him say in an almost inaudible tone, 'My pleasure indeed'. She shook her head and convinced herself that he didn't say anything else at all. Why would he?

She carried the two packages to the den and sat on the sofa to open them. They were from her brother. She loved her family dearly. Her older brother and sister were always thinking of her in some way. Her parents were just as kind. They would do whatever they could for Layla. But Layla rarely asked them to run her around because she didn't think it was fair to her mother and father. If she had listened all of those years ago, she could have been driving. But being involved in a pretty bad fender bender when she was in the car with her then teenage brother had never quite left Layla's memory.

Since that happened, she had no desire to learn how to drive at all.

The first package held a beautiful set of bath towels. The feel of them told her that they were quite expensive. The second package was a priority letter. Layla opened it and found a note from her brother reminding her how special she was to him and how grateful he was that she was his sister. Layla started to cry. Her eyes overflowed with more tears when she saw that her brother had also sent her $350. The phone rang and disturbed her one-member party.

"Hello."

"Hey, there. Where have you been? I just called a few minutes ago."

Layla was so overjoyed that she told Envy everything about her day so far. "You are not going to tell me that God isn't good. He is always right on time. I was down to my last dime and look what God did. First, he had Kacie bring her kids over for me to babysit. That was money. Then Lee sent me three hundred and fifty dollars."

Envy screamed into the phone. "I am so happy for you. Your family is always thinking about you. That is a blessing."

"Yep, it is. What's up with you? This is your second time calling in less than an hour."

"Oh, not much. I wanted to see if you needed to get out and run some errands today. I'm already out and about, so I was going to pick you up and we could go together if you need to get some things?" offered Envy.

"Sure. I do need to pick up a few things. Are you far from here?" asked Layla.

"No, about fifteen minutes."

"Well, you can head in this direction. I'm going to put on some clothes. I should be ready by the time you get here," answered Layla.

"I'm on my way. See ya." Envy hung up the phone and smiled. She was always glad to hear Layla was happy. What a family. They were closer than a glove in hand. Her mind shifted to her and Nikkei. They had never been close, even when they were small kids. It always seemed like they were trying to outdo one another. Envy was merely one year older than Nikkei, but it was no secret that Envy had gone from being her mother's favorite at an early age to Nikkei being smothered in love and affection. Then again, Nikkei wasn't exactly beautiful as Envy. She took after, God knows who. From what Envy heard from some of her friends when she was a teenager, her mother was a rolling stone. Envy never believed it, but the older Nikkei became, the less she looked like their mother or her handsome, debonair looking father Charles.

Envy arrived at Layla's house and blew the horn. She sat in the car for about seven minutes before Layla came out.

"I'm sorry to keep you waiting," apologized Layla.

"No problem. I was out here thinking. I didn't even think about the time or how long I'd been out here."

"Are you okay?" asked Layla.

"Sure. Why do you ask that?"

"Because on the phone you were talking about how close me and my family are. But you didn't even notice I was late coming out. Anybody who knows you knows how much it irks you to wait for anything or anybody." Layla focused on Envy's face.

"Naw, for real. Everything's fine." Envy turned her head toward Layla and said, "You ready to get your shop on?" and smiled.

"You got that right," was Layla's response.

Envy prepared to back up and turn in the direction of the exit when Layla hollered.

"Hold up?" she yelled to Envy. "You almost ran over Mike. Look at him, girl," Layla said as she turned her head to see him running toward Envy's car.

"Wait, hold up, Layla," they both heard him screaming. "Layla," he cursed, " I said, wait a minute. Stop," he yelled even louder.

"What is wrong with that fool?" Envy asked. "Girl, he's running after my car. Is he insane?"

"I don't know. I try my best to avoid him. I don't talk to him anymore. He's crazy." Layla said and tried to look over her shoulder but without success.

"Hey, Layla, wait up. Wait up for just a second," he yelled again. "Layla," followed by another stream of expletives. "I said, wait!" he continued to yell.

Envy slowed down. "Do you want me to stop?" she asked.

Layla paused. "No, go on. Forget him."

Envy was glad to hear Layla tell her not to stop. The two women sped out the exit gate and to the mall they went. They spent most of the day together window shopping, and they even picked up a few things.

"Poor old Mike," Envy said sarcastically while they perused the mall. "Do you think he's still out in front of your apartment yelling?" She laughed.

"If he is, I'll be sure to go in the house and call for a strait jacket for that fool. I don't know how I get mixed up with sorry men like him."

"Come on, we're not going to let him ruin our day. Do you want to go to Ryan's and eat? My treat," offered Envy. She felt like doing something to make someone else happy. What better person than Layla?

"Yeah, you know I love Ryan's. They're just getting so expensive."

"Well, today, you don't have to worry about that." Envy started the car and followed the stream of exiting cars out of the mall parking garage.

They went to the Ryan's off Kirby Parkway.

"I'm glad we came to this one instead of the one in Southaven," remarked Envy. "This one is never as crowded as that other one."

"I've only been to this one maybe twice. Me, Momma, and Daddy came here when I went to the doctor with them. It was on a weekday and they weren't crowded then either," Layla said.

"Two please," Envy told the cashier when they made it to the front.

The ladies filled their plates and found a booth next to a window. The weather outside was getting cooler as the early signs of fall approached.

"They have some of the best chicken there is."

"Girl, you just like chicken. That's all." Envy giggled and placed a forkful of green beans in her mouth.

"I didn't tell you about the postman that came to the house yesterday, did I?"

"No, you didn't. What happened?"

Layla proceeded to share with Kacie her encounter with the postman.

"Ooh, wee, wish I could have been a fly on the wall," Envy teased. "I bet you wish he'd deliver some more packages."

"You got that right." Layla tapped Envy's hand, laughed, and placed a heaping of Mac' n cheese in her mouth.

"I sure would like to see him," Envy remarked after Layla had talked about him during the entire course of their meal. "He definitely left an impression on you."

"Yeah, but too bad it's not likely that I'll see him again. He's one of those special delivery carriers, you know."

"Yeah, but there's a solution to that." Envy's brows went up in the air and a smile of mischief formed on her face.

"What do you mean?" inquired Layla, looking clueless.

"I mean, tell your brother or your sister to send you another package. It doesn't have to be much. Just send you a package and see if he'll be the one to deliver it."

"Ummm, you might have something there." Next, Layla shook her head from side to side. "Naw, on second thought, I'd better not do that. I'll be wasting my time anyway. A man as fine as he is wouldn't give me the time of day."

"Will you stop it already?"

"Stop what? Telling the truth?" Layla shot back.

"No, stop feeling sorry for yourself. You act like you're the only big girl in the world. All of that feeling sorry for yourself and thinking that the only man you can get is a bum like Mike, needs to stop. I get sick of hearing it. If you don't like yourself, do something about it."

Layla remained quiet and took a light sip of her diet soda. "Come on, let's go."

"I'm not through eating," Envy said. "Ugh, wait a minute. You sure know how to ruin a good day." Envy stopped eating and threw her napkin on the table.

The otherwise quiet drive home to Layla's apartment was nicely interrupted by a Kirk Franklin song on the radio and another song followed by Marvin Sapp.

Layla sang some of the words. "They're jamming on Hallelujah 95.7 tonight," Layla spoke up.

"Yeah, they are," Envy answered less enthusiastically. She pulled up in front of Layla's apartment. They sat in the car for a couple of minutes.

"I'll pick you up in the morning around the same time I always do, ten o'clock."

"Oh, I'm glad you mentioned that. The youth choir is going to sing tomorrow at church. So I'm going to church with Momma and Daddy since I never have a chance to worship with them that often. So since I don't have to sing, I thought I'd hang out with them. They're going to pick me up in the morning for Sunday School, which should be about eight-thirty. I probably won't be back until five or six because we're going to have dinner after that."

"Okay, then I'll talk to you tomorrow. Have a good time."

Layla opened the door, got out of the car, and then opened the back door to retrieve her packages.

"Can you make it?" Envy asked.

"Yeah, I've got 'em. I'll talk to you tomorrow. Goodnight and be careful, Envy."

"I will." Envy waited until Layla made it to her front door before she drove off. Turning outside of the driveway and pulling onto the street, Envy stopped at the red light. She looked around when she heard what sounded like firecrackers popping one after another. "Bad tail kids. Their parents need to have 'em in the house this time of night. There's no reason to have firecrackers in the middle of September." Envy shook her head in disgust and drove off toward home as soon as the light turned green.

Layla barely had time to step inside her apartment, when Mike ran up behind her. She was startled out of her wits.

"What is wrong with you?" She grabbed hold of her heart. "Why would you come up on me like that, fool?" she said furiously. "And it's night time too. So get on away from here. You are not coming inside my apartment. Not tonight and not ever."

"Shut up. You don't tell me what to do," he yelled back.

"I'm not going to shut up until you leave here. I told you, Mike. Leave me alone. I don't want anything to do with your useless, good-for-nothing tail. You don't mean me any good and anyone who has the nerve to call me terrible names the way you do doesn't have a place anywhere in my life," Layla screamed at him this time. "And look at you. You're pathetic. A pathetic loser. I don't know why I didn't see you for who you were in the first place."

Mike eased up closer and Layla noticed that his eyes appeared glassy looking like he had been using drugs, and she smelled a strong odor of liquor on his breath. She started feeling somewhat uneasy when she saw him like this. She proceeded to take a step inside and turned to close the door, but Mike used his hand to stop her from closing it up all the way.

For the first time since meeting Mike, she had become extremely frightened. Frightened by what Mike was planning, she tried to remain calm. "Look, get your hands off of my door and get away from here."

"You don't tell me what to do, you fat wench." He reached out for her hand and locked onto her wrist. Her packages dropped to the floor. "You think you're someone who can just brush me off like I'm nothing. Have you looked at yourself in the mirror lately? You're a buffalo." He started laughing.

She tried to twist out of his grip but it was of no use. "If I'm such a buffalo, then why are you trying to force yourself in the house with this buffalo? I'm warning you, turn me loose and get away from me and get away from my house. I should have known you were psychotic as they come. And maybe I am fat, but you're sorry, Mike. You're a sorry excuse for a man," Layla hollered back. That's when she saw the flowing silver piece in his hands as he raised it out of nowhere.

"Layla pushed the door even harder with the one free hand. "Help," she cried and looked around outside but there was no one outside to hear her. She pushed harder against the door, but still with one hand and now his foot inside the door, Layla was no match for Mike's brute strength. She backed up in the house.

"What are you doing with that gun? You're really crazy. Mike, get away from here and go home and sleep off that high you're on," she said in a calmer voice. She hoped if she started to talk more calmly that she could convince him to leave and she could call the police.

"I'm not going anywhere but inside the house with you. You're going to give me everything that's due to me," he snarled with slob coming from his mouth.

He barged inside and Layla finally broke free from his grasp and took off running toward the back of the apartment. "Pop." Layla went into slow motion. Her body jerked and she turned and stared at Mike.

Pop, Pop, Pop.

Her body fell limp in the middle of the floor between the den and the hallway.

Mike stood still for a second with the gun still pointed at Layla like he was daring her to move. She didn't. He kicked her. No movement or sign of life from Layla.

Mike turned away and saw Layla's purse. He started rummaging through it. He found the money Layla's brother had sent her earlier that day. He started slinging her belongings all over the house like a madman. He stepped over her still body and went into her bedroom.

Pulling out all of her drawers, he searched until he found a couple of pieces of jewelry that might be worth something and some more money, not more than fifty bucks. He stepped back over Layla's body and looked at her one more time before he rushed out of the house and into the night where he disappeared.

6

"Only in relation to our imagination can things be called beautiful or ugly, well-ordered or confused." Spinoza

Sunday morning, the youth choir sang like there would be no tomorrow. Song after song roused the congregation to a shout. People stood on their feet and gave praises to God. The church was on fire, as the pastor called every time he walked in and saw the members and choir in such an uproar.

Pastor Betts walked up to the pulpit and joined in singing with the choir and the congregation. "Let's sing praises to God. Let's thank Him for all of his goodness, grace, and mercy." When they finished singing, he instructed the congregation to turn to the scripture for the morning. Envy and Kacie followed his instructions.

Today I'm going to be talking about, "You Can't Make Yourself Look Good Before God." Envy flipped her Bible to Romans chapter eight.

Of short stature with a giant spirit, Pastor Betts preached with the power of an anointed man of God. "Making yourself feel bad for what you do wrong or have done wrong is not going to make you look good before God. It will only increase your pain and heartache. It's a form of self-righteousness. God promises if we confess our sins, then He is faithful and just and will forgive us of our sins. But when we go around holding onto our sins, wearing them on our hearts and in our minds like a hero's battle scars, then we're doing nothing but practicing a form of self-righteous indignation. No amount of pain that you hold onto for what you've done wrong will justify that wrong."

Kacie barely listened to the sermon after she didn't see Deacon. Her eyes searched around the congregation for him. No Deacon. "I wonder where he is?" she leaned over and whispered to Envy.

"Probably in the back somewhere. I don't know." Her reply was sporadic. Trying to listen to Pastor Betts and Kacie was not going to work. "Shhh, listen. Worry about Deacon after church."

Envy concentrated back on Pastor Betts. She felt the stab of conviction piercing her spirit with each word he spoke. It looked like he was looking directly at her, talking to her and her only.

"Why do some people go around holding onto self-condemning thoughts and sins when it says in the word of God, 'If God is for us, who can be against us? Who is he that condemns? Christ Jesus, who died—more than that, who was raised to life—is at the right hand of God and is also interceding for us.'"

Envy's mind yielded to a thousand thoughts of the wrongs she'd committed. When church ended, she wanted so badly to go up for prayer. Her feet were heavy as steel beams. She couldn't move from the pew.

Like they did every Sunday after church, they went to the fellowship hall for refreshments.

"I can't believe Deacon isn't here." Concern moved past Kacie's lips. "I talked to him last night and he said he would be here this morning. And where is Layla? I don't see her around anywhere either."

"Maybe he woke up late and just didn't feel like coming today. You know how that goes," Envy suggested. "And Layla went to church with her parents today."

"But he would have told me that he wasn't coming," countered Kacie.

"Okay, just call him then," Envy told her as two of Kacie's kids ran up and positioned themselves beside her with molly faces and hands.

"Go get some napkins and clean y'all hands." Kacie angrily ordered the kids between clenched teeth.

"Don't get mad at the children," Envy told her.

Kacie gave Envy a mean look. "I'm leaving. I'll talk to you later." Kacie whisked away. Envy watched with a frown on her face as Kacie grabbed hold of Kevin and Keith while screaming at Kali and Kassandra. She shoved Keshena into Kevin's arms and yanked Kendra by the hand before she stormed out of the fellowship hall.

Oh, well. There's going to be a high price to pay today in the Mayweather household. Those kids are going to catch it if she can't get a hold of Deacon," Envy thought. Envy went to her car. On her way out of the church lot, she pulled her cell phone from her small clutch purse. and dialed Layla's number to see if she had made it home from church with her parents. No answer except for Layla's answering machine. Envy left a message. "Call me when you get home, girl. Church was great. The youth choir showed out. Bye now." Envy hung up the phone and proceeded in the direction of home.

Kacie couldn't wait to get home from church and in the house. As soon as she pulled into her garage, she jumped out of the car.

"Get inside, get your clothes off, and go to your rooms," she yelled at the kids. "Kassandra, change Keshena's diaper. I'll call you when dinner is ready," she barked orders while she entered the house through the garage. The kids hurried inside and dashed to the back of the house to carry out their mother's stern orders while Kacie called Deacon and got his voicemail. She left him a worried message.

"Deacon, where are you? You weren't at church. Are you all right? Call me. Love you, bye." Anxiety loomed in her voice when she couldn't reach him. Becoming frustrated, she strode up the hallway and into the kitchen to start preparing dinner. Baked chicken with mushroom sauce, sweet peas, and dinner rolls. For dessert, she made a pan of brownies.

Kacie called the kids to the kitchen to eat but she barely ate a drop of the food she prepared. Deacon still had not called. She was frantic with worry. She didn't know if something had happened to him. Maybe he had been in an accident. She realized that she didn't even know where Deacon lived, so she couldn't go to check on him. Her head began to pound and the smell of the food she'd just fixed started to make her sick to her stomach. So sick that she rushed to the bathroom to throw up the charcoal lining in her stomach.

She dialed Deacon's cell phone at least twelve times for the next two hours before she gave up and took a hot bath. She left the kids orders to clean the kitchen, take their baths and get to bed before she disappeared behind the closed door to her bedroom.

Envy kicked off her pumps as soon as she stepped inside her apartment from church, while Fischer jumped up and down begging for attention. "Calm down, boy. Momma's here, Momma's here," she said twice and kissed him on the top of his head. She pulled off the rest of her Sunday attire and left it in the living room draped over the sofa. Envy focused her attention back toward Fischer who was following her every move with his thick tale swishing back and forth.

"Fischer, come on, boy. Let's go for a walk." Fischer jumped up and turned around and around like he was trying to keep up with his wagging tail. Envy went to the front door, removed Fischer's leash off the hanger, placed it around his neck, and they went outside.

Envy's hand flew up to her forehead when she spied Mrs. Rawlings in the front yard, checking out her small

garden. It was too late for Envy to turn around, plus
Fischer wouldn't let her anyway.

"Good afternoon, Mrs. Rawlings."

"Hello, Envy. Hi, Fischer." Fischer took the lead and
carried Envy to where Mrs. Rawlings was stooped over,
tending hiathas. She paused long enough to hug Fischer.

"We're going on our afternoon walk." Envy
explained though Mrs. Rawlings had not asked.

"How was church?" asked Mrs. Rawlings who stood
upright and wiped her hands on her garden apron.

"Good. Very good," answered Envy with a slight
smile.

"Glad to hear that. I don't go as often as I used to.
Church, I mean. But I got the word right here." Mrs.
Rawlings laid her hand against her heart. "I've been
going to church since way before you were ever born,
child. I know the Lord. Me and Him have a deep,
personal relationship. You know that?"

"Yes, ma'am." Envy allowed Fischer's tug to pull her
away from Mrs. Rawlings. Her neighbor's past was not
something she cared to hear about this afternoon. "I'll
talk to you later. Fischer's ready to relieve himself,"
Envy said and followed Fischer.

"Yeah, you go on," said Mrs. Rawlings. But let me
ask you one thing before you leave."

Here it comes, Envy thought. "Yes?"

Mrs. Rawlings had one hand on her thin hip and the
other hand held a small garden tool. "You got company
coming this evening?"

Envy pierced her lips. "No, ma'am. Why do you
ask?"

"You know why. Look here, girl. Don't try to
exchange one sin for another. It ain't right. Listen to me,
child. You can't run up in church and then come away
with the same attitude. You can't run from God and you

can't hide from your past. He already knows all about you."

Ignoring her words, Envy tugged lightly on Fischer's leash. "We'll be back shortly."

"Have a good walk," Mrs. Rawlings replied.

Envy mumbled under her breath and left. Fischer sniffed in the bushes and barked at every cat he saw like he was king of the jungle. "Fischer, that woman needs some children of her own or a husband or something. Maybe then she'll stop trying to stay up in my business. She must think she's clairvoyant or something. But she doesn't know a thing about me. Ooooh, she makes me so darn mad." Envy seethed. Fischer barked.

Envy and Fischer traveled their usual path through the neighborhood, out to the main highway where they turned left and walked half a mile until they turned left again off Elvis Presley Boulevard and onto Whitaker. Fischer did his usual barking and sniffing as they walked through the neighborhood and forty-five minutes later, they were back at their humble abode. Much to Envy's relief, when they returned from their walk, Mrs. Rawlings and her car were gone. "Fischer, we can go in the house in peace." Envy released a sigh of satisfaction.

7

"It's hard to look in the mirror these days when everyone else is everything you'd rather be." Unknown

"I'm going to put Momma in a nursing home."

"May I ask when you came to this decision?" Envy asked her sister while she paced in her second-story office overlooking the Mighty Mississippi. Envy detected the anger in her sister's voice through the phone, but then again, Nikkei always had an attitude whether they were in person or on the telephone.

"When me and T'juan had to scour the neighborhood for almost four hours looking for her. She left out of the back door while I was upstairs cleaning the house. She's never tried to unlock the deadbolt on any of the doors before. But she did today. That means she's getting worse, and I will not have her wandering around in this city for God knows who to attack her or for her to get hurt out there."

"Is she all right?" Envy's eyebrows drew together.

"Yes. We found her near the main intersection. She said she was going to meet Charles. I tell you, Envy, I can't do this anymore. Daddy's been out of her life since we were kids. Why she's all of a sudden talking and asking about him is beyond me. And for God's sake, to add flame to the fire, he has his own life with somebody else. I don't understand. But the stress is unbearable, and though T'juan is a good husband, I know it's putting a strain on our marriage."

"Maybe you're making the right decision by putting her in a home. I hate to say that I agree with you, but...hold on a minute, Nikkei. I have another call coming in. Don't hang up."

When she returned to the phone, Nikkei immediately blasted into Envy.

"Look, if you think that for some reason I was calling to get your approval, you're wrong. I was just letting you know my decision. I've taken care of Momma all this time without your help. Unless you want to call your sporadic penny donations, help."

Envy was fuming. "Look, I'm sick of you and your cynicism, Nikkei. If it wasn't for my money," Envy added emphasis, then you wouldn't be able to provide for Momma in the manner you have. You always have to call me with a bunch of attitude. You and Momma have always been just alike. Jealous and, yes, envious of me. How crazy is that? The woman who named me Envy grew to be angry and envious of me, her own flesh and blood."

"Envious? Of you? Girl, you must be sitting on stupid or something. You have nothing I want. As for Momma, she always did the best she could for you and for me. But you worshipped the ground our no-good daddy walked on. You think your money can make up for you not spending time with Momma? You think it can make up for all the times I've had to deal with her asking about you and your whereabouts when you were nowhere to be found?" Nikkei's voice rose higher and higher over the phone.

"First, let's get something straight. It's my daddy for sure," taunted Envy. "As for you, it's Momma's baby, Daddy's maybe," she scoffed. "You know what. I don't have time for your tantrums, Nikkei. Not today, not tomorrow, not ever. The good thing about putting Momma in a nursing home will be that I won't have to come to see her at your so-called perfect little castle. Let me know where she's going to be and how much it's going to cost. I'm sure you won't turn down my checks. You never have. Now, I have a meeting to attend. Goodbye." Envy pushed the button on the multi-line phone. She inhaled and exhaled, then smoothed out the wrinkles of her cadmium orange linen skirt, before she strolled out of her office to the manager's meeting.

***

The nightmare haunted Envy's sleep again. What could it be?

Terrified and uncertain about what had just transpired, the young girl throws up her blood-soaked hands against her face and screams. Easing up from the toilet, in horror she looks down at the strange object in the toilet. Surely, this couldn't have come out of me. No, God. Not here, not now. Looking at the ceramic walls of the stall, a sense of claustrophobia sets in, and fear consumed her very being. She tried with all of her might to gather her senses, and pausing, waits seconds to see if there is anyone else in the bathroom with her. She is alone. Hurriedly, she runs out of the stall, goes and locks the main door to the bathroom, and returns to the sink to clean up the bathroom stall, her clothes, and her body. Nausea fills the pit of her belly and saliva forms in her mouth. Clenching her belly, she looks around to make sure she's removed all signs of the bloody mess. Unable to look at the thing in the toilet, she rushes outside, down the side stairways, so no one can see her.

For the remainder of the night, she hides away in her bedroom. Tears like rain pellets pour from her face and soak her pillow. Sleep escapes her and she is tormented by the thought of what she has done. How could she leave her child in a toilet to die? How could she be so evil? She had planned on telling her mother about her being pregnant. She had it all worked out. She would give the baby up for adoption because she had waited too late for an abortion. Week after week, she had hoped and prayed that Stanton, the baby's daddy would change his mind, and tell her that he loved her and wanted to spend the rest of his life with her and the child they had made in love. But it wasn't the case.

Stanton was far older than her, and he didn't want anything to interfere with his college studies. When she told him she was pregnant, he blew up. She'd never seen him act this way. He cursed her and accused her of trying to trap him. But it wasn't true. She was fifteen and in love with him. She would never do anything to hurt him. But her words fell on deaf ears because Stanton told her he wanted nothing else to do with her. He warned her not to tell anyone that she was carrying his baby. How could such a smart, intelligent, kind-hearted man who loved dogs and cats and x-box games, and who smiled at babies whenever he saw them on the street; who was obsessed with his major in nuclear physics, who confessed his undying love for her, end up being someone she never knew at all? The way things turned out, he didn't have to worry about anybody finding out he had gotten her pregnant. The baby was dead and left in a toilet.

A mere child herself, she lay on her bed, frightened that any minute police would come storming inside her room, lead her out in handcuffs with her face plastered on every TV screen in America, revealing how terrible a person she was to leave her newborn child alone, in a school toilet to die. God would never forgive her. No one ever would. She would never forgive herself. Anything and everything that happened to her when people found out what she'd done would be deserving. She was a cruel, mean, wicked, wicked girl who had allowed her baby to die.

Envy bolted awake crying with her pillow over her head and her hands over her ears.

This was the first time in almost two years that she'd been plagued by night terrors as bad as this. She sat up on the sofa where she'd taken a nap. Fischer was lying on the navy-patched rug in front of the flat screen. She sat still, alone and confused. The phone rang and she made herself get up and walk over to the end table to pick it up.

"Hello. Oh, no, please no," Envy screamed in the phone. "When did this happen? Is she going to be all right? Okay, I'm on my way." Envy hung up the phone, and dashed into her bedroom. Inside her closet, she hastily pulled a pair of jeans and a light sweater shirt from the hangers and hurriedly put them on. She stepped into a pair of loafers, rushed to the front of the house, and grabbed her purse and keys. Fischer sat close by, with a look of bewilderment on his handsome dog face. Envy said nothing. She rushed out of the house and headed in the direction of the Regional Medical Center. On her way to the hospital, she managed to hit the key that connected her to Kacie's phone.

"Hello," answered Kacie.

"Kacie, did you hear about Layla?" she frantically asked.

"What about Layla? What happened?"

"She's been shot. Oh, my God. Kacie, Layla's been shot. I'm on my way to the Regional Med Trauma Center. She's in critical condition. Her mother called. She said they arrested Mike."

"But when? I thought she went to church with her parents today?"

"I don't know the details. But I do know she never made it to church. Anyway, I know it was sometime before church because her momma said they went to pick her up, and that's when they found her, sprawled in the front room just inside the door."

"I'll meet there as soon as I can. Bye," Kacie said and hung up the phone.

Tears flowed from Envy's eyes. "God, please let her be okay. Please, let her make it, dear Lord," Envy pleaded. "Please, please, please," she cried. She drove close to 90 miles on the expressway until she got off on the Union West exit leading to the Med. She parked and ran to the hospital's trauma unit.

When she arrived, Envy saw Mr. and Mrs. Hobbs and Layla's sister, Becky with her husband. Mrs. Hobbs stood and walked toward Envy with fresh tears pouring from her eyes. Envy nodded to everyone else, "How is she now," Envy asked.

"She's in surgery. She has damage to her internal organs and some internal bleeding. She's in bad shape, I'm afraid," Layla's mother cried.

"Oh, no," Envy cried again. Mr. Hobbs and Layla's sister walked over to comfort her. Mr. Hobbs led her to a seat in the trauma area while they remained standing like they were afraid if they sat down they would miss something.

"Honey, we have to stay in prayer. God is in control," he told Envy.

Envy raised her head and was met with a tissue from Becky. "Becky, when did you get in town? Layla didn't say you were here when I talked to her last night."

"She didn't know that I had already planned on coming down and staying a few days while my husband went on a mountain climbing adventure with some of his friends. But after this, he canceled his trip and drove me down here," Becky cried and her husband Alonzo, embraced her. "I asked Momma and Daddy not to say anything because I wanted to surprise Layla."

Becky's husband held her even closer and caressed her short, natural black hair.

Layla's father spoke. "Lee is on his way. He didn't know whether he was going to drive from Chicago or fly."

"Yeah, but my daddy convinced him to take a plane. He wasn't in any condition to drive."

"He should be here sometime later tonight," Mrs. Hobbs added while she twisted her hands nervously.

"And you're sure Mike did this?" Envy turned her head toward Mr. Hobbs.

"Yes. We're sure." Layla's father answered angrily. "I wish I could get my hands on him. I swear, I would choke the life out of him." Mrs. Hobbs rubbed her husband's shoulders back and forth. "Why would he do our baby girl like this? Why? I never trusted him the couple of times I saw him, but," he wiped heavy tears from his eyes while Mrs. Hobbs cried along with him and held onto his arm. "The first time we saw him," Mr. Hobbs said, "we knew he was no good for our Layla. His spirit didn't sit well with us, did it, honey?" he asked and looked down into the tear-streaked face of his wife.

Mrs. Hobbs nodded. She was too distraught to answer.

"I'm so sorry," Envy told the family.

"Come on, Daddy and Momma, sit down," Becky told them. They didn't hesitate to follow her orders and sadly they sat down next to each other. Mr. Hobbs embraced his wife and tears flowed from her eyes onto his starched white shirt. They all were still dressed in their Sunday best.

Envy started talking about the last time she and Layla had been together. "When I picked up Layla yesterday afternoon, we saw Mike running and chasing after my car. He kept calling her name and begged me to stop the car, but Layla told me to keep going. She was tired of him, she said. I remembered she leaned out the window and screamed for him to leave her alone and get out of her life. She made me speed up until he couldn't keep up with the car. But who would have thought he would have flipped out like this? I, I just can't believe it."

"Neither can we," said Mr. Hobbs and stood again when several church members from New Grove came into the waiting room, followed by one of the associate ministers and two deacons from Broadway Church.

Next Kacie appeared and Layla's family embraced her too.

Envy glanced around. "Where are the kids?" asked Envy.

Kacie responded by rolling her eyes and waved her off. "Look, I don't want to hear your preaching right now. Let me handle my own business. Now, tell me, how is Layla?" she asked, shifting her attention away from Envy and focusing on Becky.

Mr. Hobbs didn't allow Becky to speak. He shared the story of what happened not only with Kacie but with the church people who had flooded inside the waiting room.

Kacie burst into tears. "I knew that son of a..."

"Stop it, Kacie," Envy warned her and grabbed hold of her hand.

"I'm just saying, we knew he was no good. He treated her like she was nothing. I hate him. I hate him and I hope he rots in jail."

The family shared tears and Mr. Hobbs did his best to comfort the women. The associate minister talked to the family, prayed with them, and tried to do what he could to help ease the tension.

Two and a half hours passed before the doctor came to talk to the family.

"Mr. and Mrs. Hobbs," he said. "Your daughter had some extensive injuries to her intestine and a portion of her stomach. We had to remove the damaged parts and that included removing a part of her stomach and her lower intestines. We located the bleeding and sealed it off."

"Is she going to be all right?" asked Becky.

"The next twenty-four hours are touch and go. We just have to pray that infection doesn't set up in her body. We have her on an IV of antibiotics. But, if she can fight off the infection, I believe I can safely say that she'll recover. We're going to keep her in ICU for at least 24 hours to monitor her closely. She's sedated right now. But I have to tell you, she's very lucky to be alive. She took one serious shot to the belly and another shot to her shoulder, barely missing her jugular vein."

"Oh, God," Mrs. Hobbs screamed. Becky walked over to her mother to try to calm her down.

"Thank you, doctor," Mr. Hobbs reached out and shook the doctor's hand. "Thank you, so much."

"She's in recovery right now. Only immediate relatives can see her. She needs to be protected from infection, and like I said, she's heavily sedated. Two of you should be able to see her for a few minutes when she's out of recovery. After that, I ask that you allow her to rest."

"We will," Mrs. Hobbs said and hugged the doctor before he turned and walked out of the waiting room. "God bless you, doctor."

The family managed to laugh when Lee walked in.

"Lee, thank God you made it," Mrs. Hobbs said. "I thought you were going to call so your daddy could pick you up from the airport."

"No, I got a cab here. I didn't want Daddy leaving the hospital to get me. How is she? How's my little sister?"

"Your little sister is in serious condition. She had some damage to her internal organs but they've managed to stop the internal bleeding. Now if she can ward off infection, and she doesn't worsen in the next 24 hours, then the doctor believes she might just recover from this horrible ordeal. You know your sister didn't deserve anything like this. She never did anything to hurt anybody."

"I know, Dad. But everything is going to be okay. God has already spared her life." He hugged his father and then one by one he went down the line hugging and kissing his family, Envy and Kacie.

Moments later, one of the ICU nurses came in and allowed two visitors at a time to see Layla. Mr. & Mrs. Hobbs went in to see their baby girl. God is good," Mrs. Hobbs said and raised her hands toward the sky and followed the ICU nurse."

8

*"When we stop holding onto the ugly, beauty appears-
and when we stop holding onto lies, truth appears."*
L. Marquez

Layla's recuperation miraculously came quickly.
After ten days she was discharged from the hospital.
Many church folk and Mr. and Mrs. Hobbs, called Layla
a walking, talking miracle from God.

Layla was determined to be taken to her apartment to
see where it all happened. Against her parents' wishes,
they reluctantly gave in and took her. Shreds of yellow
police tape still could be seen strewn on the lawn. Layla,
with the aid of her father and brother, walked to the front
door, and with barely a nudge, it came open. There was
blood everywhere, on the walls, the furniture, and the
floor. Layla covered her mouth with her hand and almost
stumbled backward, but Mr. Hobbs managed to break her
fall.

"Sis, come on; let's get out of here," Lee urged. "I
can't believe they haven't had this apartment cleaned by
now." He tugged her by her shoulder.

Layla didn't move. She was grateful that God had
saved her life, but seeing what she'd just seen, Layla
understood that she would never be able to go back to the
place where she almost died.

Like he could read her thoughts, Mr. Hobbs said,
"Come on, baby. Let's get out of here. We're taking you
home with us," he said.

"Yes, baby, we're going to take care of you," her
mother reassured her. Layla didn't put up a fuss. She
needed to feel safe, secure, and taken care of. Her parents
were the only ones she trusted to do that.

All the way to her parents' house, Layla cried. She
didn't know that her parents had spoken to the manager

of her apartment complex. The manager immediately told them that she had already started working on getting Layla transferred to one of their other properties, but it was Layla's decision if she wanted to move. The manager explained that the other complex was well kept, with beautiful grounds, spacious living, excellent security, and more amenities than her old apartment.

Layla was visited often by Kacie and Envy. They were good at cheering her up. Kacie even brought the kids to see Layla, which she loved. While spending the next three weeks with her parents, Lee who remained in Memphis on FMLA, along with her father and several of Layla's church members moved everything out of her apartment. Becky also remained in town to help Mrs. Hobbs take care of Layla.

Every day Layla gained more strength. She began to lose weight after having the surgery because it reduced the size of her stomach and removed some of her intestines.

"Layla, honey, when you're able to be on your own, and only if you want to, the property from your apartment said they have an apartment closer to us and it's supposed to be newer and with more security too," her mother explained.

"And it is beautiful," Becky added.

"You've seen it?" Layla asked while she sat down in the family recliner. "Where is it?" Her voice was continually becoming stronger and she was moving and walking with much more ease.

"It's on Baldwin Avenue, two streets over from us. The Baldwin Apartments. Do you know them?"

Layla's eyes flickered just a tiny bit. "Yes, they are nice. I mean, really nice. But they're also more expensive and I don't see..."

"Shh," her mother said. "Stop it. Don't you think that if God brought you back from the brink of death, he can surely provide you with a place of safety? All you have to do is say the word and when you're ready, we'll take you to your new apartment."

"Are y'all trying to get rid of me?" Layla asked and held her stomach to reduce the pain when she laughed.

"You know better than that," Becky interjected this time.

"Yeah, I know. I was just kidding. But seriously, Momma. Thank you so much," Layla looked at Becky, "and you too Becky for taking care of me. I think I'll be ready soon, just not right now." Layla looked down and sadness filled her face. "I want to wait until I see justice is done. That's why, even though it's going to be hard for me today, I have to be in court. I have to," Layla cried.

"Look, sis, you don't have anything to prove to anybody, you know. This bum has already pleaded guilty. So why not stay here and rest? We'll all be there for you," Lee said and sat down beside her on her bed.

"I hear what you're saying, Lee, but I've got to do this. I have to do it or I might not ever get on with my life. I hope you understand," she raised her head and looked at her brother with solemn, but serious eyes.

"I don't know if I do, but I respect your wishes. In that case, you better get ready. It won't be long before we have to leave," he said and grabbed Layla's hand.

Layla surprisingly was right. She felt relieved when she went to court to face Mike. She believed that this was the start of regaining the life he tried so hard to end. She was still weak, and in serious pain, but she tried to remain strong. She wanted to look at him in his eyes, and hear what he had to say, which turned out not to be much at all, except the words, "Guilty, your honor."

Layla could easily have been killed that night four and a half weeks ago. As a result of what Mike had done to her, she would never be the same. She would never be able to trust a man again. The scars that were still fresh and slowly healing reminded her of the night he barged inside her apartment and did the unthinkable. The sound in her mind of the bullets aimed directly at her made her jump.

Envy looked at Layla with a worried expression, "Layla, are you up to this? You still aren't fully healed. Why not go home and I promise to tell you everything that happened."

"No, I can't leave," she spoke softly to reduce the pain she felt every time she breathed or tried to speak.

Her parents, Lee, Becky, and Alonzo, who had driven in from Chattanooga earlier that day, were there to support Layla. Envy was in the courtroom huddling close to the family as well. One last plea to convince Layla to go home went defeated.

Mike's mother, and Mike's live-in girlfriend who had mocked Layla once, were present on the other side of the courtroom. It was at the hearing that Layla found out that Mike had a rap sheet that went back to the time he was eighteen years old. He'd been in and out of jail for everything from assault, to attempted burglary, to possession of drugs, but he had never spent more than three years in prison. The judge today wasn't lenient. Mike had far surpassed the three-strikes law. The judge sentenced him to 25 years to life in prison.

Gasps and cries spilled from the courtroom from Mike's side of the family, while *Praise God* and *Thank you, Lord* were screamed on Layla's side. But Layla remained quiet. She watched as they led Mike away in hand and leg cuffs. He looked back over his shoulder and his eyes met hers.

Mike looked back at Layla when the sheriff led him away. He spoke out, "I'm sorry, Layla. I still love you." The sheriff pushed him through the door leading to the jail.

The girlfriend jumped up and screamed all kinds of expletives at him.

Layla couldn't respond. She didn't know if it was due to fear or the fact that Mike could equate love with hurt. One thing was for certain, she was glad it was over. Then a sweet, sweet spirit passed over her. Layla stared directly back at him—she was free. Free indeed to start the new life God had granted her.

"Aren't you glad all of this is finally behind you?" Envy asked as they all walked out of the courtroom and outside into an overcast day.

"Yes, I am. It's amazing how you think you know someone, but you find out you don't know that person at all," remarked Layla.

A knot formed in the base of Envy's throat before she answered. "Yeah, it is." Envy quickly changed the subject. "I don't know if you talked to Kacie, but she had to work and couldn't get here this morning." Envy paused, "And I need to go myself. Are you going to be all right?"

"Sure, I'll be just fine. We're going to go get some lunch and then Becky and Lee are leaving. Lee is going to ride as far as Nashville with Becky and Alonzo and fly out of there to Chicago."

"Oh, that's right. Becky...Lee," Envy called out and ran toward them as they stood at the bottom of the courthouse steps waiting on Layla. Envy hugged them both. "It was good to see you all again although I wish it had been under different circumstances. Have a safe trip back, and don't worry. Kacie and I will make sure Layla is well taken care of."

They returned the hugs and goodbyes. Layla walked up beside them. "I'll talk to you later on," Envy said to everyone.

"Becky, Lee, Mom, and Dad, I love all of y'all so much. I have the best family in the world," she cried with excitement ringing in her voice. "Mom, I really want to see the new apartment, and then after that, I want to get some rest and take a pain pill. I'm hurting pretty badly right now."

"Why don't you wait, then honey?" her father strongly suggested.

"No, I want to do it while I'm out. I'll be okay," insisted Layla. When her parents took her to her new apartment, Layla's blues turned to smiles. The apartment was decorated impeccably with her favorite colors. Anyone who knew Layla knew she loved color. They used tangerine, lemon, mint, and greenery to accent the otherwise white-walled apartment. There were several live plants strategically placed throughout the apartment and nice pieces of art. From the dining room table to the bedrooms, no stone had been left unturned. Layla was so overcome that she broke down and cried like a baby. Tears flowed endlessly as her family and one of her church members who'd come over to take pictures for the church photograph ministry, couldn't stop her.

Layla mumbled incoherently, but it was finally understood that she was just overcome with sheer joy and thankfulness. Several minutes later, she blew her nose, and as more tears formed she said, "God's love is amazing. He promised he would never leave me or forsake me and he didn't." She wept. "He promised that whatever the devil meant to harm me that he would make it work for my good. And look at this." She spread her arms out and looked all around. Layla lifted her head and her hands and praised God. Her family and the church visitor couldn't keep their control either. They prayed, they sang and they cried and gave God all praise, honor, and glory.

Layla's mother told her how the church pitched in and provided many of the things needed to fill her apartment. There was not one item left to remind her of the apartment she'd left behind. The blood-splattered sofa and loveseat had been replaced with a chocolate leather sofa accented with oranges, yellows, and limes.

Layla managed to tour every inch of the house including the balcony leading from her living room.

"Baby, we'd better get ready to leave so you can get some rest," her mother told her.

"Mother, and the rest of you, hear me out. I want to stay here. I'll be fine. I've cried so much that I'm in pain. I want to lie down on my new bed," Layla smiled, "and try to sleep. I have a dose of my pain medication inside my purse." She hugged her parents and the church member once more before they left.

Layla's parents appeared quite concerned but Lee spoke up on her behalf. "Mom, Dad, remember that you're just a couple of blocks away from her. Layla has a phone already installed and turned on," Lee looked at Layla who returned his look with one of total surprise. "The security is great over here and being here a few hours might help her."

Sighing deeply, Mr. Hobbs finally gave his okay. "Layla, you have to promise to answer the phone. Me and your momma have a key and if you so much as hear a creak, I want you on the phone to security. All you have to do is put in your apartment number and they'll come running.:

"Daddy, I promise. And Mom, please don't look so worried. God has already revealed how he's looking after me or I wouldn't be sitting here right now." Layla tilted her head and smiled gingerly at her mother who relented and smiled back.

"You're right, baby. I just want you to be safe. Safe and happy," her mother said. "I'll get you a glass of water so you can take your pill while you say your goodbyes to your sister and brother."

"Yes, ma'am." Layla shed tears and embraced Becky, Lee, and her brother-in-law. "Thank y'all for everything. Be safe on the highway and Lee, please make sure you call when you get to Chicago."

"I will, li'l sis. I will." They all hugged again and Mrs. Hobbs gave Layla her pain pill and a glass of water.

"Now, get you some rest. It's been a long day. And if you want me to come back and spend the night with you, just call me, you here?" Mrs. Hobbs asked.

"Yes, I will mother. I promise. Now y'all just go. I'm ready to lie down." They kissed a final time and Layla got the set of keys from her father and made sure all doors were locked behind her, and the security alarm was on.

Like she said, Layla lay back on her new bed and sleep met her quickly. She slept for the next three hours until the phone ringing caused her to wake up. It was Envy.

"You asleep," asked Envy. "I'm so sorry; we didn't mean to wake you."

"We who?" she asked groggily.

"Me, I'm on the phone too," said Kacie.

"No, I've been asleep for a few hours. What's going on?" Layla asked and walked to the bathroom to pee.

"Do y'all feel like going out to celebrate a little tonight?" Envy asked her two friends.

"Go out where?" Kacie asked.

"My job gave me a hundred-dollar gift card that's good for dinner at Charley's or Chili's. Y'all got other plans?"

"I don't think so. I've had a long day and I'm totally tired. Layla answered groggily. "Envy, why don't you and Kacie go and celebrate for me," asked Layla.

"I guess y'all forget I have kids," Kacie pouted.

"No, I was thinking you could get that teenage girl down the street from you to watch them for a couple of hours since she's watched them before."

"Yeah, girl. Go on and call her. Y'all go and have some fun for me. But I'm just not up to it. Maybe some other time real soon," Layla added.

"Kacie, we won't be gone that long. I have to work in the morning. I just wanted to do something to celebrate what happened with Mike in court, plus your new apartment, and just for everything God has brought you through, Layla. We can wait until another time if y'all want to. It's up to you two."

"Which is why I want y'all to go on and go tonight," Layla commented. "Celebrate for me," Layla insisted.

"Okay, then," added Kacie.

"Okay, we've got a plan. Where are we going? Layla, since this is your celebration where do you want us to eat?"

"Charley's," Layla answered right away.

"I agree," commented Kacie.

"Charley's it is. Long as I can get my grub on," added Envy.

"For somebody who eats a ton, you stay thin as a spaghetti stick. I hate you," Layla joked over the phone.

"Girl, puh-leeze. Since you got half of your stomach removed, you're losing weight like crazy. You keep it up and you'll be the one looking like a straw," laughed Envy. "Anyway, I have to get to this meeting and finish working on a project," Envy told her friends. "Kacie, I guess it's me and you. I'll meet you at the restaurant around six thirty."

"Bye," each one replied.

***

Kacie and Envy arrived at the restaurant almost at the same time. Kacie parked and jumped out of the car. Kacie trailed behind. Kacie stood next to Envy's car in silence when Envy raised a finger beckoning her to hold on for a moment.

"What did you just say?" Envy's face turned colors and her expression changed from relaxed to serious. "I can't believe you, Nikkei. You wait until now to call me with this when you knew you were going to do it today. See, that's what I mean about you. You do stuff like this just to be spiteful and low-down. But you know what? That's all right. You're going to get yours. Good-bye." Envy shut her phone and stuffed it inside her purse.

In total amazement, standing next to Kacie, Envy's arched brows rose and her dark eyes behind her eyeglasses, slanted in a frown. "What was that all about?"

"Nikkei's low-down behind. I swear, I know she's my sister but I can't tell it sometimes. She talked to me a few weeks ago about putting our mother in a nursing home. And I sort of agree because Momma is just getting worse. I mean she's walked off from Nikkei's and she keeps forgetting that she is not with Daddy anymore. So, like I said, I know I can't take care of her. And I know that Nikkei can't take care of her anymore either. I understand that. But the thing that makes me so mad, Kacie, is that she just called and told me that she put our mother in a nursing home up in Murfreesboro. That's four hours away. How will I have time to go see her? She never bothered to tell me she was even thinking about moving

Momma that far away from here. Momma doesn't know anything about Murfreesboro, and neither does Nikkei or me."

Kacie's lips parted in surprise. "Why would she do something like that?"

"I told you. She's spiteful and vengeful. She'll do anything she can that will make me go off. And since she's the power of attorney over mother, there's not a dang thing I can do about it. She's going to pay for being the smart-ass, conniving sister she is."

The ladies entered the restaurant and waited for the hostess to seat them. It wasn't crowded so the two friends didn't have to wait to be seated. They looked over the menu the hostess left and when the waitress arrived at their table they knew exactly what they wanted.

They spent the next two hours munching on two appetizer dishes of nachos, veggie egg rolls, buffalo wings, and spinach dip. The waitress delivered a pitcher of strawberry margarita to add to the delicious delicacies.

Laughing and talking between eating and drinking, Kacie spoke up after downing her first margarita. The light buzz she felt from the alcohol sent any inhibitions she may have remotely had right out the window. She ranted on and on about Deacon. Deacon this, and Deacon that.

"Kacie, what's up with you? You said not long ago that you had something to tell me and Layla." Envy stared without blinking at Kacie.

"Oh, nothing that can't wait. Just something about me and Deacon is all. I want to wait 'til both of my home girls are here."

"Are you sure you don't want to tell me now?"

"No. That won't be necessary. Really," Kacie answered and placed a hand over her breast.

"Come on, then. I'm ready to get home. You get home or you're going to owe that babysitter all of your paycheck," joked Envy. Kacie never revealed that she'd left the kids at home again by themselves. Everything wasn't to be shared, friends or no friends, is how Kacie often thought.

"Check you later, Kacie. We'll talk tomorrow. Tomorrow, no more excuses," Envy pointed and wobbled a bit. "I want to hear what you and Mr. Deacon are up to. For all I know, you might be getting ready to walk down the aisle." Smiling, Envy transferred her gaze from Kacie then she opened her car door and climbed inside.

Kacie brushed Envy off with her hands. She got in her car and sped off, burning rubber out of the restaurant parking lot. She flipped the radio stations until she heard one of her favorite Mary J. Blige songs come on the radio. She turned up the volume and swayed to the beat of the music A few minutes later, Kacie wore an inward smile when she thought about the new life forming inside her belly. I love that song," Kacie said when it ended.

Envy arrived home only to be stunned at the sight before her eyes. She sobered up instantly when she pulled into her driveway only to see Mrs. Rawlings outside, on her knees, tending her garden. "It's almost nine-thirty at night. What is she doing outside?" Envy asked herself.

Envy closed the door to her car. Concerned, she walked over to Mrs. Rawlings' side of the yard. "Good evening, Mrs. Rawlings. Do you know what time it is?"

"I'm not feeling too well, to tell you the truth, so I thought I'd come out here and work in my garden. I thought it would make me feel better."

Mrs. Rawlings wiped her forehead, straightened up, and then walked over and sat down on one of the steps leading to her duplex. The fall weather hadn't affected Mrs. Rawlings at all. Instead, she looked flushed and sweaty like it was a hot summer day instead of a clear, cool fall night.

Envy touched her head with the back of her hand. She felt clammy and warm. "You shouldn't be out here, Mrs. Rawlings. You feel feverish."

"I'll be all right. Believe me, I've had worse days."

"Maybe so, but I don't want you to have any more, especially when I can do something to help you. Have you eaten today?"

"I had a few peanut butter and crackers, and a cup of coffee. Didn't want it, but I made myself eat it."

"Are you in pain or aching?"

"At my age, you're always going to have pain at some time or another. I don't complain."

"Mrs. Rawlings, I understand that, but I'm asking if you feel different like you're coming down with a cold or flu?"

"My legs and head have been hurting. I thought if I came outside and worked in the yard that I might feel better. But to tell you the truth, I feel a little weak."

"Come on, let's get you inside." Envy pushed the remote lock on her car door before taking her hand and grabbing hold of Mrs. Rawlings' elbow. She helped the old lady to her feet and up the steps to her opened door.

She'd been inside Mrs. Rawlings' home twice since the time she'd lived next door to her. Everything was practically the same as she remembered. Antique pieces of polished furniture were in the living room and dining room.

The house was clean but still had what some folks called, an old folks smell. Envy led Mrs. Rawlings into the den and assisted her in sitting in her recliner.

"Where is your first aid kit?" Envy asked. I need to take your temperature."

"In the bathroom. Look in the bottom drawer of the vanity and you'll see it."

The kit was exactly where Mrs. Rawlings told Envy it was. She took her temperature. 101.2 degrees. Not good for someone of Mrs. Rawlings' age.

"Mrs. Rawlings, I'm going to take you to the hospital. Your fever is too high and you're looking listless and weak.

"Baby, I don't need to go to the hospital. All I need is a cool drink of water and a Tylenol. I'll be just fine after I take it and lie down. You go on over there and check on Fischer. You know he knows you're home. Dogs can hear good, real good you know."

"Yes, I know. And I'll let Fischer out, but then I'm taking you to the emergency room. And I don't want any arguments about it." Envy's voice was firm. No matter how much Mrs. Rawlings worked her last nerves, she cared about the old woman. Mrs. Rawlings was like a grandmother to her. She'd never admitted it, but she loved that old woman, nosy and all.

"Mrs. Rawlings, I'll be back in fifteen minutes, just as soon as Fischer does his business."

Envy gave her a glass of tap water and a Tylenol for the fever and ran over to her side of the duplex to let Fischer outside to relieve himself. Afterward, she did just as she had promised and headed back over to Mrs. Rawlings' place.

***

On the way to the hospital, Mrs. Rawlings was unusually quiet. This concerned Envy even more. There was hardly a time she'd not heard Mrs. Rawlings talking, giving her advice, or telling her about her own business. She always had something to say. Now here the old lady sat on the passenger side of the car and the only sound emitting from her lips was a raspy breathing of sorts.

Envy reached over and touched Mrs. Rawlings' wrinkled hand. "We'll be at the hospital in a few minutes, Mrs. Rawlings."

Mrs. Rawlings murmured incoherently.

A few minutes later, Envy pulled into the emergency room parking area. "Mrs. Rawlings, I'm going to go inside and get a wheelchair. I'll be right back."

Nothing.

Envy left and then quickly returned with the wheelchair, and with ease, she transferred the petite, tiny woman into the chair and headed off to the emergency station. The triage nurse checked Mrs. Rawlings' vitals and asked her a few questions, but Mrs. Rawlings was rambling. Envy told triage how she'd discovered her outside.

Two hours later, a male voice called Envy's name. "Ma'am, are you Mrs. Rawlings' next of kin?"

"No, I'm, I'm her neighbor. I look after her. She doesn't have any living relatives that I know of. How is she?"

"She's going to be admitted to the hospital. She has diabetes and her sugar level is quite high. She's also dehydrated and she has a fever, which indicates there might be some infection."

"Is she going to be all right?" Envy was shaken and her nerves were on edge.

"I believe so, but with her age and the health problems we've discovered, it can be tough to get things under control. If you want to come back to her room, you can. As soon as we get a vacant hospital bed, we'll be moving her."

"Thank you." She followed the nurse to the ER room where Mrs. Rawlings was. She was hooked up to an IV.

Envy couldn't fathom how just moments ago Mrs. Rawlings was talking and now she was on an IV, looking frail and like the wind had been sucked right out of her. "Mrs. Rawlings, how are you feeling?"

Mrs. Rawlings turned her head slowly until her sunken eyes stilled on Envy. "Baby, don't you worry 'bout me. I've told you time and time again that the good Lord has me in His hands. I'm going to be just fine."

"They're going to put you in a room as soon as one becomes available. It shouldn't be too much longer."

"You go on home now, child," she whispered weakly. "You need to see about your baby."

Envy gasped. *Baby? What is she talking about? Envy, she's feverish, incoherent. She doesn't know what she's saying,* she told herself. "No, I'm going to stay right here until you get in a room. Is there anyone you want me to call? Church member? Pastor? Anyone?" asked Envy, still reeling from what Mrs. Rawlings had said about a baby.

"No, dahlin. I want to wait to see how long I'm going to be in here first. Since you're set on staying, sit down in that chair over there." Mrs. Rawlings pointed at the chair in the corner of the room. This time, Mrs. Rawlings sounded just like herself. She acted like she knew exactly who Envy was. Envy sat down. An hour passed before an attendant came in and rolled Mrs. Rawlings to her room. Envy stayed with her until her eyes grew droopy and sleep claimed her.

On the drive home, Envy tried to make reason of what Mrs. Rawlings was talking about. "Why did she say that about a baby?" Envy decided to let it go. There was no sense in getting uptight about the words of an old, sickly woman who was confused and almost in a diabetic coma. Envy shrugged her shoulders and thought about who she should call to keep her company for the night.

***

Mrs. Rawlings had been in the hospital for three days. Every evening after work Envy stopped by her apartment to let Fischer outside to relieve himself, and then she headed to the hospital to sit with Mrs. Rawlings. She spent as much time with the old lady as she could; more than she had ever spent with her own mother. Envy began to genuinely care about Mrs. Rawlings. Not that she didn't before Mrs. Rawlings became sick, but Envy started to see her as more than just a nosy old neighbor. She slowly began to see her as a friend, or like a grandmother.

Early Saturday morning, day four of Mrs. Rawlings' hospital stay, Envy got up, fed Fischer, and afterward, they jogged through the quiet, serene neighborhood inhabited by mostly retired senior residents. Tree-lined streets, leaves falling, and the kind of neighbors who lived their lives without trying to get all up in her business. It was what she loved most about her neighborhood. There was only one exception—Mrs. Rawlings.

Mrs. Rawlings was one of those people who didn't hesitate to say what she thought. Fiercely independent, the widow often gave glory to God for being in sound mind, still able to drive and do for herself, and in fairly good health – until now. She'd been married sixty years before her husband died in his sleep from natural causes four years ago. She didn't have any living relatives, nor did her husband because both of them came from very small families who were now deceased.

Envy slowly began to understand by listening to Mrs. Rawlings that she was quite a wise, God-fearing woman. Her intentions were good, but for Envy she looked out for her a little too much, especially when she got on Envy about the flow of men coming and going from her apartment.

Whose business was it to dictate to her how to live her life? Envy was a private person when it came to her personal life, her comings and goings. But like a magnetic radar screen, it seemed that Mrs. Rawlings could tell every time a man rang her doorbell. She didn't mind lecturing Envy about her lifestyle either.

The opposite side of the spectrum was that when needed, Mrs. Rawlings was there for Envy. Whether it meant taking care of Fischer when she had to go out of town or be gone longer than usual away from home, Mrs. Rawlings never batted an eye. She would gladly step in to help Envy. There were times Envy came home and found Mrs. Rawlings, despite her age, had mowed both of their lawns and planted flowers on her side of the duplex. She was an amazing woman, if only she would stop being judgmental about Envy's chosen lifestyle.

After her walk with Fischer, Envy bathed and dressed casually so she could go to see Mrs. Rawlings.

The wind kicked at her curls when she stepped out of the car and walked toward the hospital entrance. Envy walked down the hospital corridor with calm confidence. She slowed her pace when she arrived in front of the hospital gift shop where she purchased a colorful bouquet for her neighbor. Catching the elevator to the eighth floor, she stepped out and headed to room 826. Lightly knocking, she heard the mild-mannered voice whisper for her to come in.

"Good afternoon, Mrs. Rawlings." She walked over to her bedside and set the bouquet on the table next to Mrs. Rawlings' bed.

Mrs. Rawlings' smile seemed to light up her entire face when she saw the bouquet. "Oh, Envy, these are so beautiful," she remarked and turned to smell the flower arrangement."

"I'm glad you like them. Tell me, has the doctor been in today?"

"Yes. My sugar is down to 110. If it maintains at this level, I'll be going home tomorrow. How's my house? What about my garden?" Mrs. Rawlings sounded worried.

"I told you, Mrs. Rawlings. I'm taking care of everything. Your house, the garden, even the leaves have been raked. If you get to come home tomorrow, I'll be here to get you. I'm going to check with your doctor's nurse and see what you should be eating. Then I'm going to go to the grocery store, get it, go back home, and stock your pantry and fridge." Envy sat down in the chair next to Mrs. Rawlings' bed. She grasped her hand and lightly squeezed it. "You're going to be fine. I'm going to see to that."

"You're such a sweet girl. That's why I don't understand why you do the things you do. You're pretty as a Georgia peach, smart as a whip, and you have so much going for yourself. But baby, you have to learn how to put your faith and trust in God. Can't no man, and no sex give you what you need."

Envy squirmed uncomfortably in her chair. Why did Mrs. Rawlings always have to go there? Seemed like no matter what, Mrs. Rawlings made her way to talking about Envy's business. Envy didn't want to disrespect the old woman, but enough was enough. She had to tell her how she felt.

"Mrs. Rawlings, I don't mean to sound disrespectful, but I have to say this. You cannot run my personal life. I care about you and I believe you care about me. But I can no more dictate to you about who you allow in and out of your home than you can mine. And you seem to assume that the friends who come to visit are coming to have sex with me. Why do you assume that? I'm a single, successful woman with my own. So, let me do me, Mrs. Rawlings. Let me do me."

"Honey, you might believe that you can fool me and other folks for that matter, but God's eyes are watching you. Every step you make, every breath you take, and every man you bed knowing you are not married, God sees it. One day you'll realize that I'm telling you the truth. Mark my words; something you're hiding from is going to come to light. Believe me, child. God is not one to lie and He's shown me that you've got something you're hiding. But you can't hide from Him, baby. You can't hide from Him." Mrs. Rawlings spoke boldly. "The eyes of the Lord are in every place, beholding the evil and the good."

Envy didn't respond, but the look on her face spoke volumes. She tried to force a smile of thanks for the so-called words of wisdom Mrs. Rawlings spoke, but found it impossible to do so.

"You don't have to say a thing. You know what I'm saying is coming from God. When you get ready, you can always come to me. Let me change that. When you get ready, God is waiting to hear you tell Him what He already knows. After that, if you need a servant of God to talk to, remember that I'm here for you." This time Mrs. Rawlings caressed Envy's trembling hand.

The nurse came in and Envy quickly regained her composure. She welcomed the interruption. The nurse looked at Envy. "Hello, are you Mrs. Rawlings' granddaughter?" she asked with a smile plastered on her starched white face.

"No, I'm her neighbor."

"She's a character, you know. A delightful patient. We're going to miss her when she's discharged." The nurse patted Mrs. Rawlings on her arm. "Mrs. Rawlings, it's time for me to check your insulin level." She poked Mrs. Rawlings' finger with the diabetic meter. "98. That's good. You're doing well," the nurse said.

"I'm not surprised. God has me in the palm of His hands," she told the nurse.

"Lunch will be here soon. I'll check back on you later this afternoon." She turned again toward Envy. "It's nice to meet you."

"Nice to meet you, too," Envy responded.

"The nurse nodded, smiled, and walked off. "Buzz me if you need me, Mrs. Rawlings."

Mrs. Rawlings' white skin seemed to make her beguiling green eyes sparkle like emeralds. Her wrinkled skin looked like ripples of brushing ocean waves crashing against the beach. Envy felt like the secret she'd hidden all of these years had somehow been revealed to Mrs. Rawlings. But that was impossible. There was no way Mrs. Rawlings, or anyone else, could know what she'd kept protected and sealed in her heart. She swallowed hard, momentarily, before she stood.

"Since you're doing fine, I'm going to get ready to leave. I'm going to stop at the nurses' station and see if I can get a diet plan for you. I should have asked that nurse when she came in but it slipped my mind. I'll call you later. In the meantime, if you need anything, you know how to get in touch with me." Awkwardly, Envy leaned over the bedrail, her eyeglasses slid down but she still managed to kiss Mrs. Rawlings lightly on the forehead.

"Thank you, baby, for coming to see me."

"Bye, Mrs. Rawlings." With each step she took up the corridor, Envy's stomach clenched tighter. Her mind filled with fear, panic, and the stark reality of what she'd done. Without forewarning a scripture came to her mind. *Be sure your sin will find you out.*

In her car, Envy swallowed hard. Mrs. Rawlings had struck a nerve. Without thinking, she picked up the phone and called her estranged father's house. It had been over a year since she'd last spoken to him. When his wife answered the phone, Envy started to hang up but decided otherwise. "Hello...this is Envy Wilson. Is my father there?"

"Envy, my goodness, young lady. It's been a long time since I've heard your voice. How are you?" the woman asked politely.

"I'm fine, thank you." No matter how nice and polite her father's wife sounded, Envy wouldn't allow herself to get close to her. She felt that the woman was the reason her father left them. Her mother didn't tell her that, it was just something Envy believed. She had to be the reason he left. No father could leave his children unless some other woman out in the streets made him. She focused her thoughts back on what his wife said.

"Envy, it's good to hear from you. I wish you wouldn't wait so long to call. You know your father's getting older and he misses you. He talks about you all of the time, you and Nikkei."

"Is he there, please?" Envy asked without responding to anything her stepmother had said.

"Yes, he's here. I'll go get him," she said.

Silence.

"Envy, baby. How are you?" her father asked after getting on the phone. He sounded like he was glad to hear from her. "I haven't heard from you in a while. Is everything okay?"

"Yea, Daddy. I was just thinking about you." She spoke somberly. "Daddy, Nikkei is putting Momma in a nursing home next week up in Murfreesboro, Tennessee."

"Yes, I know. She came by and brought the grandchildren to see us. They're growing like wild

94

weeds, aren't they?" Envy could hear the sound of joy in the tone of his voice.

"Yes, sir. They sure are."

"I can't wait until a man snags you. You're such a talented and gorgeous girl. I'm proud of you, Envy. I know I don't get a chance to tell you that as much as I should, but I am, you know. I wish you'd come around, Envy. I miss seeing you, baby."

"Thanks, Daddy, but I hate to disappoint you. You see, I don't plan on getting married or having children. Not ever." She spoke with emphasis and a mild harshness in her voice.

Her father didn't return his thoughts about what she'd said. He shifted the conversation back to Envy's mother. "I hated to hear that about your mother. From what Nikkei has told me, your mother has gotten worse. I know you don't like the idea of her being in a nursing home, but it's too hard on your sister. She has a family you know."

Envy grew angrier with each word spewing from her father's mouth. It was just like Nikkei to call and tell him her sob story. Nikkei was always vying for their father's attention. Every time Envy looked at Nikkei, she saw something of their jealous mother in her. Now here she was, beating her to the punch by calling him and making herself sound like an angel.

"Daddy, when am I going to see you?" Envy sounded like a young child.

"Honey, you know you're welcome to come to our home any time that you want to. Your stepmother, Carol, and I would love to have you. Your sisters and brother would love to see their big sister too," her father, Charles said and chuckled.

It wasn't the answer she wanted to hear. She didn't want to see her stepmother or her little sisters and brother. She wanted to see him. It had been like this since her father left. How could she dare go around that woman and his children? No way, no how. "I'll see, Daddy. So much is going on at work that I barely have any free time. Anyway, I'll talk to you later, Daddy. I have another call coming in."

"I love you too, baby. I hope we see you real soon."

Envy hung up the phone. Tears trickled down from her eyes. She turned the ignition, put it in reverse, turned, and drove off the hospital parking lot.

9

"Truth is beautiful, without a doubt. But so are lies."
Emerson

For the fifth day in a week, Kacie couldn't muster up an appetite, not even for Coco Puffs, her all-time favorite cereal since she was a little girl. The very thought of milk and cereal sent her to the bathroom heaving. Having given birth to six children, she didn't have to go to a doctor or run to the drugstore for a pregnancy test. There was no doubt about it. She was pregnant. Kacie freshened up and when her stomach settled, she drank a glass of pineapple juice. Sitting alone at the kitchen table, Kacie stared outside at the orange and gold leaves as they fell to the ground. The site was beautiful to her. The leaves fell gently, one by one, some two by two. Kacie folded her arms inside each other and hugged herself like she was warding off the cool wind blowing through the trees in the front yard.

Standing, Kacie retreated to the living room and started picking up behind the kids. She paused a moment and massaged her belly. Looking down; she smiled at the idea of giving birth to the child of the man she loved – the man God had finally sent her way. "You're going to have a wonderful daddy," she whispered. "And, unlike the rest of the bums I've had in my life, this time, everything is going to be different. I wouldn't be surprised if your daddy asks to marry me." She drew back into the living room and leaned against the spotless wall. She turned with a start when the phone rang.

"Speak of the devil," she said when she looked at the caller ID and then down at her tummy. It was Deacon. Kacie beamed with joy.

"Good morning, beautiful." The voice on the other end of the phone forced her to smile.

She loved Deacon. The four and a half months they had been seeing each other seemed like a lifetime to Kacie. It was like she'd known him all of her life. Except for the times like yesterday when Deacon seemed like he'd fallen off the face of the earth, their relationship was good. Maybe he didn't tell her he loved her like she told him, but Kacie believed he did.

"Actions are better than words," Layla reminded her from time to time.

Kacie retained Layla's words in her mind to retrieve whenever Deacon didn't call or when she wanted to hear him say those three special words.

"Deacon, honey. I've been so worried. You weren't at church yesterday and you didn't answer my calls. Are you okay?" Kacie asked with grave concern.

"What have I told you about getting yourself all in a tizzy when you don't hear from me every day? I got called out of town at the last minute late Saturday evening after we talked. You know how those trips can be. Quick, exhausting, and spur of the moment. I'm sorry. I wanted to call you, but I was up half the night with a client trying to kiss up to him so he would sign a contract with our company. It was late by the time I convinced him to sign on the dotted line and I was exhausted. I didn't make it back to Memphis until after midnight. I wasn't about to wake you up then, knowing you had to get up early yourself to get your kids off to school."

Kacie exhaled. "I was so worried. When I talked to you Saturday, you said you were going to see me at church. I just started going out of my mind thinking all kinds of crazy thoughts when I didn't see you. I forgot how your job keeps you on call twenty-four-seven."

"Well, now that, that's settled. How's my favorite girl doing?" he asked.

"Perfect, now that I'm talking to my favorite guy," she answered. Kacie walked around the sofa where she spotted one of the boys' wrestling figures on the floor.

"I was thinking about coming by before going to the office this morning. You up to seeing me?"

"Do you have to ask?" Kacie sat on the back of the sofa.

"Do you want me to stop somewhere and grab you a sandwich?" Little thoughtful things like that made Kacie adore Deacon. He was such a considerate man.

"No, I'm not hungry this morning. I just want you. You'll be my breakfast," she crooned into the phone.

"Hey, hey, I like that. I'll see you in about ten minutes, love."

Kacie hurried through the house, making haste to pick up around her already clean house. Except for the wrestling figure she'd found, everything else remained in perfect place. From the crisp, freshly washed, and ironed window treatments in each room, to the dust-free plantation blinds and shining waxed hardwood floors.

Next, she took a bird bath, just to make sure her body was fresh. It didn't matter that she'd already taken a morning shower right after the kids left for school. As usual, Keshena was still asleep and would be for at least another hour.

Kacie slipped into a pair of crystal blue leggings and an oversized matching top. Not a minute too soon, because she heard Deacon's key turning in the door leading from the garage into the hallway. Deacon rushed up behind Kacie and swooped her off her feet until she faced his stare. "Oomph, oomph, oomph. You are drop-dead gorgeous. You know that." He smothered her in kisses starting with her ear and whispered a string of sexual innuendos into her ear while he continued to embrace her and sit her down on the sofa.

It didn't take long for the couple's need for satisfaction to take over. Their eyes met, their breath grew louder and heavier, and Deacon made himself more familiar with the one underneath his weight. Sounds of passion traveled through the vents and up and down the hallway of the house. Enjoying to the fullest, Deacon's expert loving making, Kacie did not doubt that he would be in seventh heaven when she told him the news.

***

Holding her against his sweaty, spent body on the narrow black printed sofa, Deacon nibbled on her ear until Kacie eased back as much as she could.

"Come on, let's take a bubble bath." She jumped up and giggled while running through the house in her birthday suit. Deacon laid back for a few minutes until his strength returned.

"Come on," Kacie yelled from the back bedroom.

"Hold it down before you wake up Keshena," Deacon answered back and strode his lean, chiseled body to Kacie's bedroom.

She gasped at the sign of his returning desire. "Uh, huh, not until you get in this bath.

"So it's like that, huh?"

"Yep, certainly is." She stood at the side of the master bath and stretched out her hand. Deacon followed. He patted her on the butt, and Kacie squealed.

Soaping each other down in the garden tub, Kacie turned and then laid her braided hair against Deacon's chest. "I have some good news," she said feeling like she was in seventh heaven.

"Umm," he moaned softly as his manhood pressed against the small of her lower back.

"Deacon, you know I love you, right?" she said in a serious voice, but without turning around to face him.

"Uh, uh, sounds like an episode from the Maury Show. But yeah, I know you love me, sweetness. What's up? Where is all of this gooey stuff coming from?"

"I know you haven't told me that you love me, but you do, don't you?" For just a while, Kacie was afraid of what Deacon's answer might be. She shifted slightly and tilted her head back so she could see Deacon's expression.

"Sure, you know that goes without saying. I'm not big on words. I like to show you how I feel about you. And I thought I did just that."

"Baby, of course, you do. You've shown me in the most special way a man can. And a woman for that matter."

"What are you talking about?" Deacon sat up slightly in the tub and swung her around so he could see Kacie's face like he was sizing her up. A spot of soap was on her cheek and her forehead. He grinned and then kissed the soap off of her jaw.

Kacie took hold of his free hand. It was massive. He eased the other one under the warm bubbling water, almost taking her mind off what she was about to tell him. A gentle, low moan pierced her lips and she bit her bottom lip lightly and twisted her butt against the soapy tub surface. Barely able to speak, she managed to say, "Deacon, baby," again she moaned. There was no turning back. Deacon had her where he wanted her. She was under his spell, and until she released her desire, there would be no use in trying to tell Deacon anything.

Stepping out of the tub, Deacon grabbed the bath towel and began drying off while Kacie followed and did the same. Deacon had a way of getting her to succumb to him. When she was with him, she got a thrill. She lost control and her world was all about the man she loved.

Nevertheless, Kacie understood that she had to find a way to tell him about their lo

"I'm going to the office," Deacon told her after he finished dressing. I have a meeting at ten this morning and then an afternoon meeting with some prospective clients. I won't get a chance to talk to you until later this evening, so don't go worrying about me." He pecked a robed Kacie on her wet hair and then her lips.

He leaned against the bedroom door frame and looked at her intently. "Hey, you all right?" he asked her.

Pausing at first, Kacie thought she ought to just come right out and tell him. But on second thought hesitated, believing that it wouldn't be such a good idea to share such a personal thing with him when he was on his way to an important meeting. No, she had plenty of time to tell him.

"Yes, I'm fine. I'm just drained. You do me good, Deacon," she moaned and kissed him at the door. "You do me real good. Now get to work. Call me when you can," she said and then yawned.

"You get yourself some sleep, precious." He straightened his camel-colored three-button suit that seemed formed for his perfect body. Kacie's cheeks turned colors. "I will, but only if you leave now before I pull you back inside and strip you out of that suit, boy.

"I can't let that happen, you'll get me fired. Look, for real, I'm outta here." Deacon strolled in his sexy stride until he reached his car.

Kacie stood at the door until she saw his car take off and race out of sight down the street. Touching her stomach, she caressed it again. "Don't worry. Momma's got everything under control. Don't you worry about a thing."

Kacie turned, closed the security door behind her, and went to take Deacon's advice. She slept an hour or so when Keshena stood in her crib and began to cry to get out of it.

The remainder of Kacie's day was great. She'd been with the man she loved and everything for now was good in her world. She busied herself cleaning the house. She was going to work for four hours today so she prepared the kids a light meal for them to have when they got home from school.

The afternoon came quickly. The kids came in from school and Kacie passed off Keshena to Kassandra.

"Y'all be sure to get your homework done. Dinner's on the stove and remember, no cooking unless it's something you're warming up in the microwave. I should be back home by 9:30 tonight. Bye now," she told them and hugged them one by one.

Her cell phone rang just as soon as she got in her car and backed out of the driveway.

"Hello," she answered.

"Hey, I just called you at home, but no one answered."

"I know. I was so glad to see you this morning that I forgot to tell you I had to work this evening. I'm on my way there now."

"And the kids?"

"Deacon, you know the kids aren't allowed to answer the phone when I'm not there unless they look on the Caller ID and see that it's me."

"I know that, but I'm talking about them being at home by themselves."

"My kids are trained. They know what to do. I cannot afford to pay three hundred bucks a week for someone to keep my kids for a few hours a day. It's ridiculous, highway robbery. They know how to call me on my cell phone, and I work only five minutes from home. So now that we have that understood, will you let me handle my kids," she said, "and tell me the real reason you called."

"I just got hold of some tickets."

"Tickets? What kind of tickets?" Kacie asked as she made the turn into the store's parking lot where she worked.

"A stage play. It's this Friday night. Do you want to go with me?"

"A play? What kind of play?" Kacie asked.

"It's called *Sinsatiable*. It's going to be at the Orpheum. I heard it's an outstanding Christian-themed adaptation from a novel."

"Oh, yeah, I've seen the previews about it on television. It looks like it's going to be good. I'd love to go." Kacie's voice rang with excitement.

"Great." Deacon sent a kissing sound to her through the phone. "Let me get back to work. Remember I have a trustee's meeting at church tonight. Say a prayer for me. I think Pastor may talk about inducting me as one of the trustees. One of the other deacons gave me a heads up." Deacon sat on the edge of his desk.

"Wow! That would be great, honey. You've been committed to this church for a long time. You deserve the position." Kacie suddenly started laughing uncontrollably.

"What's so funny?" Deacon asked.

"I was just thinking. What are they going to call you? Your name is already Deacon," she continued laughing. "I guess they'll say Trustee Deacon Riggs."

Deacon started laughing too. "You are too silly. 'I'm glad I have you in my corner." His voice revealed a sound of surety and confidence. "Bye, bye."

"Deacon, hold up." Kacie nervously said.

"What is it, baby?"

"I, I'd like to talk to you about something. But it can wait until we talk later."

"Okay, but I may not talk to you tonight, so don't get bent out of shape. I don't know how long tonight's meeting is going to last."

"Sure, that's fine. I love you," said Kacie.

Deacon hung up the phone without responding.

10

"A person is only beautiful, when their own beauty, is reflecting on to others." Tara Grady

Layla returned home from choir rehearsal like she'd performed eight hours of hard labor. Like most Tuesday nights, rehearsal was full of drama. Soloists argued over who would lead the new song. Some of the members thought that Layla led too many of the songs, and maybe she did. But it wasn't their decision to make; it was the director. After two hours of practicing and bickering, another choir member took her home after rehearsal was over. Layla was delighted when she stepped into the sanctity of her apartment.

She turned the key to the door and stepped inside the warmth of her apartment. It wasn't too cold outside but it was easy for anyone to know that fall was about to give way to winter. She slipped out of her pantsuit and into a warm shower. Her weight had plummeted an additional twenty-eight pounds. She felt better physically than she had in a long time. If only she could forget the reason she was losing the weight so fast, then she would be so much better mentally and emotionally. She knelt on her knees, next to her double bed and folded her hands in prayer.

"God, my father, thank you for every good and perfect gift you're given me. Thank you for loving me even when I don't love myself. Thank you for my family and friends, my church, and my pastor. Lord, I ask you to watch over those who are homeless, sick, and in prison. Forgive me for my shortcoming, and for my sins. Forgive me for still holding onto my past and the fears of the terrible crime Mike did to me. Help me to learn how to forgive him, like you have forgiven me countless times. Help me to remember that You saved my life for a purpose and that You have not given me a spirit of fear,

Father. You said that I should not fear what man can do to me, Lord so please remove the fearful thoughts from my mind. Make me to be the person you want me to be. Amen." Struggling to pull herself up, she stopped and allowed herself to rest back on her knees. "And, God, there's one more thing I want to ask you. I do want a man in my life; if it is your will. Not just any man, Lord. I want a man who loves me for me and who I love too. Amen." She used the bed to help her get up off of her knees and climb into bed. The cool sheets felt good against her skin and mixed with the warmth inside her apartment, she was able to fall asleep quickly.

"Layla, are you ready? We're going to be late, baby."

"Honey, here I come. I had to put on the last touch of makeup."

"How many times have I told you that you're beautiful just the way you are?" The man walked up to her, gathered her tenderly in his arms, and held her snugly. Layla felt his heart beating against her full chest. When he reluctantly pulled away, she caught the heart-rendering stare of his gaze and the pull of his sexual magnetism aroused a sense of urgency inside her.

"Baby, you just said you don't want us to be late." She could hardly speak.

"I know what I said, but I can't help it. You do this to me every time. Layla, I'm so thankful you came into my life. Who would have thought that our lives would turn out like this? I love you, girl."

"Don't you know I've waited on someone to say those words to me for such a long time? I prayed to God for a man like you." A knot rose in her throat. Her body trembled. "I love you too.

He stopped her words by moving his mouth over hers, demanding more of her. In return, Layla gave in to the passion of his kiss and the heat of his touch as he explored her body.

"Baby, baby," she spoke in a whisper.

Her eyes, heavy with drowsiness, roamed the surroundings with curiosity. Her heart beat wildly and her gown clung to her moist skin.

Layla eased herself up in bed once she became fully aware that she was dreaming. She turned over on her side and opened the drawer next to the bed. She pulled out a chocolate candy bar and took one nibble from it before she threw it in the waste basket next to her bed. Her mind slowly relived the memories of her dream.

***

The following afternoon, Layla saw the mail truck headed down her street. She had been up early, bathed, and gotten dressed. The shawl collar sweater and one-pocket jeans gave her a boost of self-confidence. She opened her front door and walked down the walkway like she was perhaps going to visit a neighbor.

The postman pulled up beside her and got out of his vehicle. "Hello." His voice was as charming as she'd dreamed about last night. He placed a couple of pieces of mail in the mailbox he passed but continued to walk alongside her.

"Hello." She tried her best to act flippantly but was sure it wasn't working.

"You look lovely today, Miss, uh, uh, don't tell me. Hobbs. Right?"

Impressed, Layla stopped in her tracks, and for the first time, she really looked at him. It was as if she felt blood surging from her fingertips to her toes. "You're right. But too bad I don't have the same privilege."

"The same privilege? And what exactly does that mean?" He flashed a beguiling smile and popped his fingers. "Oh, I get it. You don't know my name. May I start over?"

"Start over?" It was her time to look at him in amusement.

"Yes. Let me introduce myself. I'm Dennis, your friendly neighborhood postman," he grinned. This time his even, near perfect white teeth transfixed her. "Dennis Parker."

She extended her hand out to his. "It's nice to meet you, Dennis."

"May I ask where you're headed?"

"Oh, nowhere in particular. I decided since the day is so beautiful that I'd take a walk. It's not too cold or too windy, and I wanted to get out of the house for a while."

"Oh, I see. If I'm not being too presumptuous, I thought you lived in another apartment on the other side of town?"

Layla stood still again. "I think you are being a little nosy."

"I'm sorry. I didn't mean to be. It's just that I notice that your mail is no longer coming to that complex and I thought I remembered your name when I put your mail in the box, that's all. I didn't mean any harm." He looked truly sorrowful, so much so that Layla felt bad for coming off so strong, but she was not going to take a chance with anyone – not after Mile.

"Yes, I moved over here not long ago."

"Oh, I see. This is my regular route, so I hope to see you more often," he said with a beautiful smile.

Layla said nothing. She turned around and went back inside her house. Her heart raced and she felt a light twinge in her stomach, which happened from time to time since the shooting.

"Hey, Layla."

She turned around before disappearing from her balcony. "Yes?"

"Hey, I forgot something."

"What?" she asked.

"Your phone number," he replied.

Layla smiled. "Sure."

He put her number in his phone and turned to walk away. "I usually go to lunch when I finish this route. I thought if you didn't have anyone to report to at home, you might let me take you to lunch."

Did he say lunch? No, he didn't just ask me to go out with him! "

"I really would like to, Dennis, but I already have some other plans. What about a rain check?" She couldn't believe she'd said that.

"Okay, I'll call you."

11

"I'm stronger, I'm wiser, I'm better." Marvin Sapp

Since the shooting, Layla had lost thirty pounds in one month. Her appetite had diminished dramatically since they removed part of her stomach and intestines. She often became queasy if she tried to eat more than her stomach could hold.

Layla looked in the mirror. "God, thank you for saving my life. Thank you for taking a bad situation and making it work for my good. I'm healthier, I'm stronger and I'm wiser. I owe it all to you, Lord."

***

"It's going to be fun having a girl's night out. Seems like forever since the three of us have been able to spend some time together just to have fun. So I say, before we go to the Orpheum, and since we're downtown, let's do some wild and crazy shopping for you, Layla. You need to show off that new figure." Kacie laughed. "Who knows, you just might see Mr. Postman again one day." This time Envy and Layla laughed along with Kacie.

Envy added, "Now, you're talking with sense. I agree. Layla, we are going to get your shop on, baby."

"All right, since y'all insist," screamed Layla in the car. "Y'all know something?" she looked from Envy to Kacie.

"Naw, but I bet you're about to tell us," chuckled Kacie who had ordered tea, something unusual for her.

The two women chattered away on the phone on three-way. Envy was extremely elated for Layla. Maybe he would help Layla take her mind off the horror of what Mike had done to her.

Layla, suppose this one is the one," Kacie added.

"Kacie, why do you always have to look at a man like he's the next meal ticket or something?" Envy chastised her.

"I don't. But the truth is the truth. We all need a good man in our lives. What woman doesn't like love, attention, and affection and a few dead presidents to go along with it," she chuckled over the phone.

"With all of those kids you have, I guess you have a point," Layla teased on the sly.

"You got that right," agreed Envy.

Silence.

"Layla, just go and have a good time. Don't be acting shy and all quiet like you've never had a good man before. Although you haven't," Kacie said with a twinge of bitterness.

"That's enough, Kacie," Envy warned.

"I'm sorry, Layla. I was only joking."

"I know you, Kacie. I'm too high on excitement to let anything you say bring me down."

"Since I have y'all on the phone, I guess I better go on and tell you what it was I had to tell you." Kacie's tone turned from silly to serious.

"Do you have to tell us now?" asked Layla

"Yea, can't it wait?" Envy agreed. "I have a meeting in about ten minutes. We can talk tonight if we're still going to the Orpheum."

"Oh, yeah, that's right. What time do y'all want me to be ready and who's driving you or Kacie?" asked Layla.

"I'll drive," Envy volunteered. "I'm going to get out of here a little early today, go home, let Fischer out and check on my neighbor's place."

"Are you talking about that nosy old neighbor who lives next door to you?" Kacie asked.

"Yes, I'm beginning to have a change of opinion; she's not so bad after all. She's a nice woman. I know I complain about her a lot, but when it's all said and done, she looks out for me. She reminds me of a grandmother. She's in the hospital. So I plan to stop by and visit with her to make sure she's doing okay. When I leave from there, I'll pick you up first Kacie and Layla. I should be at your place around seven-fifteen. And will the both of you please be ready? Kacie, as for you, I hope this time you have a babysitter. You're going to keep leaving those children at home alone and CPS is going to ride down on your tail. So get that together for tonight or you won't be going with me. And I'm serious. Now I've got to go. Bye, y'all."

The three of them hung up the phone. Layla checked her light makeup and added a dab of her favorite cologne that Envy had bought her for her birthday. She restyled her hair and put on a pair of hoop earrings and a different sweater top. The time flew quickly and before she had a chance to settle down, there was a knock at the door. It was Envy and they set out to pick up Kacie and then out for the evening's events

Kacie was standing at the door when Envy pulled up with Layla in the car. Kacie locked the door behind her and joined her friends and got inside the Saturn.

"First stop, a restaurant somewhere close to the Orpheum. I am starving," Envy told the other two girls.

Kacie agreed right away, while Layla merely nodded.

"Guess what?" Layla said to them on the way to the restaurant. "I found out that the postman who brought that package a few weeks ago is on my regular route in my new complex. Now, how weird is that? I can watch his fine butt every time he delivers the mail. And you better believe the brother's got it all. Well-groomed, dark hair, hickory bronze skin, features so perfect that he looks too good to be a man." Layla laughed. She opened a piece of sugarless gum and popped it in her mouth.

Kacie leaned over a little toward the front so she could see Layla's face.

"Then the brother has a smooth-lined beard, and when he talks, he shows off a pair of even white teeth. Oooh-weee. What did Marvin Gaye use to say, 'mercy, mercy, me?'"

Envy laughed so loud that some of the customers from the other tables looked their way. But it appeared that neither of the girls cared. "Have you stepped to him?" asked Envy.

"What do you mean by stepped to him?"

"You are still green as grass, Layla," Kacie added. "What she means is have you flirted with the man or let him know you have some liking for him?"

"No, are y'all crazy? I'm not about to come on to some stranger. That man probably doesn't know I'm alive."

"That's the reason you should, you silly woman." Envy bit her lip and leaned forward in the chair.

"I wouldn't know where to start anyway." Layla's face suddenly turned bleak.

Envy ignored Layla's change of expression and instead threw her head backward and laughed until it spread to Kacie. "If that's all you're worried about, let me fill you in on how to get a man's attention. "

Envy began rattling off a list of what to do to impress a man. "For instance, pinpoint the time he usually delivers the mail. Make yourself visible. Not all the time but every so often, you can just happen to be outside when he pulls up in his mail truck. And of course, don't sound too forward or act like you're desperate. Just be nice, cordial and please don't come outside in one of those oversized dusters you wear when you're at home." Envy curled her eyes up in her head.

"Shoot, I know she better know better than to do something like that," Kacie said and rolled her neck.

Envy found a parking space on the downtown street close to the Orpheum and Beale Street. They walked along Beale and settled on B.B. Kings Blues Café.

The hostess sat them at a table near the window while the three of them continued to talk. Layla swished in her chair and looked at each of her friends like she was frightened to death. "Y'all are scaring me now. Maybe I'm making a fool of myself, thinking that I can get somebody like him."

"Look, Layla. Don't start that mess tonight. Get over it," blurted Envy. "Don't start acting like you're all insecure and self-conscious. No man wants a woman who doesn't feel good about herself."

Kacie spoke up. "Yeah, Envy's right. Do you think because you're overweight that you're not attractive? We're sick of that lame excuse." Kacie's temper flared. "First of all, if you don't like yourself the way you are, then do something about it other than stick fast food and fried chicken in your mouth. That's all you do is tear yourself down."

Curses poured from Kacie's mouth, but she couldn't stop. She was on a roll. "I'm tired of holding back and trying to pacify you. Either you love yourself like you are or you do what it takes to change it. Either way, I, for one, am sick of your whining and insecurity."

Layla stiffened.

Envy's eyes loomed large. "Kacie, that's enough," she said in a critical tone. Deep down inside she agreed with everything Kacie said, but the way she said it was unacceptable.

"Kacie, we do not belittle our friends. You, of all people, should know better." Envy clenched her mouth tighter while Layla turned away and fought back tears.

Layla, without warning, jumped to her feet and exclaimed, "No need to chastise her, Envy. She's right. Everything she said was right." She spoke soft enough so that hopefully no one else in the restaurant could hear her. "I am fat. I mean how can I forget that? I have to deal with it every day. Sure, I've lost a few pounds since my surgery, but the fact remains that I'm still a big girl. Everyone in my family is fat. We've always loved to eat. There wasn't a day that passed that my mother wasn't cooking us three huge meals a day, and that didn't include the snacks we had."

Layla eased back down in her chair but her words continued without pause. "I try to love myself just the way I am. I tell myself over and over again that God made me this way and that if anyone wants me, they'll just have to accept me just the way I am. But," tears fell, blinding her eyes and choking her voice. "It's hard to deal with. Seeing the postman and having him be so nice to me aroused me."

Kacie and Envy both reached across the table and took hold of Layla's trembling hands.

"There was just something about him. Nothing like anything with Mike. This man, without touching me, made a tingling go through my stomach."

Kacie smiled and squeezed Layla's hand tighter. "I mean, y'all just don't know." This time, Layla smiled. "He looked like a gift from God, perfect in every way. Devastatingly appealing. A ripple effect. Bold looking, black as midnight eyes. Barry White voice. Hershey bar skin color. Oh, my gosh, I can't help but think about him every day all day."

"Kacie, I think this girl's got it bad," advised Envy and her smile broadened. She petted Layla on the back. "Looks like it's time for the three of us to do a little shopping."

They paid the tab and proceeded to the downtown stores. Layla was glad that she'd fixed a few heads of hair earlier in the week. She may not have had her cosmetology license, but she could hook up a sister's hair when she wanted to. Using the money she made to purchase nice, sexy outfits for herself, however, was something new for Layla.

Layla was especially crazy about an eye-catching V-neck dress with the collar turned up and elbow-length sleeves with single-button cuffs. The A-line silhouette showed off her curvaceous full figure in a pleasing sort of way. Kacie helped her choose a pair of satin slings and a textured clutch to go along with the dress while Envy looked around the store for other outfits.

"Hey, come over here, Layla. Check this out, girl. This is gorgeous. You can wear this when you go on your date with Mr. Postman." Envy waved her hand to call her over to where she stood.

"I don't know what I'm going to do with the two of you," Layla laughed out loud. "I don't even know the man and he certainly doesn't know me, and here I am buying new clothes like a fool."

"You're no fool," snapped Envy. "Whether it's the postman, some other man, or no man, you're doing this for you. Remember that." Envy pointed her finger at Layla and pursed her lips.

"You're right again. And I have to admit that I feel like I've been awakened, that I've come to life for the first time since God knows when. And I owe it all to the both of you." She reached out to Kacie and Envy and they shared a group hug.

"Okay, okay. Enough. Look at this." Envy removed a stunning, black, three-piece pantsuit from the hanger. The pantsuit included a sheer, button-front duster with hanging lace appliqués and a handkerchief hem, a square neck tank, and elastic waist pants.

"It's hot. I love it. I can't believe it. But how will I look in either of the outfits you guys chose?"

"Great," Kacie encouraged her. "Go try them on. Then come out and model each one of them for us. You know we aren't going to tell you a lie."

Layla followed their suggestions. Each outfit made her face glow like a cluster of stars. She felt her level of confidence soaring above the clouds and the smile that filtered her face was irreplaceable. After listening to Kacie and Envy's oohs and ahhs, she purchased the outfits, plus matching shoes and accessories.

After visiting almost every store that sold plus size wear, Layla came out of the stores satisfied with the outfits and lingerie she'd chosen. On their way outside of the mall, the three of them sang, *"Hey, wait a minute Mr. Postman...Hey, hey, hey, Mr. Postman."* Between singing, they laughed, ignoring the weird looks some people gave them.

"Thank y'all for the best time ever," Layla told them. She paused before going to the passenger's side of Layla's van. "I just thought about something."

"What is it, Layla? We are not going back in there and buying that red thong," Envy teased.

Layla and Kacie burst out in laughter too. "You know better than that. But Kacie said she had something important to tell us. But then we started talking about me and forgot all about you, Kacie." Layla turned and looked at her friend and Envy stood still in front of her car door.

"Come in, we don't want to be late for the play," insisted Layla and they left and struck out for the car to place Layla's packages in Envy's trunk and then they made the short walk to the Orpheum.

The three friends laughed and cried during the play. Once it ended they proceeded to leave the Orpheum and continued to talk about the play.

"Y'all, I'm telling you, Harpo was a fine brotha, totally unlike the one who played Harpo in the movie version."

"Yes, indeed. He was that. And Sophia acted her butt off." Layla added as they walked down Main Street.

"My favorite was Shug Avery. She really played her part well. And the church ladies, y'all they had it going on," Kacie laughed and the others along with her.

"Envy, thanks again for inviting us. Your job has some good perks," Kacie exclaimed.

Envy smiled and said, "That's what friends are for. My company sponsors the section where we were sitting, which means we always get tickets to the shows. It's just that I can't get them all the time. Non-management employees have to have the same opportunity as management does, you know. It wouldn't be fair otherwise. It's still early yet. Come on, let's go walk back on Beale and have a drink?" suggested Envy.

"I don't think I'll go," Kacie said. "It's already late, and I left the kids at home. But y'all can come and hang out over my house. I have some wine coolers in the fridge."

"I hate it when you do that, Kacie. You were supposed to call the girl down the street. So much can go wrong when you leave small kids at home by themselves."

"Look, I told y'all I wasn't going to miss this play. Plus, I don't do it all the time and y'all know it. I don't wanna hear your lectures tonight."

"You know she's right though, Kacie." Envy pushed her eyeglasses up on her nose. "You do it all the time."

Layla agreed with Envy and said, "Yea, and you know it."

Kacie did her usual wave of the hand and started to talk about her favorite part of the play again. They chuckled and talked about the Broadway show, and Layla even got a chance to talk a little bit about her lunch proposal from Dennis. The girls made it to the car and struck out to take Kacie home so she could check on her kids.

Layla couldn't help but grin from ear to ear for almost the entire time Envy drove to Kacie's house. When they got there, Kacie unlocked the door and found the kids in the living room watching *Pirates of the Caribbean III* for what was probably the tenth time since she'd bought them the DVD. Keshena was laid out asleep on the couch, one leg hanging off the pillow. Kassandra sat in the corner of the sofa while Kenny and Keith lay on the floor with their heads resting in their heads.

"Kenny, where are Kali and Kendra?" Kacie's voice was stern.

"They're in their room. They're sleeping already," Kenny replied without taking his eyes off the television.

"Well, y'all turn that television off and go to bed. Me, Layla, and Envy are going to chill for a minute."

"Hey, you guys," Layla said first as the kids slowly moved from their stilled positions.

"Hello, Auntie Layla. Hi, Aunt Envy." They spoke one by one.

Kassandra picked up Keshena and carried her to the back along with them. The baby didn't wake up at all.

Kacie went to the kitchen and pulled out a six-pack of wine coolers. They gathered around the table and the ladies continued where they'd left off in the car.

"Tell us about what's going on with you, Envy?" Kacie asked as she sat the coolers on the table.

Kacie opened one and took a swig of the ice-cold cooler. "Yea, you always playing the field but you don't ever seem to be trying to settle down." Envy's eyes evaded Layla and Kacie.

"I don't know what y'all talking about." Envy cracked a slight smile. "I'm not getting involved and falling head over heels for some man. I don't care how fat his bank account is or how good he looks. Nice conversation, a light dinner, and dancing, and that's it." She followed up with a gulp of her cooler.

"Don't you ever, you know?" Layla hunched over and rested her elbow on the table and the side of her face in her hand. An unwelcome blush popped out on her chubby cheeks.

"Ever what? Cat got your tongue now?" Kacie pressed.

"Leave her alone, Kacie. You and I both know what she's asking. Do I ever want some is what you want to know, isn't it? Like do I ever have the desire to make love to a man?" Envy spoke confidently. "To answer your question, of course, I do. And when I feel like that, then I take action."

Kacie, surprised at Envy's bold response said, "Oooh, lawd have mercy. No, you didn't just say that." Both Kacie and Layla threw their heads back and exploded in laughter.

"I sure did. The truth is the truth. Men do it all the time. They hit it and quit it. So I figure, why can't I do the same? I mean, it's not like I do it often, just now and then." Envy added that lie because men came in and out of her humble abode like roaches commuting from one apartment to the next.

Layla's burst of laughter stopped as suddenly as it had started. "But let's get serious for a minute here. We profess to be Christians. None of us have the freedom to use our bodies the way we want to. We're supposed to present our bodies as a living sacrifice, holy and acceptable to God."

"Preach, girl, tell her all about it." Kacie wound a finger through her hair.

Envy crooked her neck to the side, tilted her glasses down, and focused her gaze on Layla. "Look, Kacie, I know you aren't saying amen to anything. You probably have asked God for so much forgiveness for all the children you got that it's one of the longest on God's prayer list."

"Ha, ha." Kacie faked the laugh. "I could care less what any of y'all think. God knows my heart. And I am a Christian; so don't try to judge me. And another thing, so what if I have children with no good daddies? It's not my fault."

"Not your fault?" Envy bucked her eyes at Kacie and said, "Are you crazy? Don't you know that if you're going to mess around with every Tom, Dick, and Harry and Harry's brother, then you should at least use some form of birth control, stupid?" Envy's anger was obvious. "Better yet, you need to stop having sex altogether 'cause you know you're a baby-hatching machine." Envy scorned her.

"Look, we're not here to argue, y'all," interrupted Layla. "God knows we're human and we're carnal minded. I wasn't trying to be judgmental anyway; all I was saying is that we need to exercise more control and discipline over our bodies. When Dennis asked me to have lunch with him, I felt like I wanted to lie right on the concrete pavement and say, *here I am, baby, signed, sealed delivered, I'm yours*," Layla sang.

The girls giggled again and calmness returned to the table.

"That is too funny, Layla," remarked Envy. "And, Kacie," Envy said, "don't take things so seriously. We've all done wrong and we all have some dirt in our lives. I know I do. And maybe I don't have kids and baby daddies running around, but I kid you not like I said. I have had more than my share of sleeping partners."

"I can't talk either," Layla added. "Mike didn't just come over once or twice a month for money." Kacie and Envy appeared stunned. It was the first time they'd heard Layla admit that Mike came to see her for money. "I gave him money. He gave me sex. I hate what I became with him. Nothing more than a whore. And when he couldn't use me anymore, he wanted to see me sprawled out on the concrete dead." Tears that crested in Layla's eyes streamed down her face and onto the table.

Envy teared up as well. "It's all right, Layla." The friends embraced her with love.

"Yeah, you have needs too. And sometimes we get caught up when we don't mean to. Next thing you know, we find ourselves in a vicious cycle with no idea of how to get out of it." Kacie's eyes darkened with emotion. "So, don't feel bad about yourself or what you've done. God has given you the strength to move past what happened with Mike."

"Yea, and who knows. Dennis might be the one to show you the brighter side of life and maybe even love," Envy encouraged her. "I don't know, but whether he does or not, really doesn't matter because God has you, me, and Kacie. That's what Mrs. Rawlings tells me and I believe it. I just wish I had better control over me, you know.'

"But today, there's no one really walking around who hasn't indulged in some form of sex outside of marriage. Even preachers. What do we do? Men don't even want to fool with you unless you give up the booty," Kacie said and plopped both hands on the table.

Layla looked at Envy and then Kacie, and said, "Thanks, y'all. That's why I love you two. You're always here for me."

"And the same goes here," Kacie remarked. "That brings up what I wanted to tell you. But you have to promise that what I'm about to say doesn't go outside of this room because no one other than the two of you will know about it until I decide to tell someone else."

"Okay, okay, you know you never have had to tell us to keep a secret so don't act like you do now," Envy reminded her.

"Come on, tell us. I'm tired of the anticipation. When is the wedding date?"

"I hope it's soon. But that's not it." Her eyes were radiant. She gracefully stood from her sea and looked at her friends. Sighing with a smile, Kacie said, "I'm pregnant with Deacon's child."

Layla stared blankly at Kacie with her mouth open.

Envy remained mute with a mask of stone replacing an earlier smile.

"Okay? What's wrong? I don't hear any congratulations." Kacie got up and strolled around the table with her arms folded.

"Congratulations? Girl, are you crazy or on drugs? Did you just hear what we were talking about? What is wrong with you? What makes you think we would be happy about your tail being pregnant? You know what? You're a work of art. A stupid work of art at that."

Envy jumped up from the chair, threw her hands up in the air, and turned toward the door. "Layla, you going or what? Because I am not going to stay here and listen to this fool one minute longer. Then she got the nerve to talk about God this and God that. You're nothing but a hypocrite."

"Wait just a minute. Who are you calling a hypocrite?" Kacie stepped up in Envy's face. "Just who do you think you are? You're the last one that should be judging me or anybody else."

"Wait up, y'all." Layla stood and moved in the middle of the heated argument. "Listen, Kacie, all Envy is trying to say is that you and Deacon haven't committed to each other. What does he have to say about it? Is he going to marry you?"

"I...I haven't told him," she said with her head slightly down.

Envy chuckled hysterically. "I bet you haven't. I wanna know how soon this so-called man from God is going to hang around when he finds out you're pregnant, let alone marry your delusional butt. I guess you don't realize that forty-five percent of black women with children are unmarried. What makes you think you're going to be the one that tilts the statistics, especially with your track record with six million children growing up in single-parent homes?" Envy spoke angrily. "You don't even take care of the six you already have," Envy yelled.

"Kacie, you need to tell him. I mean, how do you know he wants a child? And you already have six kids. Dang. This isn't right. It wasn't a wise decision on yours or Deacon's part."

"I know how many children I have. And you know what. Y'all don't know what you're talking about. Deacon loves me and we are going to get married. I'm telling him about the baby tomorrow. Then I wanna see your cracked faces. Things are different this time. God sent me this man. He's decent, he's kind and he treats me well." Kacie cried.

Envy got even closer in Kacie's face like she was about to strike her. "What do you call treating you well, Kacie? I guess you think that means bringing you a sausage and biscuit sandwich when he comes over here in the morning to get his rocks off before he goes to work? And when has he ever tried to form a relationship with the kids you already have? What has he done to help with them or to take time to spend with them since he's so good to you?" Envy jerked her hand back like she was about to strike Kacie.

Kacie moved in closer and as upset as she was, she almost lost her balance.

"I'm so sick and tired of y'all bashing me and downing me. Just go. Y'all get out of my house. Right now." Kacie walked to the door and yanked it open.

Envy rolled her eyes. "With pleasure. Let's go, Layla."

Layla followed Envy in silence with tears in her eyes.

"You're pitiful, Kacie. And you have the nerve to wanna give advice to Layla. Seems to me you need to look in the mirror and learn to love yourself for who you are and for how God made you." Envy turned around and pounced out of the door. Layla followed.

Once in the car and driving off, Envy couldn't hold back. "Layla, I know you want to be the nice and sensible one, but even you have to admit that the broad must've lost her marbles. Pregnant? This will make seven children. No father or should I say fathers in her case."

"I don't understand her either. But I'm praying that Deacon loves her, and I hope to God he wants this child." Layla massaged her forehead. "This is too much to take in. I think Kacie has low self-esteem. It has to be hard living with the crippling effects of cerebral palsy. It has to be hard having to deal with the way some people stare at her. And she told us more than once how much kids used to tease her when she was growing up. Shoot, Envy, I don't have cerebral palsy or a house full of kids but I'm self-conscious because I'm fat. Not obese. I'm fat. And it hurts. It makes me feel bad."

"But you can do something about it if you exercise, change your diet, and work on yourself and your health. And that's exactly what you've been doing. You should congratulate yourself on the weight you've already lost. I know it came by means of a horrible crime against you, but you're making it work for you, Layla. You're not walking around like you used to do having a pity party. But Kacie, having baby after baby, by one man after another, does not do anything to improve her self-esteem issues. It makes her look like a slut, plain and simple. I don't feel sorry for her anymore. And not only is she sleeping with men as they say, 'in the raw' and getting pregnant, dang, Layla, she doesn't care enough about herself to insist that he use protection? It's downright irresponsible."

Disgusted, Envy shook her head. Drew in a deep, unsteady breath and pushed her eyeglasses up on her face.

"We have to pray for her, Envy. Only God can help her."

"Yeah, I guess you're right, but God has His work cut out for Him."

They arrived at Layla's apartment. They got out of the car and Envy helped Layla with her packages.

Envy sat the packages inside the door.

"I guess I'll talk to you tomorrow. Thanks for taking us to the play and for bringing me home."

"Yeah, sure, talk to you later."

Layla closed the door and disappeared.

Envy clicked her Bluetooth on and dialed a number on her cell phone before pulling off and going in the direction of home.

"Hey, what's up?" She asked the person on the other end. "I need some company tonight. You game?"

She listened to the man's reply.

"I thought you would be. Be at my place in an hour," she commanded and clicked off her Bluetooth.

Envy rushed home; walked Fischer, and checked on Mrs. Rawlings' house. Hopefully, Mrs. Rawlings would be discharged tomorrow which would make things easier for Envy. After her tasks were done, Envy bathed and waited on her playmate for the night.

***

At home, Kacie flopped down on her bed and cried.

"Hey, sugar plum." Deacon's voice soothed her.

"Hi."

"How was the play?"

"It was good. Layla and Envy just left." She sniffed. "They came over and we had a couple of wine coolers. I was just about to call it a night. Unless you're coming over here," she managed to say while she wiped the last few tears from her eyes.

"I wish I could, but I'm beat. It's been a long day. I hung out with the boys, shot some hoops, and played a few rounds of pool, something I haven't been able to do in quite a while. I just wanted to tell you that I miss you." He sent a kissing sound over the phone.

Kacie almost cried again. "I miss you too," she paused. "Deacon?"

"Yea, baby?"

"I *will* see you tomorrow, won't I?"

"I plan on it. I have a meeting at the church at one o'clock and then a few errands to run after that. So we'll see how it goes. I told the boys I might meet them again tomorrow afternoon for a rematch at the hoops." Deacon laughed.

"Just call me and let me know. But first, I want to ask you something, and please don't get upset," Kacie added.

"What is it?"

"Deacon, we've been together almost five months and I still haven't been to your apartment or house or whatever it is. And I don't have your phone number, just your cell."

"Baby, please don't start this again." His voice sounded disapproving of her questioning.

"I've told you more than once that it doesn't make sense for me to have a home phone. My cell phone is my home phone, my business phone, and my social phone. As for visiting my apartment, I don't see what the big deal is. I don't like it when you get upset with me," he said in a tender voice.

"You're right and I'm sorry. I didn't mean anything by it."

"You must mean something about it because you're hassling me about it." His voice turned from tender to rough. "As for coming to my crib, I haven't pushed that because of your kids. I know it's hard getting a babysitter all the time. I don't mind paying and you know I've done that before. But why pay a babysitter when you have a nice place, and when the kids are asleep, hey we make our own fun." He tried to remove some of the edge from his voice. "Do you think I enjoy disappointing you? This job is so stressful, Kacie. I can't seem to get from under it. I know this isn't the time to tell you, but Friday night is off. I know you're probably sick and tired of me making plans with you and then having to go back and renege on them, but my boss insists that me, him, and two other executives spend Friday, and probably Saturday morning, catering to these executives coming here from Japan. I didn't want to tell you, especially when I call and you jump all over me. I know how much you wanted to see *Sinsatiable* and I'm sorry."

"Deacon, everything you've said is right. Please, forgive me, baby. I'm just feeling lonely for you tonight. I should know better. You work hard and being an executive for a large corporation isn't easy. It's me. I'm being unreasonable."

"Look, I tell you what I'll do."

"What are you going to do?" Kacie asked in a sorrowful voice.

"I'm going to make dinner for you – at my place. Just give me a few days so I can make sure I don't have to go out of town for work or have anything that will interrupt us. Okay? Does that make my baby feel better?"

"Oh, Deacon. Are you serious?" she asked happily

"Have I ever lied to you?" he asked.

"No."

"Well, it is what it is," he said. I don't ever want you to be angry with me. I promise I'll try to do better. Please, just tell me that you forgive me."

Immediately, her uncertainty subsided. "Oh, I love you, Deacon. I love you so much. And I forgive you." Relief filled her. She would show Envy and Kacie how wrong they were about Deacon.

"I know you do, baby. Now look, I'm about to pull up to the apartment. I'm going to hit the shower and then jump in bed and dream about you. I want you to sleep well and have dreams about me too."

Kacie went to bed and almost on cue, she drifted off to sleep and began to dream about her and Deacon and their bundle of joy. He was with her in labor and delivery, encouraging her, wiping the sweat from her face, kissing her face, and telling her over and over again just how much he loved and adored her.

***

Layla prepared for bed. She still felt mild effects from the coolers. Drinking alcohol was something she didn't make a practice of doing, but having a cooler every now and then wasn't a sin in Layla's book.

She relived the day's events and her body shivered at the thought. When she finished undressing, Layla saw the flickering light on her answering machine. Unlike Kacie and Envy, she didn't own a cell phone. She had six messages. Three from her mother, calling to make sure she was doing all right and one of the messages was to see if she had made it home yet. The fourth message was from her brother who said he was just calling to chat with her since he hadn't talked to her in a few days. The fifth message was the choir director reminding her about the special choir rehearsal Saturday morning. But it was the last call that made her stumble and fall back on the bed, breathless with excitement.

"Hi, Layla. It's Dennis. I know you're out with your girls. I hope you're having a great time. I just wanted to let you know that I enjoyed talking to you today. Have a good night. And if you have caller ID, this is my home number that I'm calling from, so if you want to talk when you get in, hit a brother up. If you don't, then I'll understand. I hope to talk to you and see you tomorrow. Sleep tight."

Layla hit the delete buttons one by one but saved Dennis's message. She picked up the phone to dial his number but had second thoughts. "I don't want to come off like I'm desperate. I'll talk to him tomorrow," she said.

Getting down on her knees, she prayed a prayer of thanksgiving and gratitude. She sent up a special prayer for Kacie. When she climbed into bed, she turned over and picked up the phone to let her mother know that she was safe and at home. Then she called her brother and talked to him for almost an hour until her eyes became droopy and her voice slurred from tiredness. Just before dozing off, she told God 'Thank you" again and smiled herself to sleep.

*****

While Kacie was at home crying about Deacon, and Layla was enjoying the newness of having someone interested in her, Envy was at her apartment fighting off the psychological line her guest was trying to lay on her. She had faults that much was true, but being stupid like Kacie, Envy was not. She was not about to be any man's fool. She called the shots.

"I don't need you trying to get all serious with me. It is what it is," Envy explained to her gentleman guest.

"Why do you do me like this? I got feelings for you. Real feelings, Envy," Leonard admitted to her." He sounded like he was pleading and it caused Envy to shut down her heart even more.

"Look, I've told you time and time again that I'm not the serious kind. I don't believe in falling in love and I don't want commitment. You don't have to take care of me, and you don't have to wine and dine me. All I want is what I got. I'm satisfied and I know you're satisfied," she said with the voice of a kitten and the stance of a lion.

He stepped forward, reaching out toward Envy just as she moved away. "Come on, it's two something in the morning. Way past my curfew for visitors," she said sarcastically. "You've got to go."

He stiffened like she had prodded him with a branding poker. The executive put on his designer clothes, stepped into his soft leather shoes, and slowly, like a whipped puppy followed Envy to the door with Fischer wagging his tail beside Envy.

"I don't understand you. One minute you're ringing my number off the hook. All you want from me is sex. There are other times you've called and I've listened to you, Envy. Listened to you like a true friend. You mean a lot to me, girl. I only hope you allow the ice around your heart to melt before it's too late."

"Thanks. Drive safely." She closed the door. While she showered, Fischer lay on the bathroom floor.

Following her routine, she removed the soiled sheets and replaced them with fresh ones.

Fischer jumped on the bed and cuddled at the foot of the bed while Envy swiftly drifted off to sleep.

12

"Beauty is not in the face; beauty is a light in the heart."
Khalil Gibran

"Come to the altar. All you who are burdened and
heavy laden. If you want to come and intercede on behalf
of someone else, please come. God wants you to come."
The lay pastor of the nine o'clock a.m. service beckoned.
Most of the congregation followed his prompting and
gathered around the front of the pulpit while the pastor
prayed.

Like she'd done once before, Kacie looked around
with her head bowed, searching for Deacon. *He really
has it coming. Where is he?*

"Hug somebody while you return to your seats," the
pastor ordered. Kacie walked past everyone, ignoring the
pastor's instructions. The kids were in the newly started
children's church and nursery. She was glad they had
finally opened a nursery during this service. Bypassing
her seat, Kacie went out the side door leading out to the
hall where the restrooms and fellowship hall were. She
walked around the circumference of the church, peeping
in as many doors as she could, all except the one marked
Private and Pastor's Office. Her anger rose and she went
back inside and reclaimed her seat next to Envy.

"Where were you?" Envy whispered.

Kacie waved but didn't say a word. The sermon went
on in slow motion. She was anxious to leave when the
pastor ended his message and extended an invitation for
people to join the church.

Kacie whispered to Envy that she was leaving. She
went to the children's church to gather four of the kids,
but before she could make it to the nursery for her other

two children, the words from the intercom stopped her dead in her tracks.

"For those of you who have to leave, we understand. But today we are installing three trustees and two deacons."

Kacie's face glowered. She gave the kids a *do not say another word* stare while walking back toward the sanctuary.

The seat next to Envy was vacant along with enough room for the kids since several people had departed.

"I thought you were gone."

"I thought I was too. I came back when I heard them say they were inducting trustees and deacons today. Deacon didn't tell me anything about it. I bet that's why I haven't seen him in service. He's probably going to be inducted today. He said the pastor had a meeting with him again yesterday." She tried to whisper as softly as she could. "He must've wanted to surprise me. Ooh, I love that man." Kacie smiled and kissed one of the kids on top of the head.

Envy's mouth turned upwards like she was equally happy for Kacie.

The pastor and deacons made their usual round of speeches as they prepared to ordain trustees and deacons.

Kacie's smile was equally as broad when five men, including Deacon, paraded into the sanctuary and down to the front of the church. They stood firmly and quietly next to each other facing Pastor Betts and his board of trustees and deacons. The ceremony was spiritually inspiring to Kacie, so much so, Envy looked in her direction and saw glitters of tears falling down Kacie's face.

For the next hour, each man was asked a series of questions which they answered individually before the congregation and pastoral ministry, and deacons.

Afterward, each newly ordained deacon and trustee was called and along with his wife and family, presented with a Bible and Certificate of Ordination.

Kacie seemed to glow at the thought that soon she would be the wife standing next to Deacon to pledge her support for him, along with their child like the other two wives and children.

"Deacon Riggs," the pastor called.

In her mind, Kacie pledged to be a faithful, loving, and supportive wife.

The choir began to sing the gospel hymn, *We All Can Do Good*.

Layla could barely maintain her stance at the shock of seeing the look on Kacie's emaciated face.

Kacie's eyes filled with liquid as the congregation walked around and extended congratulations.

The woman next to Deacon had her arm entwined in his. With apparent ease, she shook each person's hand that passed by her and thanked them for their congratulatory remarks toward her husband.

Envy approached Deacon and said in a rough tone, "Congratulations - Trustee Riggs."

With relative ease, Deacon replied, "Thank you, Sister Wilson."

"Hello, I'm sorry, how are you?" Envy addressed the woman and coldly extended her hand toward the woman's heavily bejeweled hand. "I'm Sister Envy Wilson."

"I'm Martha Riggs," the lady answered confidently.

Deacon's face reddened. "Sister Wilson, this is my wife." He embraced his wife tightly around her waist. His introduction of his wife sounded like he intentionally said it loud enough for Kacie to hear him as she stood in line behind Envy, trembling like she was standing stark naked in a snowstorm.

Kacie gave Deacon a blazing stare while tears took up residence at the edges of her eyes. "Congratulations, Trustee Riggs." Her bitter voice all but died away.

His reply sounded like an echo from afar.

Before Kacie had time to say anything to Deacon's wife, she felt the tug of a person's hand on her wrist. It was Envy's firm grip pulling her right past Deacon's wife before the chance of trouble could break out.

Layla met Envy and Kacie at the other side of the church exit.

Kacie, still in disbelief, caved into the hurt that penetrated her heart. Her knees already naturally buckled, but with Layla and Envy planted on each side of her, it halted her total collapse.

"Oh, my God. I can't believe this. I can't, I can't, I can't." She cried into her hands. Several church attendees watched closely as did Kacie's older children who had no idea why their mother was in tears.

"Come on, Kacie. Let's get you out of here. I'll go get Kali and Keshena." Layla looked back over her shoulder as she passed by the open sanctuary. She caught a clear glimpse of Deacon. Like a true professional actor, she saw the shimmer of his smile and how he embraced... Mrs. Riggs. *May God have mercy on your rotten soul, Deacon.* Layla turned back around and concentrated on her destination.

"Kacie, there's no way you can drive. I'll take you home and get a friend to come back and get your car. Or I can use my roadside assistance service to have it towed to your house."

Bawling, with dribbles of snot forming under her nose, Envy hurriedly grabbed a piece of tissue from her purse and passed it to Kacie just in time. "I can drive myself. I don't need your help, honestly. I don't."

"No, listen, Kacie. Envy's right. You're in no condition to drive. You're too distraught," Layla told her.

"No," Kacie insisted. "I can drive. Come on, y'all," said Kacie as she reached toward her kids.

Envy looked at Layla and Layla returned the gaze. "Look, I'll follow you home then," Envy demanded.

"And I'll ride with Kacie," Layla remarked. "That way, I can make sure she's going to be okay."

"All right. But let the kids ride with me. Let me get their car seats." Envy walked toward Kacie. "Kacie, the children are riding with me. Kenneth and Kassandra help me get the car seats, please," Envy asked."

Kenneth and Kassandra obeyed and once the car seats were in place in Envy's car, they all climbed inside.

Kacie got to her car, and with Layla rushing behind her, she jumped inside and sat still for several seconds. With streams of tears falling, the heavy sobs poured and sounded like a gushing waterfall.

Layla reached over and placed her arm around Kacie's shoulders and cried with her. "I'm so sorry this happened to you. God knows I am."

"I don't understand. I had no idea Deacon was married. How could he do this after all these months? How could he lead a double life?"

"I don't know. I wish I had the answer, but I don't. All I know is that you have to get yourself together. You have six children who need you."

Kacie looked over at Layla. After a long pause, she swallowed hard. "He's going to pay. He's going to pay dearly," she said in a defiant voice before she started the car and pulled out of the parking space.

The women made it safely to Kacie's. Envy had stopped at McDonald's to get all of the children Happy Meals so Kacie wouldn't have to worry about preparing food for them.

The children, excited they had Happy Meals, happily climbed out of Envy's car one by one. One of the older kids picked up baby Keshena and carried her up to the porch where they waited for their mother to unlock the door.

Kacie's eyes were almost swollen shut by this time. Weak. Broken. Stunned. How could pain hurt so bad? How could love that was right turn out to be wrong?

Once inside the house, Layla and Envy helped get the children settled at the kitchen table, then refocused their attention on Kacie.

"Did you have any idea about this? Any idea at all?" asked Envy like she believed Kacie knew all along about Deacon having a wife.

Kacie tossed her head and stiffened defiantly when she heard Envy's question. Her unsteady legs forced her to hold on to the nearby recliner. "How could you ask me that? Do you think I would have allowed myself to fall for somebody else's husband?" At that moment, she felt a mild contempt for her friend. "I'm not you, Envy. I don't make a habit of dating just anybody's man, or should I rephrase that and say any man?" She bit back sharply.

Envy placed both hands on her curvaceous hips. "Look, don't get bent out of shape with me. I'm not Deacon and I sure as heck am not his wife. I was just asking."

"Let's not argue about this. We don't want the kids to hear any of this," Layla whispered. "I'm just shocked at the nerve of that guy. But I must say, I have to give him his props."

"Props? What does that mean?" Kacie asked bitterly.

"He managed to fool a whole lot of people," explained Layla. "Think about it. I've never heard anyone at church mention him having a wife. And I mean never. Have you, Envy?" Envy shook her head, no. "What about you, Kacie?" Kacie tearfully shook her head, no. "That's what I'm talking about. People at church can be some of the worse gossipers, but I've never heard anything about the, oh so perfect, Trustee Deacon Riggs." Layla laughed sarcastically. "What a name to go with such a slimeball."

The three of them managed to laugh slightly before Kacie returned to a serious look. Her pulse beat wildly. Confused. Baffled. Bewildered. Her emotions spun out of control. "I'm pregnant with Deacon's child." It was as though she suddenly remembered her condition.

"What are you going to do about it? He doesn't know, does he?" asked Layla.

"No. I never had a chance to tell him. I planned on telling him last night but he didn't call me back."

"It explains why he never took you to his place," commented Envy.

Kacie spoke up almost like she was defending him. "But he said that was because he didn't want me to be away from the kids, and he was usually in and out of town, or getting home late at night."

"Sure, and you fell for that line. But now it all makes sense. And people say the devil is a liar. Sounds like Trustee Deacon just might have the ole sly devil beat," Envy said with a smirk on her face. She removed her glasses and started nibbling on the end of the frame.

"Are you still planning on telling him that you're pregnant now that you know he's married?" Layla looked confused.

"No, the question is, are you still going to have the baby? How far along are you?" inquired Envy while she twisted her glasses around in her hand, apparently agitated at Kacie's excuses.

"I'm four months pregnant for your information. And what kind of question is that? I don't believe in abortion. I could never imagine killing my child."

"Yea, you don't believe in abortion, but you sure don't have a problem lying down with one dog after another and popping babies out like a rabbit-making machine," snapped Envy. "You're doing nothing but talking and living a double standard. You're fooling no one but yourself, because you're sure not fooling God. You better check your salvation, baby, because you're living an outright lie."

"A lie?" Kacie yelled. "I am not."

"In a way you are," Layla said in her soft, kitten-like voice. "I don't condone abortion either, but God says that adultery and fornication are wrong too. Maybe Envy didn't exactly say it lovingly, but what she said is true, Kacie."

"Whatever," Kacie stormed back. "Two wrongs don't make a right, and I am not aborting my baby. And for your information, Miss Church Lady," Kacie focused her gaze on Layla. "God says gluttony is a sin too, but I see you're still feeding your fat...oops, I mean your face," she quipped. "The only reason you're losing a little weight is because you got half your belly yanked out because of that no-good Mike," Kacie said with hatred.

Envy played advocate and stopped the heated exchange between them because things had gotten out of hand. "Now you know you were wrong for that, Kacie."

Surprised at Kacie's callous comments, Layla bowed her head in silence like a scared sacred calf. "Do whatever you want to do. It's your life."

"Kacie, sleep on it," Envy advised. "It's been a wild and crazy Sunday. When he calls, you don't have to talk to him until you're ready, you know."

"Do you honestly think he's going to call after this?" asked Kacie. "If he does, he's going to get cussed out, and I mean it. Y'all talking about me living a double life, well I'm telling you already that my religion is out the door tonight. That dog is going to bark like mad when I finish destroying him."

Come on, Layla," urged Envy. "Let's go. Don't do anything stupid, Kacie," Envy told her while Layla walked toward the door in hurtful silence.

Kacie stood up. Her legs quivered uncontrollably when she stood; something that was often intensified when she was nervous. She supported her shaky legs by holding on to the wall, the chair, and finally the front door. "Thanks, y'all. I don't know what I'd do without you."

Envy hugged Kacie. "Sure," Layla said and walked past Envy and outside the open door.

"Layla," Kacie said in a pleading tone. "I'm sorry about what I said. I never meant to hurt you." Kacie's eyes shined with the sparkle of fresh tears as did Layla's.

"I know." Layla cried. "I know."

Kacie was in her room crying a river of tears when the phone rang. She saw Deacon's name pop up and refused to answer. She didn't want to hear anything he had to say. He had been lying to her all of this time and nothing could make up for that. Now, here she was, pregnant with his child. What was she going to do? The phone stopped ringing for only a few seconds before it started ringing again. Once again, Kacie refused to answer. She undressed and put on a pair of PJs and curled up in her bed. She turned her phone off and called out the names of her kids and instructed them to come and get in the bed with her. It was something she did from time to time, especially when she felt unloved, alone, and forsaken. No matter what went wrong in her life, she could rely on her children to be there for her. They loved her despite the mistakes she made, no matter how angry she got, or how many men she slept with. They loved her because she was their mother. They depended on her and no one else.

***

"Do you believe she's going to tell Deacon about the baby?" Layla asked on their drive home.

"Layla, you and I both know that it's hard to tell what Kacie is going to do. Who would have thought she would get pregnant again? And why, for God's sake, won't she get her tubes burnt, tied up, twisted, and in knots? Whatever it takes. Kacie is one person that I have never been able to figure out. I'm not going to try anymore either." Envy sighed and kept driving. A look of downright revulsion formed on her face.

"But, Envy, I still feel sorry for her. I mean she can barely provide for the six kids she already has. From what she says, only one of her kid's daddies pays child support, and I don't think that amounts to much of anything. If it wasn't for food stamps and that part-time job she has, the girl would be homeless."

"You're right. But did you know that she applied for SSI benefits for Keith?" Envy asked and looked at Layla like she knew that Kacie hadn't told her.

"What for? The boy is not mentally or physically challenged. He's just a typical five-year-old kid. How could she even think she could get benefits for him?" Layla became perfectly tuned to what Envy had just said.

"He's been tested at school, and then they sent him for a psychological evaluation. They've determined he has a learning disability. She's waiting to hear from the disability determination section. If he's approved, then she'll get a little over six hundred dollars a month."

Layla spoke in a harsh tone after hearing what Envy told her. "Sometimes, Envy, I don't know about Kacie. She acts like she wants to be stuck in the welfare system forever. I mean, she's not dumb. But then again, she keeps having all of these children. She lives off of section eight and makes just enough money to keep getting benefits. Now if she puts that poor child on disability, she's going to reap even more benefits. As for a learning disability, all he needs is some one on one time, someone to sit down with him and go over his work with him. Instead, she treats those children like they can do everything on their own."

"I agree with everything you've said. But what can we do about it?" Neither of them answered. The car was filled with silence until Envy dropped Layla off at home.

Layla got out of the car and said her goodbyes to Envy. Layla turned the doorknob and heard the phone ringing when she walked inside her apartment. When she answered it, she immediately forgot about all of the day's events. Dennis's voice invoked calmness in her.

"Hello there, lady," he said.

"Hi, Dennis."

"What's up with you this evening?" he asked.

"I just walked into the house. I went to church. Afterward, we had a special installation service for new trustees and deacons. When that was over, I went to visit one of my friends."

"Umm, friend, huh? May I ask if he's a steady friend?"

Layla giggled. "She, not he, is a longtime friend," she quickly made plain.

"I heard that. I'm relieved," he said flirtatiously.

"So, you are, huh?" Layla walked to the living room and sat on the peach print sofa. With shyness in her voice she asked, "And why are you relieved?"

"Because I want you all for myself," he replied boldly. "Can I see you tonight?"

Caught off guard, Layla didn't know what to say. "Uhh," she stammered. "I don't know about tonight."

"So you're saying you don't want to see me?"

"No, I'm not saying that."

"Oh, so you do want to see me?" he spoke jokingly.

Layla laughed. "Yes, I want to see you, but tonight isn't good." Her laugh turned into a voice mounting with uneasiness. Perhaps the cutting words of Kacie still weighed heavily on her mind.

"Okay, I guess I'll let you slide this time. But I do want to see you. I'd like to get to know you better. And of course, you can get to know me better."

"I'll agree to that." Layla's tension eased.

"So why don't I give you a call tomorrow."

"Sure, sounds good."

"Have a great evening, gorgeous."

Layla felt somewhat self-conscious when Dennis called her gorgeous. She wasn't used to such flattering remarks. Mike never called her anything but cutting words. She shook at the thought of Mike. She raised her blouse and glared at the protracted, hideous scar on her belly. The thought of how it got there, made her want to break down. Mike had meant to kill her. When she felt tears trying to fall from her eyes, she quickly released the shirt and focused on her conversation with Dennis. Mike was gone out of her life forever. Not only would he never torment her again, he would never be able to do it to any other woman.

Layla vowed never to allow a man to mistreat her again. She was far too special. God loved her and He wanted everything good for her. She wanted her own treasure, which reminded her; she had to make sure Dennis wasn't carrying any hidden baggage himself.

13

"Everything has its beauty, but not everyone sees it."
Confucius

Mid-morning Kacie woke up to the kids arguing. It took a minute for her to remember they were out of school for the next two days for teachers' conferences. She turned back over in the bed and closed her red, puffy eyes. The past days' events smothered her mind. Deacon was going to pay. Somehow, someway she had to make him feel as much pain as he was causing her. Envy was right. She was stupid and deserved everything coming to her. Now she would have another mouth to feed and no one to help but her. Her family would be angry enough. Rarely did they see the kids and they never volunteered to keep them.

It wasn't until close to one o'clock in the afternoon when Kacie stumbled to the front of the house. Her hair was all over her head and she didn't stop by the bathroom to wash her face or brush her teeth.

"What y'all doing?" she asked the kids.

"Watching TV," Kassandra spoke up.

"Well, y'all clean up the kitchen. Make sure you bathe Keshena too, Kassandra."

"Yes, ma'am," Kassandra answered.

Kacie turned around and ambled back down the hall. She sat back down on her bed, picked up her phone, and then turned it on. Eight messages. Envy had called a couple of times and the other times it was Deacon, pleading for her to talk to him so he could explain. Each message he left, sounded more pitiful than the one before. So much so that Kacie felt compelled to talk to him and hear him out.

Maybe I should at least entertain listening to what he has to say. On second thought, forget his lying behind. Some Deacon he is.

The doorbell chimed.

"Momma, Mr. Deacon's at the door," Keith ran to the back of the house and told her.

"What have I told y'all about opening the door?" she chastised him and popped him on his back.

"But it's Mr. Deacon. You said not to open it if we didn't know who it was," Keith pitifully explained and tried to hold back his tears.

Kacie got up and walked on her tiptoes more than ever. She rushed to the front and met Deacon head-on coming down the hallway. Due to limited muscle restriction in her lower legs caused by her medical condition, Kacie almost lost her balanced when she stopped suddenly. "What are you doing here?"

"We need to talk," he demanded.

Kacie swished around and stormed back to her bedroom. "I don't want to hear what you have to say. Shouldn't you be at work?"

"Don't worry about that. I'm here and we need to talk, like I said," he spoke with furrowed brows.

"I know all there is I need to know. You are a liar." She yelled at Deacon and pointed a finger in his face. "A married liar at that," she fumed.

"Believe me, baby. I planned on telling you, but the time was never right." He broke out into an apology. "Kacie, please, forgive me. I was wrong. I didn't intend for you to find out like this. It's been over between me and Martha for a long time. That's why you never hear about us as a couple. She goes to her home church and I go to mine. We share a house; we have no children or anything else." He lightly grabbed hold of Kacie's elbow as he sensed her body beginning to relax. "What keeps us together is the fact that we share quite a bit of property, stock, and real estate. It would be disastrous for us to divorce just like that." He snapped his fingers.

"Oh, poor, Mr. Riggs. He has so much money that he has to stay in a loveless marriage. Poor, poor Deacon," she said with bitterness ringing through her voice.

"We can work it out, please, just give me time to work everything out." His voice was less brusque.

"And here I was, happier than I'd ever been in my life. You have no idea what you've done, Deacon." Unable to hold back any longer she spoke with desperation in her voice. Holding on to her already baby-fat belly, she blurted, "I'm pregnant. I'm pregnant with your child, Deacon."

The color drained from Deacon's face. He jerked her hard and she held on to his other arm to keep herself from falling.

"How dare you grab me like that. Are you crazy?" Her eyes darkened and displayed a look of fury that Deacon had never witnessed.

He quickly loosened his grip and she flopped back on the bed.

"Pregnant?" He ran his hand through his thick head of naturally reddish-brown hair. "And you want to sit here and go off on me when you've been screwing around on me? Is this your sick-minded way of revenge?" His voice was hoarse with harshness and he took two steps away from her.

"Cheating on you? Why, you good for nothing, fake, wanna be..." Expletives rolled from her lips. "I'm pregnant with your child. I've never cheated on you."

Kacie was so angry she grabbed hold of a pillow and threw it at him.

"Don't get mad now. I know the truth must hurt, but the surprise is on you." Deacon chortled. "You see, baby girl, I can't have children. Not that I owe you an explanation, but I had a vasectomy years ago because I've never wanted kids. So you better add your name to the Maury Show. Maybe he can go through the list of men you've been sleeping with and figure out who the father of this one is. The joke is on you, sweetheart. That kid," Deacon pointed at her slightly swelling tummy, "no way that's mine." He spoke so loudly that there was no doubt he was enraged.

"Get out; you self-righteous, deceitful liar. I *am* pregnant. And you're the father," she screamed, pointing at the door.

He didn't hesitate to follow her commands. His steps were sure and his broad shoulders appeared to stretch the fabric of his shirt as he walked up the hallway.

She stood, her hair disheveled and she frowned with a cold fury.

Kacie caught the kids peeping through a barely open door. "Get back in that room and shut the door," she yelled an octave louder. "Get out of my house," she repeated to Deacon.

Deacon halted when he got to the door. "Even if I could have a kid, do you think I would want it by you? Your children practically raise themselves. I don't know how you tripped them, other dudes, up, but this is one you ain't trapping with your bull crap. I'm outta here. Stay away from me, and if I see you again, it'll be way too soon."

***

Deacon's wool jacket was more than enough to keep him warm against the cold. The heat that had evolved inside him had him hotter than a day in July. He climbed into his car and sped off.

"Dang, I can't believe that I've gotten myself caught up like this. What am I going to do if she starts going around telling folks that lie? Stupid, stupid me. I slipped up one or two times and didn't use protection; that's why she thinks she can blame that baby on me. That's what I get for letting my body control my mind. Dang," he said and gunned the accelerator as he hit the interstate. There was only one person whom he deemed close enough to talk to; his long-time high school friend, Floyd. He called him on his cell phone and Floyd picked up quickly.

"Whuzzup, man?" Floyd answered.

"I need to talk to you. I've got myself into a suckified situation – at least I think I do. You got a minute."

"You at work?"

"Naw, man. Work has to wait. I'm in a suckified situation so going to work is the last thing on my mind."

"Sounds bad, man. Yea, come on over. I'm here by myself, chillin.' My ol' lady's gone with her sister."

Deacon arrived at Floyd's house. He didn't waste time telling him about everything that had happened.

"Man, what were you thinking? A broad like that and you don't use protection? I hate to bash you, but the truth is the truth. You have got yourself in more than a mess. And now you're a deacon at church? All of that is going down the tubes. Vasectomy or no vasectomy, man you need to put a stop to that female and her big mouth. It's bad enough you've been sleeping around on Martha. When she finds out about Kacie, it could lead to the end of your marriage. And then the broad is saying she's pregnant by you, too."

Floyd shook his head in wonderment. "And you know how females are, man. If Martha hears that this chick is pregnant, she's not going to be thinking about you having a vasectomy. That's gone out the window, with the wind, and you know it. It's something about ladies, man.

Martha is probably going to think that you never had a vasectomy, or that you had it reversed. She might even think that you said you had a vasectomy because you didn't want to have children with her. The list of possibilities when it comes to the female psyche is endless."

Floyd stood up from his leather sofa and started pacing across the hardwood floor. "I'm telling you, they believe what they want to believe. I don't know what to tell you, man, except you better get to Martha and tell her everything before that broad gets to her. If that happens, your marriage is probably blown for sure," added Floyd with a wrinkled frown.

Deacon stood up too and took Floyd's place by pacing back and forth. His right hand massaged his stubbled chin. Then he placed both hands on the sides of his head like he was in the throes of a migraine. He stopped and looked at Floyd. "The kid is not mine, that's for sure. She could be lying about the whole pregnancy thing." Deacon's mind was a flurry of confusing thoughts. "You know I never wanted kids and Martha knew it before we got married. My mother used to babysit kids day in and day out and I promised myself that when I became an adult, married, or whatever, there would be no brats running around under my feet. The closest I'll come to claiming a kid is if I'm an uncle."

"I guess the one smart thing you did, for now, is to tell the woman you had a vasectomy. That was good." Floyd laughed lightly. "If she's lying about being pregnant then she'll probably tell you that she had a miscarriage. On the other hand, if she is pregnant, then she's more than likely going to set out to ruin your life. She won't care if it's yours or not because your marriage, your status at church, all of it will be ruined. Dang, man, I feel bad for you." Floyd told him and then placed a hand of sympathy on Deacon's shoulder.

"You don't know Kacie. I don't think she's the kind that will up and disappear. She can cause trouble, and don't forget she goes to the same church as I do; it's not going to be as easy as you might think."

"*Shooo*...man you got yourself into a full-blown mess. I say, give her some money, you know like pay her to shut her mouth. She got at least five baby daddies already, which says right there that she ain't 'bout nothing. Now she wants you to up and believe that what she says is gospel. I say, no way."

Floyd lit a cigarette and pulled on it. He stood with his arms folded and his brow ruffled and remarked, "Whatever you do, from this point on, be smart, man. No more dumb or stupid moves. You're in deep enough already." Floyd patted his friend on the back. He took another pull from his cigarette and squashed the nearly whole cigarette in a nearby ashtray.

"Let me go, man. I'm going home to think and pray. It's wild how life can get screwed up so quickly." Slowly and looking downward, Deacon turned and walked toward the door to leave. "Thanks for listening."

He grabbed his wool jacket off the coat rack by the door and put it on.

"Think about what I said. You know this baby isn't yours. It's not like you haven't had a chick or two on the side before. Did any of them come up with this, 'I'm pregnant' story? No, not one, so that's even more reason for you to know that this female is lying. She's in revenge mode after finding out you're already spoken for."

Floyd and Deacon stood at the front door. "Women are worse than the devil himself when you cross them. You know that for sure," Floyd added and then opened the door.

'I'm outta here. I'll let you know the outcome."
Deacon walked off quickly, trying to hurry to get in the
car to escape the dropping temperature. Just before Floyd
closed the door, Deacon stopped, turned, and said, "One
thing's for sure, I'm not going to let some slut mess up
my life; that you can bank on."

Floyd nodded his head in agreement. "Now that's
what I'm talking about. Check you later, man." Floyd
closed the door and Deacon got in the car with refreshed
confidence.

When he drove into the garage at his home, he went
inside, not fully knowing what to expect. He was a little
paranoid, unsure of what to think. Would it be like in the
movies? A man walks into the house. Mistress and wife
are sitting in the kitchen sipping hot tea or coffee? He
shook his head quickly from side to side to bring himself
to reality. He had to keep it together. Though it had been
only hours earlier when his life changed, it felt like
someone had been watching him the entire time of his
infidelity. He exhaled when he found Martha dressed in a
lounging outfit, reading a book in her favorite gingham
bedroom chair.

"Hello, sweetheart." He knelt over and kissed her
hair.

"Hi. Where have you been? I thought we were going
to spend today together celebrating yesterday's
installation. We barely had enough time yesterday with
everyone pulling at you and then we had dinner with the
other inductees, and on and on. So you can imagine my
disappointment when I woke up, to find you were gone."
She glanced up at him, with acceptance, not anger,
engraved on her face.

"I know. And I'm sorry. But, like always, they called
me to the office to put out a blaze that could have turned
into an inferno. One of our clients was raising cane about

some of the additions he wanted for his office design that he had already signed off on. But all of that's taken care of and now it's just you and me," Deacon said and gingerly removed the novel from his wife's soft hands and gently pulled her up from the chair.

"Well, I want you to know that I'm proud of you for how hard you work to make our life as comfortable as it is." Martha scanned the huge, lavishly furnished master bedroom and smiled. "I'm proud that you are a loving man, a man who treats me like a queen. I'm proud," she continued to talk sexy, "that you are my king. And I'm definitely proud that you are a man of God, Trustee Riggs." She lifted her head and leaned it back. Puckering her lips, he leaned over again and this time kissed her with more passion.

"Thank you, baby. God is good and I pray that I will live up to what he has assigned me to do. Right now, I'm going to take a shower. I want to be nice and fresh for our celebration," he grinned and winked his eye. He kissed her forehead. "Want to join me?"

Martha smiled. "Not this time, honey. I've already had mine." She refocused on the book she was reading and Deacon retired to the bathroom.

Underneath the jet spray, he pondered what to do. "God, I've messed up. I need your help, please. Show me what to do, Lord." He toweled off and then came out of the bathroom in his birthday suit.

Martha's eyes widened when she saw him. His body was muscular; his legs, deep brown. With each step he took toward the bed, she watched him until their eyes connected.

"Like what you see?" he asked.

"Always have," answered Martha. Without saying anything else, Martha stood up and allowed her loose satin gown to fall from her shoulders down to the floor.

The eight steps it took to make it from the chair to the bed proved long enough for Martha to meet her husband in her full nakedness. She stood on her tiptoes and kissed him with her own driving need of desire.

Deacon yielded to his need to be touched and his body craved hers. He gently took control and laid her down on the bed. For now, there were no more thoughts but those of pleasure, passion, and satisfaction.

14

"Beauty is the gift from God." Aristotle

Weeks passed and Kacie hadn't seen or heard from Deacon. She hadn't been to church since the installation service. She couldn't trust what she would do if she saw Deacon serving in his newly appointed capacity.

Kacie met her doctor's appointment before it was time for her to report to work. She only had to work a five-hour shift today. The kids were at school, which made the day even more perfect. Now that Keshena was one year old, according to the Department of Human Services she could go to daycare.

When she was called back to the patient area where the doctor performed an ultrasound.

"Your baby is growing. A big baby too." The heavy accent of the nurse practitioner made her difficult to understand.

Kacie took her time replying. "All of my children were big babies when they were born," she said nonchalantly.

The practitioner's mouth turned slightly upward. He wiped all remaining gel from Kacie's protruding belly.

"Do you want the image of your baby?" the practitioner asked.

"Yes," answered Kacie with a show of happiness on her face for the first time since she'd been in the room.

"You must take vitamins because of low iron," he explained.

"Is the expected delivery date still the same?" Kacie asked as she removed her legs from the stirrups and sat back on the table."

"Yes, middle of May. Sometimes come early. Sometimes late. Up to baby." The doctor laughed.

Kacie left the doctor's office and pinned the ultrasound picture on the top of her sun visor. *Deacon, things will change when you see your child.*

Of all days, when she arrived at work, the store was busier than it had been in a long time. But she still kept thinking about Deacon's stinging words. Here she was, pregnant by a married man.

Kassandra's daddy was married when they messed around too, but at least she'd known it from the beginning, because he was straight up with her. But Deacon, Deacon had purposely deceived her. She was going to do some investigating. She would find where he lived somehow, someway. He didn't know who he was messing with, but Deacon Riggs was going to find out.

She spoke aloud to herself, "If he thinks he's just going to disappear out of me and our child's life, then he's in for a rude awakening. Not this time. This baby's daddy is going to pay, and pay handsomely."

Kacie not only had plans to find where Deacon lived, but she was going to tell Martha Riggs that she and Deacon were in love. Deacon may have refused to accept the fact she was having his baby, but she wanted to hear for herself how his wife would feel once she told her.

Envy, much to Kacie's surprise, came inside the store. Kacie was rearranging stock on one of the aisles when Envy saw her. "How are you, girl?" she asked when she noticed Kacie.

"What are you doing here?"

"I need some panty liners, so I thought I'd run in here on my way to the office. Are you all right? You look a little spaced out."

"Naw, I'm not doing well at all. I'm still perturbed that I haven't heard from Deacon since he popped up over my house a couple of weeks ago raising cane." She whispered to make sure other customers couldn't hear what she was telling Envy. "Remember I told y'all he had the nerve to not only deny the baby, but he wants nothing to do with me."

"I hate to say it, but…"

"Then don't say it. I already know. But I'll take care of it." She forced tears to stay back while she followed Envy to the Health and Hygiene aisle.

"I hate to see you like this." Envy leaned closer to Kacie who nervously started arranging items on that aisle as well, "but I've got to get to work." She squeezed Kacie's hand in support. "We'll talk this out later. Until then, please, Kacie, don't do, or say, anything that you'll regret," Envy pleaded.

"That's one promise I don't know if I can keep."

"Look, I've got to get to the office, but please think about what I said. We'll talk later, "said Envy and touched Kacie's arm in a show of sympathy. "Bye."

Envy turned away and walked off.

"Bye," mumbled Kacie in return, while she continued to nervously fiddle with the items on the shelf.

***

Envy stepped into her car and ignored the cat calls from a couple of guys entering the drugstore. She was used to men flirting with her so much that it had become a regular part of her day. The drive to the office didn't take very long. She parked in the office garage and caught the elevator to her office.

Envy spoke to the administrative assistant and informed her that she would be in her office answering emails, and phone calls, and completing paperwork. Envy's mind, however, continued to center on Kacie's problem. She truly felt sorry for Kacie, but there was nothing she knew to say or do that would help her through this crisis.

"Excuse me, Envy. You have a call on line one," the administrative assistant conveyed through the intercom.

Envy picked up the phone. It was Leonard, one of her *bedtime friends*, something she'd started calling them when the number of men outnumbered their names.

"Good morning, Leonard. It's rather early for a booty call, don't you think? Plus, I'm at work. You, of all people, know that I don't talk about nighttime pleasures when I'm at work. "

"It's never too early when it comes to you." His bold voice hinted at a smattering of laughter. The mere sound of your voice gives me pleasure."

"Whatever, Leonard." Envy continued to scan through her emails.

Leonard was the only one of the numerous men she bedded who meant something to Envy. She liked his style, his cockiness, and he was quite a successful, confident, and kind man.

"I want you to have dinner with me this evening. It's part business and after business is over, I promise to give you all the pleasure your heart desires." His voice was sexy, tender, and empowering. If anyone was capable of transforming her into a love-sick chick, it was Leonard. He was the only man she could easily fall in love with if she didn't keep her guard up - she kept her guard up well.

"So what you're really saying is that you need someone tonight to compliment that Breitling on your wrist." She spoke with assurance and rested the palm of her hand on her desk. She turned in her swivel office chair away from her computer and toward the picture window.

Her response sounded like it amused him because he laughed lightly before he responded. Ahh, Breitling – extravagant and expensive. Envy – well, let's just say, you're exquisite and priceless."

159

"Since you realize that nothing compares to me, I'll take you up on your offer. What time will your driver arrive?"

"Seven. I can't wait to see you," he responded.

"You'll have to." Envy hung up the phone. *Victory.* Envy smiled, turned back toward her desk, and continued working.

Her day was full of clearing her desk of several projects. She shuffled through a few more folders of paperwork and then a call came from the hospital informing her Mrs. Rawlings was being discharged. She looked at the time on the monitor. 2:54 p.m. She wouldn't have much time after picking up Mrs. Rawlings to get ready for her date with Leonard, but she had no choice; she had to.

She finished a memo, passed it to her administrative assistant to deliver, and left the office for the day.

Much to her surprise, it didn't take long for Mrs. Rawlings to be discharged. On the way to take Mrs. Rawlings home, Envy stopped to get Mrs. Rawlings' prescriptions filled and to pick up a vegetable plate from a nearby restaurant.

"I am thankful God sent you my way," Mrs. Rawlings said out of nowhere.

Envy turned and looked at her for a second before she looked back at the road. "There is no need to thank me, Mrs. Rawlings. You're my neighbor, like a grandmother to me." Envy cracked a small smile. "Even though you can be a little nosy, I love you." Envy reached across the seat and squeezed Mrs. Rawlings' age-spotted hands.

"I only do what God tells me to do. Part of that means looking after you and telling you the truth. Now, quit all of this talking and just get me home. I miss my plants and my garden." She gave Envy a weird look. "Did you take care of my garden and my house?" She looked like she was expecting Envy to say that she didn't have time.

"Yes, ma'am, I did. Before I stop talking, I want to tell you that I already made plans tonight; I didn't know you were going to be discharged. I have a business meeting this evening. I'm not sure when I'm going to get back. Would you like Fischer to stay at your place for the evening? I'll make sure I walk him before I leave, and if he acts like he just has to go out before I return, let him in the backyard, but not for long. Twenty minutes max."

"Who are you telling about taking care of Fischer? Child, I know all about that dog. I miss him too. He'll be good company. But don't try to be slick with me. What you're trying to say is that you won't be coming back home from your, uh, business meeting." Mrs. Rawlings frowned.

The expression on Envy's face was one of a thief being caught in the middle of her thieving act. "That's not what I mean at all. I thought you would enjoy seeing Fischer since it's been almost two weeks that you've been away. I know he's going to have a fit when he sees you. As for coming home tonight, I plan to…but if I don't, you know how to call me, right?"

"Humph," Mrs. Rawlings said and turned her head to look at the passing cars and scenery as Envy drove along.

***

Leonard's driver rang the door promptly at seven.

Mrs. Rawlings hovered at her window, while Fischer jumped up next to her and pushed his wet nose against the window. Probably still weak from her hospital stay, Mrs. Rawlings didn't bother to open her door and take a good look at the man to see if it was the same man, but it sure looked like the same limo.

Watching her intently as she approached the open door of the limo, Envy could feel Leonard's gaze. The side look she caught from the limo driver as he escorted her to the limo reassured her of just how good she looked – not that she needed reassurance. She had no doubt she'd chosen well when she decided to wear a midnight black, form-fitting, strapless dress over black, sheer leggings. Metallic silver double-beaded hoop earrings. Snakeskin platform sandals with ankle strap fasteners and a large metallic buckle. Crystal-hinged bracelet. Chanel, of course; together she knew her attire made her irresistible.

Like a sleek runway model, Envy strolled to the limo with confidence clinging to her like a second layer of skin. She gathered her waist-length jacket to shield her from the coolness of the night and seductively scooted into the seat next to Leonard.

When they arrived at the downtown bistro, the business meeting was intriguing to Envy. She loved sitting in on meetings that had the chance of leading to big decisions and risk-taking changes. While she sipped on a cape-style martini, Leonard's financial savvy was evident and toward the close of the business meeting, potential clients had signed on the dotted line as clients. Another achievement on Leonard's ladder of success as a top executive financier.

Envy eyed him with desire when he stood and extended his gratitude and goodbyes to his new clients. She studied his firm mouth that always seemed curled slightly upward in a smile stance. Muscular. Sinewy, classically handsome features and dark coffee skin like he'd been kissed by the sun.

Hypnotic was an understatement when it came to describing Leonard Stein.

For several more minutes, Leonard and Envy remained in the restaurant and shared intimate conversation and club soda.

"Why don't we continue to celebrate my conquest by going to my condo?" With each word he spoke, Envy was drawn in more. "We can make the evening more romantic and fun by riding the trolley if you'd like," he suggested.

"I'd like that," answered Envy. His gray temples and dark hair sent shivers up and down her arms.

Leonard pulled his cell phone out of his inside coat pocket and told his driver about the change of plans.

"Ready?" Leonard asked.

She nodded. Words no longer necessary. Leonard stood, pulled her chair out, and lightly took hold of her soft as cotton hand. Helping her with her jacket, they left the restaurant hand in hand and `ran a short distance to catch the downtown trolley to his Madison West Condo.

Leonard wasted no time going after dessert. Once inside his lush condo, he eased Envy's jacket from her shoulders and slid it down her slender arms. In one motion, she was in his arms. She put up no protest, allowing him to explore the hollows of her back. He ravished her and hungrily covered her mouth with his. Envy felt like she was being transported on a cloud when, with one swoop, Leonard eased her into his arms and carried her into his bedroom. She curled into the curve of his body and teased him with light kisses while he undressed her with skill, removing any barriers of fabric between them. The silk sheets served as an aphrodisiac and her desire for him escalated. She arched her body toward his. Leonard pulled back gently and used one hand to search for protection in the Victorian nightstand drawer.

The coolness of his fingertips brushed against her body. *Be careful, don't even entertain the idea of this relationship being anything more than what it is, friends with benefits.*

Envy sensed that he was just as captivated by her as she was by him when she saw his dark eyes fixed on hers.

Envy gasped as he lowered her body atop hers. For now, everything felt right and good in Envy's world. If only for one night.

15

"I never saw an ugly thing in my life: for let the form of an object be what it may—light, shade, and perspective will always make it beautiful." John Constable

The following Friday was the girls' night out. The three of them sat in Layla's cozy living room, eating caramel popcorn and sipping on sodas. They laughed at the old DVD starring Vivica Fox, *Two Can Play That Game*. At the end of the movie, they began to talk about what was going on in each of their lives; something they routinely did on girls' night out.

"It's not much that's changed since our last girls' night out. I'm working like a speed demon. Oh, and I interviewed for a director's position in my department. I feel confident about it. There's nothing I don't know about quality, whether it's at work or play," Envy proudly stated and took a swig of her soda.

"You know you can be so cocky at times," Kacie told her. "I understand that you should have confidence and faith in yourself and your abilities. But, girl, you can come across as one of them uppity, know it all witches."

Layla listened to the two of them. She was used to their bantering.

"Don't be jealous, Kacie. If I got it like that, then I got it like that. See, the problem with you is that you lack self-esteem. You think you're lucky if a man looks your way and gives you some time. Just because you have cerebral palsy doesn't make you any less than the next female. You're supposed to be the one that has the drawing power. But with you, it ain't so. You're the one that has what a man needs and wants. Didn't God, say that when a man finds a woman he finds a good thing?"

Layla held up her hands. "Hold up, there. That's not exactly what the Bible says, Envy," she interrupted. "It says, "He who findeth a wife, findeth a good thing. Get it straight now."

"Yea, yea, yea, Missionary Hobbs," Envy commented sarcastically. "Speaking of a good thing, what's up with you and Dennis?"

"We're friends. I think we have a pretty solid relationship. We spend a considerable amount of time talking and laughing. We go on walks along Tom Lee Park, when the weather permits. We talk on the phone, and sometimes we go out to eat or take in a movie. You know, just simple, fun things. He's living a celibate lifestyle and so am I. But y'all believe in giving up the booty. I'm sorry to say this, but that's what's got you in the trouble you're in now, Kacie."

Kacie's eyes narrowed. "Don't even go there. Not having sex does not make you a saint, just that much hornier. You're still making out with the guy. As for bringing up me and my children. Lemme tell you!" Kacie swirled her neck, her stomach seemed to swell even bigger than it already was, and then she pointed her longest nailed finger at Layla.

"Hold up, Kacie, she didn't say anything about your children," interrupted Envy.

"When she all but calls me a whore, she's talking about me and my children. When she points the evil finger at me, then she's pointing the finger at my children. And if you had any sense, you'd know that. But you walk around like you're some prized possession yourself. Look, Miss Hot Shot, don't think that me and Layla don't know you're an undercover freak, Kacie said in anger.

"You don't know a darn thing about me." Looking at Layla, she added with force, "And neither do you. So think what you want to think," Envy said with contempt in her voice. "I'm not the two of you. I keep my business

to myself. I don't care how close we are. So think what
you want to think." Envy yelled.

"Sure you don't. You mean the fact that you sleep
around more than half the women in Memphis, doesn't
matter to you?" Kacie's voice raised and she stood from
the sofa like she was ready to fight.

"Stop it! Just stop it, y'all," Layla told them. "We're
friends. None of us are perfect. We all have our faults."

Kacie jumped in again. "You're right, Layla. At least
one of us does." She stared with a creased forehead at
Envy. "But it seems like Envy doesn't know that we
know that she's probably been with more men than she
can keep up with. I bet if she tried to write down the
names of every man that's been in her bed, she'd use up a
full ream of paper." Kacie folded her arms and rudely
giggled

Envy turned crimson. On one hand, she was annoyed,
but it changed quickly to someone who acted like a
demon-possessed woman gnashing her teeth. How did
Layla and Kacie find out about the life she'd tried so hard
to keep hidden? She looked ashamed and cowered like a
two-bit streetwalker who'd been caught goofing off on
the job by her pimp.

"Let's watch another movie, y'all. We're supposed to
watch a thriller now. Remember?" Layla said.

No one said anything.

"Come on, y'all. We're friends and we have been for
a long time. So stop all of this arguing and let's have
fun." Layla tried to persuade the two of them. Instead, the
night came to a swift end.

Envy jumped up and left Layla's apartment without
saying a word. "See," Layla's hands flew up in the air.
"This is exactly what I didn't want to happen."

"It wouldn't have if Envy didn't come across like
she's so high and mighty all of the time. Just because she

has a good job and no kids doesn't make her better than me, or you." Kacie pointed her finger at Layla for emphasis. "She's no better than either of us. I'm sick of people like her looking down on people like me." Without warning, she went into a spill. "So what if I have CP, it doesn't make me less than anybody else. I've dealt with girls like her teasing me and looking at me like I'm some kind of freak, all of my life. I've been made fun of all of my life. I'm constantly being taken advantage of by no good men like my children's daddies."

Layla was silent like she was weighing what she was going to say. "Look, Kacie. Envy has a good heart, and so do you. Just because she has a great job and a little extra spending cash than the two of us, doesn't mean that she thinks she's better than we are. I've never gotten that impression. I've never heard her say anything negative about your disability. All she's ever said is that you should get your tubes tied and stop having baby after baby." Layla quickly covered her mouth with her hand.

"Don't you see? It's none of her business how many children I have. She's not taking care of any of them. Who knows, she's probably had her share of abortions."

Layla gasped at Kacie's accusation.

"Don't look so shocked. I wouldn't put it past her. I can't prove it, but I don't care what you or Envy say, she's had her share of men. Believe that. Anyway, I'm leaving. I'm beginning to feel sick to my stomach. I don't know if it's from this baby I'm carrying or the mess I've had to deal with tonight."

"You don't have to leave, Kacie. Stay a little longer until you're feeling better," suggested Layla.

Kacie hugged Layla. "Thanks, but no thanks. I'll talk to you tomorrow." She went to the door and turned slightly before opening it. "You're a good friend, Layla. I hope you have better luck with that postman than I did with Deacon. G'nite."

"Nite, Kacie. Be careful," Layla told her and walked to the door to lock it behind Kacie.

Layla went into the kitchen and grabbed another diet soda and the remaining bowl of popcorn. She glanced sideways at the clock on the kitchen wall. "Nine o'clock; umm. Should I call and talk to Dennis? I don't want him to think I'm a come-on kind of girl." Munching on the popcorn and drinking the fruit soda, her level of confidence suddenly dropped. "He probably doesn't like me. He's probably another guy like Deacon. I'm too fat and I have to do something about myself. I hate being fat. Not obese; fat." She looked up, "God, what's wrong with me? Why don't I practice self-discipline over my body? And Dennis is so handsome, then me, well Lord, I'm nowhere close to being pretty like Envy and Kacie."

The next move she made was her hand going into the bowl of popcorn again without thinking about it. She turned on the movie that the three of them were supposed to watch and shifted her mind from her weight and Dennis to the movie.

While Layla was watching her movie, Envy arrived home, still furious at Kacie's tongue-lashing. She took a look in the rearview mirror at herself before glancing over at Mrs. Rawlings' apartment. All of Mrs. Rawlings' lights were off, except the light in the living room. That usually meant Mrs. Rawlings was already in her room asleep or maybe watching her favorite show.

Envy met Fischer at the door and petted him until she could get hold of his leash to take him for his last walk of the night.

The air was breezy; not too cold. The season was about to change, she could tell just by the way the stars nestled in the sky and the way the air planted one cool kiss after kiss on her delicate skin. It didn't take long for Fischer to handle his business. Tonight she was thankful for that. Her mind wasn't on a lengthy walk.

Envy went inside the house and prepared for bed.

Fischer jumped up and rested on the foot of the bed and lay quietly.

Envy said her nightly prayers and climbed in the bed but sleep didn't come easy. She picked up a novel she had been reading for the past couple of days.

"You're going to jail for the rest of your natural life. You're a murderer; a baby killer. How could you?" her mother cried. "I never in my life thought you would do something like this."

Nikkei sobbed. Envy couldn't explain how she felt. Had she done what they accused her of? Could she somehow have blocked it out of her mind? The day the police came to her job and handcuffed her in front of everybody was the worse day of her life. When they drug her downtown to Homicide, the first thing they started doing was grilling her about a dead newborn baby left in a bathroom toilet. They showed her pictures of the tiny, barely recognizable baby. Its body was grotesque and yet Envy knew it was her child. The child she'd delivered prematurely at school. "Oh, God, please forgive me for committing such a horrible crime; for killing my child." She cried so hard until she made herself sick, but the homicide detectives did not pity her whatsoever. Envy placed both hands over her ears and screamed over and over again.

Barking furiously, Fischer woke her up. He was standing over her like he always did when she had a nightmare. Her face was flushed. She sat up in the bed and stroked Fischer along his back to let him know she was fine. It took almost half an hour for the effects of the nightmare to dissipate. In the kitchen, she prepared a warm cup of sugar-free hot cocoa. Taking it back to her bedroom, she flipped on the television until she saw something interesting on Animal Planet. *You can run, but you sure can't hide,* her mind said to her.

***

The following day, the friends acted like the argument from the night before never happened. They talked three-way for about fifteen minutes before they each hung up the phone to go their separate directions for the day.

Dennis called and invited Layla to spend the afternoon with him. She told Envy and Kacie about it. After finishing her conversation with them, she started going through her closet and settled on one of the pants and shirt outfits she'd purchased a few days ago.

Kacie spent most of the day in bed while the kids ran in and outside the house. She had to come up with a plan to make sure Deacon's wife found out about her pregnancy. She made several calls to some of the church members and got bits and pieces of information. Just enough to put together some facts about Mr. Deacon Riggs.

Kacie had a way of getting information when she really wanted to. The girl could have been a detective. By the time she hung up the phone a few hours after starting her search, she had a home address for Deacon and a phone number. She also discovered that he had no children. She smiled naughtily, believing this would give her an advantage over his wife. *Every man wants a child, especially a son,* she thought. She guessed by the way she was carrying her baby, that it was a boy.

The children happened in the house for at least the seventh or eighth time. Kacie got out of bed and chastised them, instructed them to fix sandwiches for lunch, and turned to go back to her detective work. Keshena, a late bloomer, had started walking about a month and a half ago, so she could now try to keep up with her older brothers and sisters.

Next Kacie called Deacon's cell phone. "Didn't I tell you not to call me anymore?" he roared into the phone like an angry grizzly bear

Ignoring him, she asked. "What are you going to do about our baby? It's a boy. He'll be arriving in late spring. So I suggest you get to breaking the news to Martha about our love child." She spoke with a sneer in her voice. "Unless you want me to pay her a little visit and tell her myself."

"You don't want to cross me, Kacie. I'm telling you. You'll live to regret it."

"So, you're threatening me now? My, my, my. Sounds like you're a tad bit upset that I'm having your baby and not Martha. What is it? She's infertile or something?" Kacie's laughter traveled through the cell phone line.

"If I weren't a man of God, I'd tell you exactly what I think of you and your little charade. But for now, all I have to say to you is you need to find your baby's daddy, because it sure isn't me. And believe me, if I wanted a child, I would have had one by now. Think about it?" he snarled and hung up in her face.

Kacie chased the kids back outside after they finished eating. She searched for a composition notebook. Finding one inside Kassandra's desk drawer she pulled it out, grabbed an ink pen, and back to her bedroom she went. Sitting on the edge of the bed in silence, she began to write.

Dear ~~Mrs. Riggs~~, Martha,

I know you do not know me and I regret that we have to become acquainted like this. First of all, before I go any further, I want to tell you my name is Kacie Mayweather. Deacon and I have been having an affair.

He has confessed many times that he loves me. I would never have given him the time of day had he been straight up with me from the beginning and told me he was married, but he chose not to. I also want you to know that I don't make a practice of coming between anybody's marriage or relationship, for that matter. But what I have to say must be told to you because Deacon refuses to do so. I did not know he was married until the day of his installation at the church where he and I both belong. You can imagine my surprise when I saw you standing by his side and being introduced as his wife.

Deacon came to my house to beg me not to leave him, but I told him that I could not be the cause of a broken marriage even though we are having a child together. I have enclosed a copy of the ultrasound, not to be mean, but so you will understand that I am not being cruel or lying. Deacon and I are expecting a baby in late May. You can imagine my torment about what to do. I am a Christian woman who committed fornication, but I am no harlot or adulteress.

I have spoken to Deacon on more than one occasion and pleaded with him to tell you everything rather than continuing to deceive you. But each time he goes into a rage and tells me that there is no way he is going to tell you and jeopardize his position at the church. He also told me that you were unable to have children but he wanted to have our child more than anything. He asked me not to tell you, but I can't live life like this.

I'm sorry you had to learn about us this way. Please forgive me. All I want now is for Deacon to take care of his child. I can't stand the fact that the child I am carrying will not have the same love and support as my other children. From one woman to another, please talk to Deacon and let him know the importance of taking care of his son. I hope the two of you will survive this news because I certainly do not mean to cause separation or trouble. I just want to know that Deacon will be there for our child when he comes into this world. I hope you can find it in your heart to forgive me and Deacon too. May God bless you, Kacie Mayweather

Kacie swirled the last 'r' in her name and folded the letter. Her hands were shaky but her mind was going a hundred miles a minute when she placed the stamp on the envelope. Going to the back door, she made the kids come inside and ordered them to get in the car. Before she could change her mind, or have second thoughts, she drove to the post office and dropped it in the mail. Afterward, she smiled, almost gloating. She took the kids to the grocery store and brought groceries before returning home.

The baby inside her belly squirmed and Kacie jumped. *I know your daddy is going to be here for you. Don't you worry about a thing,* she said to the child growing rapidly inside her. *God is on our side and so is the child support system.* She patted her belly and then massaged it gently. *You picked the wrong woman to mess with Deacon Riggs. The wrong one.*

The kids and Kacie carried the bags of groceries inside the house. The phone rang and Keith rushed into the den to grab it.

"Hello," Keith said in a clear voice. "Yes, ma'am. Momma, Aunt Envy is on the phone for you." He approached his mother with the gray, mini cordless phone.

Kacie purposely took her time taking the cordless phone out of Keith's hand. "What is it?" asked Kacie in a grumpy voice.

"My momma's sick." Envy got straight to the point. "The nursing home called Nikkei. Momma's dementia has worsened. She's had a stroke and they're testing her for a pulmonary embolism. It's serious," Envy cried into the phone."

"What are they going to do? Have you talked to her?"

"Not yet. I'm leaving later this afternoon to go up there."

"Is Nikkei going?" Kacie placed a sack of groceries on the floor while talking.

"Yea, we're leaving from her house. I just wanted to tell you. I tried calling Layla but I didn't get an answer. Will you tell her just in case I don't reach her before I leave? Right now, I can't promise that I'll call too much."

"Don't worry. I'll make sure she knows."

Kacie hung up the phone and swore under her breath when the baby in her belly started squirming around again like he was trying to get out. Kacie made the kids put up the groceries while she called Layla.

Layla answered the phone like she was out of breath.

"You all right?" questioned Kacie.

"Yes, I'm fine. I just came from the walking track. Girl," she said between deep puffs," I thought I wasn't going to make it back home. It seemed like it took me an eternity to walk around it, and I only did it once."

Sounding surprised that Layla had taken such an initiative, Kacie praised her efforts. "Envy had been trying to call you. Her mother has fallen ill. She's getting ready to go to Nikkei's house and they're headed to Murfreesboro," explained Kacie.

"Thanks for telling me. I'll try to call her back as soon as I sit down for a minute and unwind."

"Okay, I'll see you at church tomorrow."

"Okay. Bye."

Layla slowly walked into her kitchen and grabbed a bottle of flavored water from the fridge. Flavored was the only way she seemed to be able to drink it. The ice-cold berry-flavored water was refreshing. She took a few gulps, went to sit on the couch, and then tried contacting Envy.

Envy happened to answer her phone. "Hello."

"Hey, I'm sorry to hear about your mother."

"Kacie must've called and told you, huh?" asked Envy.

"Yea. I want you to go and do what you have to do; check on your mother. We got your back," Layla reassured her.

That's one of the things Layla loved about their friendship. No matter how many times they fussed or fought, argued or disagreed when it came down to looking out for each other, they laid all of the small stuff aside and stepped up to do whatever needed to be done.

"I don't know exactly how long I'm going to be gone. But I assume we'll be back sometime Sunday night. Nikkei and I both have to work Monday."

"We're going to be praying for y'all."

"Thanks, Layla. I love ya." Envy teared up and her voice quivered.

"Don't start boohooing. Go see about your mother. It's time for you to be strong. I'm praying for you, Envy."

16

"Much that is beautiful must be discarded so that we may resemble a taller impression of ourselves." J. Ashbery

The trip from Memphis to Murfreesboro was a mixture of pleasantries, arguing back and forth with each other, bringing up issues about the past, and what more could be done for their mother.

Ten minutes outside of Murfreesboro, the two sisters were silent as a snowflake floating in the air. Maybe both of the women were in thought about what they would be faced with as they drew closer to their Momma's care home.

Envy pulled open the window flap in front of her and viewed herself in the mirror. Inside her purse, she removed a tube of lip gloss and painted her lips.

They pulled up to Adams Place Long Term Care Health Center.

"I sure hope Momma is doing all right." They were the first words Envy had spoken to her sister and it broke the silence.

"Momma hasn't been in the best mental state for a while," Nikkei responded and looked at Envy like Envy wasn't aware that their mother hadn't been well.

"I know that," Envy snapped back. "But with all of these new health developments, it makes me uneasy. For the first time since I was a child, I think she could be at the end. We've had our differences, me and her, but she's still my mother, and nothing will ever change that." Envy's voice took on a sad tone and she looked downward while Nikkei found a parking space and pulled into it.

Nikkei turned off the ignition and faced Envy. She reached out to her sister and laid her hand on her shoulder. It was the first sign of compassion and sisterly affection shown between the two since they were in their late teens.

"Momma's a fighter. You know that, Envy. She's not leaving here until she's good and ready." Nikkei grinned.

Envy returned the grin. "You're right. I apologize." Envy's eyes locked on her sister's and her tone sounded grim. "I want to tell you, that you've done a great job taking care of Momma. I know I could have done more to help you. I'm sorry about that."

"No need for apologies. We're family. I know you, Envy, remember? I'm your sister. You and Mother wouldn't get along long enough to close the door behind you if she had moved in with you. I know she loves you and you love her, but the two of you are too much alike. So it worked out just the way God intended. You've contributed finances and I know you would come running, just like you did when I called this time, had Momma needed you. So what if you didn't come by to see her every day? She understood you, Envy."

Nikkei's words were soothing to Envy's spirit. Envy fought against the tears that formed. She hated crying. She believed crying revealed far too much of what was going on inside a person's heart.

Envy hugged her sister, and for a few minutes, they sat in the car like they were contemplating what they were going to do when they saw their mother.

Envy's phone rang just as she opened the car door and stepped out. It was Leonard. For some reason, the sound of his voice brought comfort to her troubled soul. "Hi, what's up with you?" she asked, trying to sound like the hard, tough Envy that she often displayed.

"You and me, I hope. Where are you? I'd like to see you later this afternoon. Maybe we can have dinner or just go to the park and hang out," he suggested.

"No, I can't. I'm out of town."

"Out of town? For how long?" he asked without sounding like he was badgering her.

"I'm with my sister in Murfreesboro. Our mother is in a long-term care facility up here. She's taken a bad turn health-wise."

"I'm sorry to hear that. Is there anything I can do? Do you need anything?" He sounded so sincere, so caring. His words seemed to draw her closer to him than she wanted to be.

"Thanks, Leonard, but I'm fine. I've got to go now. We're on our way to her room. I'll talk to you when I get back to Memphis. Bye," she said and snapped the phone shut.

"A friend?" Nikkei asked.

"More like an acquaintance."

"Envy, when are you going to allow someone into your life, into your heart?" Nikkei asked as they walked inside the center. "Any time I ask you about a man in your life, you always say the same thing; 'no friend or boyfriends for me, only acquaintances.'"

"It's safer that way, Nikkei. You lucked out and found a great husband and a good father to your children. But those kinds of men are becoming extinct. I don't like test driving to see if this one is the right one, or if that one is the wrong one. You know, all of that game-playing. I've played it long enough. Now I'm content doing things my way."

They caught the elevator to the second floor and walked along the clean-as-a-whistle corridor.

"Plus, believe it or not, I like my life just the way it is," said Envy.

"Yeah, I just bet," said Nikkei, not convinced.

They came to their momma's room. She was asleep.

Nikkei approached her bedside first while Envy looked around the room. It looked like a small efficiency apartment; the kitchen to the right, the living room area toward the back, and to the far left was the bedroom. A door next to the bedroom led to an accessible bathroom. A large picture window near the living room furniture made the room appear lively and full of life. Live green plants were strategically placed throughout the space. Her mother always had a green thumb.

Shame crept up and Envy could barely stand the thought that she had never been to the nursing facility since the three months Nikkei had taken their mother there.

Nikkei was a great daughter. Something clicked in Envy and she began to see her sister in a different light. She watched her as she gingerly stroked her gray hair and spoke softly to her. Though her momma didn't answer, as Envy walked over and stood on the other side of the bed, her mother slowly turned her head toward Envy.

"Hi, Momma." Envy leaned down and kissed her on the side of her soft crinkled cheek. "How are you feeling?" Her mother stared without answering before shifting her gaze back to Nikkei.

"I'm going to go to the nurses' office and see what they can tell me about Mother. "I'll be right back." Nikkei was her mother's power of attorney and executrix over her estate. Envy used to be upset about it, but the more she saw Nikkei in action when it came to their mother, the more Envy understood why her mother placed her over everything.

Nikkei was capable and she was going to handle their mother's business, no matter what. It wasn't like that for Envy. Envy thought of how busy she was, doing her. Her life mirrored that of her mother when her mother was a young woman. Beautiful. Secretive. Selfish. Self-absorbed. Successful. Like her mother once did, Envy used her looks and her brains to get what she wanted out of life. She attended church to make sure she stayed on God's good side, something her grandmother taught her to do before she died when Envy was twelve years old.

"You can do what you want out in this world, Envy," her grandmother would often say, *"but you can't make any of it last if you don't keep God in your life. Always find time to spend some time with God. No matter how many men come knocking, make sure God is always the first one you let inside."*

Envy pulled up a chair and sat next to her mother.

"Momma," Envy whispered. "It's me, Envy. Your baby girl." She squeezed her mother's ice-cold hand. "Momma, I love you. I love you so much. I know you're going to get better. You're a survivor." Slowly her mother shifted her head toward Envy. She didn't speak but she did turn up her mouth in a barely noticeable smile. "I'm glad to see you smile, Momma. This time when you get better, you're going to come home with me. I'm going to take care of you. I promise. Okay?"

The door to her mother's room opened and broke the moment of silence. It was Nikkei.

"The nurse practitioner wants us to come to her office. She needs to talk to us together. They have a monitor in here so they can see what's going on with her around the clock. I'm glad Momma's here. This is one of the best long-term care facilities in Tennessee. I was lucky to get her in here. She looks very well taken care of, don't you think?" Nikkei eyed her sister with curiosity.

"She does. Everything is clean and so is Momma. She looks like she's being cared for in the manner which she deserves. That's a blessing."

"Yes, it is." Before leaving the room, Nikkei explained to their mother that they would return shortly. The woman met her daughter's explanation with blank

181

eyes. Nikkei kissed her and squeezed her hand, then pulled the covers up around her neck.

The sisters walked at the same rhythmic pace to the nurse's office.

Using her hand, the nurse gestured toward the seats in front of her desk. "Have a seat," the nurse practitioner offered.

They sat down. "What's going on?" asked Envy right away.

"Your mother's tests for a pulmonary embolism returned positive. Unfortunately, it is a large clot in her lungs. We're working on trying to stop the blood clot from getting bigger, as well as keeping new clots from forming. Right now we have her on medication to thin the blood, hoping it will dissolve the clot faster.

"I still don't understand." Envy began to cry and Nikkei wrapped her arm around her sister.

The nurse practitioner was patient. "The risk for PE doubles every 10 years after age 60. She's been experiencing shortness of breath, chest pain, and coughing, which is why we suspected a PE. The fact that she has hypertension and dementia makes her condition much worse. I'm sorry." The practitioner's expression went grim. "I can tell you that we're doing everything for your mother, but she will have to be transferred to Murfreesboro Hospital ICU where she can be treated more effectively. A transport ambulance should be arriving any time."

"Code blue," the lightweight male voice on the intercom invaded their conversation loudly. "Code blue, Wilson F234," he announced again and medical staff raced toward the room.

"Excuse me," the practitioner mumbled and rushed off in the same direction.

The sisters followed her into their mother's room.

"Envy, what's going on?" Nikkei squeezed past Envy and saw the bluish-gray skin of her mother.

She screamed, and so did Envy when she stole a space next to her sister.

A defibrillator was pulled out, and like a suction cup, it jerked their mother's limp body up off the bed when they placed it on her weakened chest.

Envy placed both hands over her mouth and bit on one of them.

Nikkei had tears streaming down her face. They suddenly grabbed hold of each other's hands and they were forced out of the room. Shaking like they were standing outside in a blizzard, they held on to each other outside their mother's room while fear danced around in their heads.

"Lord, please heal my mother. Bring her through this," Envy pleaded out loud.

Nikkei turned and faced Envy. "What are we going to do if she doesn't make it? What are we going to do?" Nikkei's cries escalated until other residents started opening the doors and coming out in the hallways, poking their heads out the door.

Someone in blue scrubs came outside of Mrs. Wilson's room and escorted the ladies to a waiting area.

"Everything will be fine. The doctor will be in shortly to talk to you." Her voice was consoling. She closed the double glass doors and exited the room.

An eternity passed during the next sixteen minutes.

The doctor entered the room and pulled the scrub cap off of his blonde head of curly hair.

"How is she, doctor?" Nikkei spoke up first. Her face was engraved with furrowed fear and hopeless faith.

He averted his eyes toward Envy. His words moved in slow motion, or at least they seemed like they did. The hollow sound of his bold voice told them what neither of them wanted to hear.

"I'm sorry, we did all we could..."

***

Like the late great Mahalia Jackson, Layla's voice rang out the old spiritual hymn, "Amazing Grace." Her voice had the same hypnotizing, spirit-filled effect it always did, even though this was a funeral.

Soft cries could be heard as people stood around the coffin underneath a funeral shed. A light mist of rain fell and the clouds were overcast. Kacie positioned herself as close as possible near Envy.

Envy looked in a daze at her mother's coffin, probably unaware of who was or wasn't at the graveside service. Leonard stood toward the back of the cluster of people.

So much of Envy's life had been spent resenting her mother for the things she didn't do while she was alive. She resented her name for one. How could a mother name their child, Envy? How could a mother become jealous of the very child she gave that name to? Her mother always seemed to favor Nikkei.

Envy couldn't help it if her father left her mother for his secretary when they were small kids. It wasn't her fault that her mother began to get out of shape, and the once strikingly beautiful face and figure had meshed into a figment of imagination.

Envy was too busy pulling boys and older guys into her world using out-of-control sex as a means of self-gratitude. It was her mother who showed Envy through her actions how to use her beauty and body to get what she wanted from the opposite sex. Anything from money to food to clothes. Just about anything she wanted, her mother could con a man into getting it for her, and Envy learned well how to do the same. Envy watched, tearfully, as the funeral directors lowered her mother into the cold, damp ground. Her beauty had faded away like dust.

Envy wondered if her father was at the funeral. She couldn't remember if anyone mentioned that they had called him or not. She had not, though she would have informed him had her mind been more stable. But her mother's death stole a piece of her life away and she didn't know if she would ever recover to the point of one day looking back on this day without being sad. Someone passed her a green plant and kissed her on the cheek when the funeral was over. Her eyes were too glazed over with tears to see exactly who it was, probably one of her mother's few real friends.

Envy held on to the plant and the beautiful obituary Nikkei had printed. It was full of happy memories from the time they were children all the way to now. If anyone didn't know any better, they would think they were the perfect family. But the secrets ran deep. So deep that Envy wasn't sure if her mother was in heaven with God and the angels like the pastor preached.

Envy rarely heard her mother talk much about God unless it was included in a line of expletives. She'd never forced Envy or Nikkei to go to church and she sure never took them. If it wasn't for Layla inviting her when they were younger, Envy imagined she would probably be a replica of her mother. Her emotions were mixed, but the grief tugged at her harder than in the days of old when Envy felt left out and kicked aside. Tonight she needed to be held, to be comforted. She would call one of her bedfellows after the repast.

Envy arrived home exhausted and mentally drained. Just as she turned the key to step inside her apartment, Mrs. Rawlings met her at the door.

"Baby, I'm sorry I couldn't make it to your mother's homegoing."

Homegoing? Where is her new home? Who knows? Envy's mind raced with one confusing thought after another.

"Thank you, Mrs. Rawlings. I know you were thinking of me. That makes me feel better," Envy lied. She still felt lousy. She didn't want to be bothered with Mrs. Rawlings' preachy words, not after today. *Too much pain, too many wounds, too much.*

Fischer popped his wagging head from behind Mrs. Rawlings' red and white skirt. When he saw Envy he almost knocked Mrs. Rawlings down trying to get to Envy. He jumped up on Envy and licked her face all over.

"Hey, Momma's big boy," Envy said in baby talk. "You always make Momma feel good." She gathered his huge head inside her hands and gave him a big Eskimo kiss. "I'll take him for his walk, Mrs. Rawlings, after I get out of these clothes and heels. I'm drained."

"Honey, I know you are. But everything is going to be all right. God is with you whether you realize it or not. And your mother is in a better place, child."

Envy cringed when Mrs. Rawlings said 'better place'.

"And Fischer just came in the house about thirty minutes ago. I let him in the backyard for a long while. So you shouldn't have to worry about walking him. He's just glad to see you. I am too."

"Awe, thanks. I'm glad to be home. I want to get in my bed and go to sleep. Maybe when I wake up, all of this would have been a bad nightmare, something that never happened." Envy's words were heavy and her face was visibly saddened.

"Have you eaten?" asked Mrs. Rawlings.

"Yes, ma'am. That reminds me. I made you a plate. There was so much food at the repast. Let me go get it out of the car. We should have enough food to last us at least a day or two."

Envy opened her apartment door and kicked off her shoes before she turned around and went back out to her car to retrieve the bag of food. She gave Mrs. Rawlings two plates of food covered with thick aluminum foil and carried the other two plates with her.

"Envy, you're a sweet young lady. I wish you would see what I see in you. God loves you so much and He wants to do so much in your life. But you have to get right. Confess your faults and let go of whatever is keeping you bound."

"Thanks, Mrs. Rawlings. But the only thing that's got a hold of me is the death of my mother. The woman who birthed me gave me my horrendous name and showed me how to make it on my own. I miss her, but I don't think it's in the same way my sister misses her." Envy hunched both shoulders. "Anyway, I'm going inside. I'll talk to you tomorrow."

Envy walked inside her apartment with Fischer wagging his tail against her black feathered dress. When she closed the door behind her and sat the plates in the kitchen, something inside her felt like it was bursting wide open and she started to cry.

She cried so hard that her stomach caved in and her head felt like it was being pounded with a hammer.

Fischer stood in front of her and barked in slow, whiny barks as if he understood her pain.

She sat on the living room couch and cried until she heard the shrill ring of her home phone. She didn't want to talk to anyone. She would talk when she was ready, on her own time. The phone stopped ringing and then started up again.

Next, the cell phone started to ring. It was Layla.

"Hey, Layla."

"Hey," said Layla

"I'm on the phone too," Kacie chimed in.

"Hi, Kacie. Thank y'all for being at the funeral. And Layla, you know you were spectacular, as always," Envy complimented.

"We didn't call to bother you, Envy," was Layla's gentle reply.

"Yea, we just wanted to tell you that we love you and that we're here for you," added Kacie.

"Thanks, y'all. You don't know how much I appreciate that."

"Envy," Kacie spoke up. "Did you happen to notice the man dressed in a three-piece gray suit standing toward the back of the crowd of people?"

"I told you that she's not going to remember anything like that. There were so many people there, how could she notice one somebody in particular?"

"How did he look?" Envy asked as she sniffed loose tears up her nose.

"All I can say is that he was suave, handsome as Denzel and that suit that clung to him wasn't from the Men's Wearhouse. Brother was bronze like the sun had planted light kisses evenly over his face. He wasn't tall as Deacon but he wasn't short like Kirk Franklin either. Brotha was just fine." Kacie laughed over the phone and Layla lightly snickered.

Envy's mind played like a recorder on autoplay. *Sounds like Leonard. But how would he know about my mother's death? I haven't talked to him since last week when I told him she was sick.* "I can't say who that was."

Envy was not about to reveal that it was possibly one of her mates. "It could have been one of my brother-in-law's friends or co-workers; or Nikkei's co-workers or church members. I don't know. And right now, I don't care to try to figure out who it was." Envy's tone changed to that of agitation.

"See, Kacie, didn't I tell you that Envy wasn't up to talking about a man? You need to be concentrating on getting your life together before you drop that baby. No sense in trying to hitch on to another man until you get things straight with Deacon...and his wife," snapped Layla.

"Look, heffa..." said Kacie.

"Stop it," Envy yelled into the phone. "I don't want to hear this tonight. Y'all settle it between yourselves. I'm out. I'll talk to y'all tomorrow. I need to get some rest." Envy hung up the phone quickly after Layla and Kacie apologized to her for causing a ruckus.

The home phone rang just as she hung up the cell. "Dang, who is it now?" she said to Fischer.

She got up and walked to the phone sitting on the hallway stand. The caller ID read, L. R. Swift. Envy thought for a couple of seconds and answered the phone just as it was about to go into voice mail.

"Hi, Leonard. What's up?" she asked with slight surprise.

"Just thought I'd call to see how you were doing. I'm sorry about your mother," he said. "Is there anything I can do?"

"How do you know about my mother?" Envy muttered in a broken voice.

"It's not important how I found out. What's important to me is you. You sound so sad. I can't imagine what you're going through, but I can let you know that I'm here for you." His voice sounded calming.

Unsure how to respond, Envy forced her tears to stay back and gained control of her voice before she spoke. "That's nice of you. But I'm fine. I'm going to try to get some sleep. This has all been draining. One minute I'm looking at my mother and she's alive; she's sick but alive. The next moment, like a motion picture script, crash carts, and code blues, nurses and doctors are rushing to her room. Then the worse words that I can imagine were next. 'Your mother didn't make it.' How crazy is that?"

"Do you want me to come over?"

"Nah, I'm fine."

"Why won't you let me be there for you? For once, let someone in your life, Envy. If only for a while." His words rang with insistence.

Envy hated it when people thought they knew her, especially men. No one knew the real Envy. No one understood what thoughts rushed through her mind, what demons she fought against every day. Did people like Leonard think she enjoyed closing herself off from the world and men like him? She had no choice. The past was a constant reminder of that.

"Look, I don't know why you're trying to come off like you're so concerned about me. I don't want to play mind games, not tonight. I want to be left alone to be me. I can't think of satisfying you tonight and I sure don't think you can satisfy me. So let's leave it at that." She spoke harshly, hoping her words stung him enough to make him back away.

"I don't want to come over there for my gratification. I want to come and be with you, comfort you, and hold you because you're my friend. It's not about making love. Just let me come to see you for a few minutes. Please."

Envy paced from the hall to the kitchen. Fischer lay on the sofa with his head resting on his giant paws. She succumbed to his pleading. "Okay, you can come by. But only for a few minutes."

"I'll be there in about twenty minutes. Do you want me to bring you anything? Food? Soda? Anything?"

"Yes, white wine," she told him and hung up the phone.

Envy's phone rang about the same time as Leonard pulled into the driveway. It was Mrs. Rawlings.

"Mrs. Rawlings, is everything all right?" Envy said into the phone.

"I'm fine, but I called to ask you the same question. I heard a car and when I peeped through the curtains, I saw that black jaguar pulling in the driveway. You know the one I'm talking about. One of your so-called friends got out."

"Hold on just a second, Mrs. Rawlings. The doorbell is ringing." She held the phone to her ear and walked to the door. "Mrs. Rawlings, I tell you what, we'll talk tomorrow. Goodnight," she told her and welcomed Leonard inside after hanging up.

"Hey, there," he said sensuously.

"Hi, Leonard. Come on in." She extended her hand as a guide and closed the door behind him.

"I'll open the wine if you want," he offered after grazing her cheeks with his soft lips.

"Sure. Look in the cabinet opposite the sink. You'll find the wine glasses."

He followed Envy's instructions and filled two glasses with wine. He walked back into the living room. Empty.

Like she could read his mind, she called to him, "I'm in the bedroom."

191

He went straight to her room. She was laying in the bed in the fetal position. A coral panty and bra set covered her private places.

"Here you go," he said without noting her skimpy attire.

"Thank you." She sat up and accepted the glass of wine. Immediately she took two rather large swallows. "This is good."

Leonard remained standing like he was waiting on an invitation before he proceeded further. He didn't have to wait but a nanosecond.

Envy patted her hand on the bed and he sat down. "You know you didn't have to do this. It's not like I need looking after or anything. I'm a big girl. I know how to deal with the ups and downs of life."

"You don't have to tell me that. I noticed that practically the first time I met you. You proved yourself at the business meeting between my company and the one you work for. I think I fell for you right on the spot. You were hot," Leonard flirted. "Just like you are now," he said calmly while observing her with a full body scan.

The two of them laughed and exchanged friendly banter as they reminisced. "That was three years ago, but who's counting?"

Envy laughed. It felt good to momentarily exchange her grief for happiness. With every word Leonard spoke about their friendship, she realized that he had been a constant in her life when all the other men she'd been with came and went. What made Leonard hang around? She'd never really thought about it. Whatever it was, she wasn't going to begin trying to figure it out tonight. Tonight she was thankful for him being there.

He exited the bedroom in between changing subjects and brought back the bottle of wine. They enjoyed another glass. After the start of her third glass, she nestled her body beside Leonard, and with a slight nudge from her, he fell backward on the mattress.

Envy inhaled his scent. In quietness, he wrapped his ripped bicep around her delicately, like a blossoming flower. She didn't know if it was the mixture of wine, the comforting assurance in the way he held her, or her grief that allowed tears to flow. But they did.

Leonard used the back of his free hand to gingerly wipe tears that tread along her face. He held her close as her sobs broke free. Envy had never allowed herself to show emotion of this kind around any man. She had promised never to allow a man to have any control over her thoughts, actions, and definitely decisions. Crying was for babies, and she wasn't a baby by a long shot. As if recognizing suddenly what she was doing, Envy pounced up and away from Leonard's loving embrace. She reached for a tissue on her night table and wiped her face. She blew her nose and excused herself.

"I'll be back in a minute," she said and headed for her master bathroom.

After several minutes passed and Envy had not come out of the bathroom, Leonard undressed down to his boxers. His six-pack was pronounced and his calf muscles ripped from obviously working out.

"You okay?" he asked when she returned.

She halted her steps when she saw that he was undressed. "I'm fine. I'm sorry about that. You know that's not me," she spoke apologetically.

"No need to apologize. That's what friends are for. I'm glad you allowed me to be with you tonight." He reached out his hand to beckon her.

"Leonard, please put your clothes back on. I'm not in the mood for getting my groove on. Not tonight." She shook her head and folded her arms. Not bothering to make another step toward him.

"Neither am I. I only wanted to feel comfortable. I had to get out of that monkey suit. So come on, you know me enough to know that I don't bite that often," he joked.

Envy slightly smiled and accepted his offer. She walked over and climbed into the bed next to him. They lay back again.

Envy popped up, turned toward him, and rested her body on her elbow. "Leonard? Were you at my mother's funeral today?" she asked like the thought had just popped into her mind.

"Yes. I hoped you didn't see me. I didn't want to make you uncomfortable. I know how you treasure your privacy; that's why I believe we do so well together."

Envy rested back against him and the pillow without responding. A slightly upturned expression came on her face.

Fischer plopped onto the foot of the bed like he was claiming his space no matter who was there. Envy usually kept the door closed when her mates came to visit, leaving Fischer out, or she'd make him stay in the guest room. But so many things about today, tonight, and this very moment had changed. She didn't know what it was, but for her, she understood that life would never be like it was before her mother died.

Envy fell asleep in Leonard's arms. A man of his word, he didn't try to make love to her. He simply held her and kissed her hair before he fell asleep.

"Breaking News! Tot's mom was arrested and charged with murder, the caption read. News correspondent, Nancy Grace broke the news about the despicable young woman who left her toddler to die in a bathroom. While her baby lies in a toilet, this so-called mother leaves and goes to class. Yes, you heard me viewers. She leaves her baby to die in a bathroom toilet

and doesn't look back. I hope she gets the death penalty. How inhumane can a person be, especially a mother?"

Envy tossed and turned in her sleep. The torment of all that had happened replayed in her mind. Bad dreams, the loss of her father to another family, and her mother's death. All of it zoomed through her mind like a presentation on loop. Her eyes opened wide, pointed toward the ceiling as she relived the nightmare. *Lord, won't you have mercy on me? Please?* It seemed like she could hear an almost inaudible childlike voice replying, "Why should God have mercy on you when you didn't show mercy toward me?"

She looked around like she expected someone else other than Leonard to be in the room. There was no one else. Leonard lay beside her still asleep, one arm underneath the nape of her neck.

Envy closed her eyes, hoping somehow she could drown out the words that sounded over and over in her head. *You didn't show mercy toward me.*

17

"Most people tend to think the best of those who are blessed with beauty; we have difficulty imagining that physical perfection can conceal twisted emotions or a damaged mind." Dean Koontz

The following afternoon, Dennis arrived to pick Layla up for Bible study at her church. Afterward, they were going to dinner. It was Layla's idea to invite Dennis. During the time they'd been seeing one another, she'd learned quite a bit about Dennis. His parents were ministers, but Dennis was not a regular churchgoer.

During one of Dennis and Layla's long night conversations, he told her how he was burned out from going to church. When he was growing up he spent seven days a week attending some type of church function with his parents. He had vowed when he became an adult he was going to attend church when he chose to, and he'd kept his word.

Dennis's father and mother didn't have their own church, but they were ministers at a church in Brownsville, Tennessee where they had served for over 13 years. His father was an ordained minister and Minister of Pastoral Care. His mother was a licensed evangelist. To this day, they still attended church faithfully.

Layla looked in the mirror. She was starting to love herself more and more. Since meeting Dennis, she'd lost close to seventy pounds. Though the reason for her dramatic weight loss was unpleasant, it had truly made a difference in her life. Dennis never complained or acted like he disapproved of her size, but she wasn't feeling this because of Dennis. She had made up her mind after what Mike did to destroy her, that she was going to use it to make a positive change in her life, which included eating healthier and exercising. In time, she hoped to start to love herself the way God always loved her.

When Dennis picked her up, the look on his face showed that he was very well pleased with the sight before him.

Layla's Pacific blue empire tunic, navy pants, and matching slingbacks and accessories enhanced her beauty. Her steps were more assured and confident and the smile she wore on her face was for real. She allowed Dennis to easily take hold of her hand and lead her to his Sedan.

"Not only do you look fabulous, you smell like a field of the best-smelling flowers." Dennis opened the passenger door for Layla. After she got inside, he leaned in and kissed her with delight on her polished lips. She returned his kiss with equal eagerness.

"I am so excited about you coming to church with me tonight," Layla told him with a huge smile on her face.

"Like I told you, God is my savior. And I know that when my time is up on this earth, I am going to be with Him. But as for going to sit in church every Sunday, I don't do that. I don't have my name written on any church roll, but I do visit various churches frequently. I don't choose to do it every Sunday," he explained with gentleness.

"I understand. I have no problem with that."

"Good, but I do want to let you know that tonight won't be my last time. I have to come one Sunday so I can hear you sing."

Layla blushed. "I'm going to hold you to that."

The mid-week service was led by the associate pastor. It was a sermon about Christians and worrying. Pastor Byrd spoke with power and conviction.

"There are many of God's people wallowing in self-pity, anxiety, and worry. They walk around depressed,

197

anxious, confused, fearful, and trouble-minded. I don't
understand this when we serve a true, living God. God is
the creator of everything. No matter what troubles you
face, God is able. He is our provider, our healer, and our
deliverer. The cattle on a thousand hills belong to him."

Pastor Byrd moved around the pulpit with ease. "If he
cares for the birds and takes time to provide water and
food for them, how much more do you think he cares
about us?"

Dennis squeezed Layla's hand and looked at her with
great affection.

"This evening I want to remind you that God is bigger
than any problem you are facing. There is nothing too
hard for him. Absolutely nothing," Pastor Byrd
emphasized. "As I close this message, I want to leave you
with this; do not fear. Do not fret. Do not be discouraged.
Trust in God. God's promises are yes. His word tells us
in Psalm chapter thirty-four and verse nineteen, 'Many
are the afflictions of the righteous: but the Lord
delivereth him out of them all. Now that's enough to
shout on.'"

Several people stood and waved their hands in the air,
while others shouted, "Praise God" and "Amen." Layla
nodded in agreement.

"God said that He will deliver his children out of
every single solitary one of them, not some, but all of
them. Whatever your problems. No matter how big, how
small. God promises to deliver you out of them all." He
balled his fist, and raised his arm in the air each time he
said the word *all*.

"Thank you for your word," Layla said.

"Let us take to memory, Ephesians chapter three, and
verse twenty as I take my seat. *"Now unto him that can
do exceeding abundantly above all that we ask or think,
according to the power that worketh in us.* Stop

worrying, people. You are children of God, and God takes care of His own. Go forth from here and walk in God's blessings."

The congregation began to mingle and talk as they left out of the sanctuary and headed to their cars.

"How did you enjoy the service?" Layla asked as they slowly processioned out of the sanctuary and into the parking lot.

"It was quite good. He knows the Word. He preaches where I believe just about anyone can understand where he's coming from. That's what I like rather than some of those preachers who use words that they don't even know."

"Our Senior Pastor is the same as he is," Layla happily replied, "only better."

Ten minutes after leaving the church, they turned into the parking lot of Olive Garden. Being that it was midweek, they didn't have to wait in line to be seated. The hostess seated them right away and placed them at a table near the center of the restaurant. They chose their food items and drink and then concentrated on each other.

Dennis reached across the table and caressed Layla's supple hand. His expression grew serious.

Layla looked uncertain about what he was about to do or say. *My God, he doesn't want to see me anymore. I knew it. I should have seen it coming.*

"Look, baby, after spending time with you these past months, I think it's time that I tell you what I'm feeling. I mean, really feeling," Dennis said.

Layla licked her licks nervously after chewing the tender buffalo strip.

"You know I've been thinking about us, and what you mean to me. And I'm not going to even lie. I love you, Layla."

This time Layla's lips parted in total surprise at Dennis's confession. Love? Did he love her? Was she dreaming? She'd never heard those words from any man other than a family member.

Dennis continued to talk and Layla hoped she didn't have a stupid look plastered on her face. She did feel her hand starting to tremble.

"I don't know where you are when it comes to me, he continued, "but that doesn't even matter. All I can say is that I can't keep hiding my feelings. The more I see you, the more I want to see you. The more I'm with you, the more I want to be with you." Dennis's words sounded sincere and the look in his unwavering eyes revealed a look of total sincerity.

Layla swallowed but this time it wasn't from swallowing a buffalo tender. Somehow she seemed frozen, seduced by the words pouring from his lips.

"Just to make it clear, what I'm saying is that I just don't love you but I'm in love with you, Layla."

Layla shook her head and moved her hand away from his. "I don't know what to say. How can you say you love me? We've just started hanging out and spending time together as a couple. I don't want to play games, Dennis. I'm too old for that."

She observed the somewhat awkward look that appeared on his face. His brows closed in together and a line appeared between them while his mouth opened ever so slightly.

"Game? Is that what you think this is? I know it seems like more time should have passed before I started talking seriously to you about love, but I couldn't hold it back. I used to be one who scoffed when others talked about love at first sight. Now, I believe in it for myself because the first day I laid eyes on you, I felt a stirring within."

Dennis touched his mid-section. "I couldn't explain it then, and so I tried to push it out of my mind. But each time I saw you, it returned. I found myself thinking about you on my mail route, anxious to turn down your street; hoping I'd see you coming out the door, anything just to get to see you."

He reached across the table and used his hand to cuff underneath her chin. His touch made her a little sensitive. Part of her felt the strength in his hard-working hand as he caressed her chin. The other part of her tried to focus on the turkey giblet drooping from her neck. But Dennis never seemed to act like he was uncomfortable when it came to her size. All of her inhibitions were self-imposed. If she was going to return his love, she had to learn how to love herself first and foremost.

"Dennis, that's sweet of you to say." She eased back just a little out of the reach of his hand and he pulled it back across the table. "This is all new to me. Please listen and try to understand."

She wanted to be as sensitive as possible. No way did she want him to think that she didn't care for him because she did. "I like being with you. I like talking to you and laughing with you. I like watching you and just being in your presence. I want to hear your voice every day," she confessed. She reached for the napkin on the table and used it to twiddle. But to be honest, to say that I'm in love with you, I don't know how to respond." She admitted with lowered eyes and her body appeared to stiffen.

"Didn't I just tell you that I don't know where you are regarding me? It might take time for you to feel the same way. If that's the case, then I want you to know that I'm going to spend every moment I can, showing you how much I love you. I'm going to pray that one day you'll know how wonderful it is to love another person unconditionally. I want that person to be me, Layla. One day you will love me just as much as I love you. Until that day arrives, I won't pressure you in any way. But I ask you to do one thing for me?"

"What is that?" Layla's emotions felt out of whack suddenly as she tried to digest all that Dennis had confessed.

"Just let me love you. Don't worry about loving me back. Do that for me?" He looked so endearing.

His open admiration and admittance of love for her brought out a smile.

"Yes. I'll let you love me." She pushed away the remaining plate of food like she'd lost her appetite.

In a joking manner, Dennis pushed it back toward her. "Uh, uh, you're going to eat that. I'm not paying for you to eat a buffalo strip and push the rest away. It's time to celebrate. Now eat up."

Layla laughed and tilted her head back. Then she picked up her fork and they started eating, laughing, and talking again.

On the way from the restaurant, Layla felt exuberant. When he arrived in front of her apartment, Dennis stepped out of his car. Layla was used to remaining in her seat until he walked around to open her side of the door. He followed the routine and he extended his hand out toward her. He didn't release it but used the other hand to close the door. Hand in hand they walked to her apartment.

Layla pulled her key out of her purse and unlocked the door. Like he'd done many times before, Dennis led her inside the cozy apartment. This time, when he closed Layla's door behind them, he turned and pushed her up against it. He rushed forward and his lips covered hers hungrily. His hands explored her flesh with expert execution, like a skilled surgeon. She embraced him, unable to resist the passion emanating from him.

With one swift move, he turned her around. While he continued to kiss and caress her, he walked her backward to the sofa and gently eased her back until her knees touched the sofa and she sat down. Planting himself beside her, she listened to his string of love moans and his desire for her was sure.

Unlike Mike, Dennis was loving, gentle, and sensitive. He took his time. True to his word, though she enjoyed his affection, she didn't feel under pressure to engage in sex with him and he didn't try to force himself on her. He seemed to be content kissing her face, her eyes, her neck, and her cleavage. His enjoyment was more evident when she felt how tenderly he caressed her body.

"I love you," she heard him tell her. His voice sounded enticing and sexually charged. "I love you so much," he said again as he lightly pulled on her bottom lip. He leaned back and exhaled. "Let me get outta here." His smile was broad.

He stood and Layla viewed the depth of his excitement as he reached down and pulled her up. She stood against him and once more he bathed her in kisses. When he stopped this time, she could see how flushed his face had become, and could only imagine how hers must have appeared.

She could see in his body language that he wanted to take things all the way.

He wanted to show her how much he loved her by making love to her. But he wouldn't, although she knew that if he insisted, he might be able to push her beyond the limits she wanted to go with him. Their time would come. And when it did, she believed there would be no turning back for either of them.

Dennis stopped kissing her and grabbed hold of her hand again, and walked toward the door. "I had a good time with you tonight." He touched her hair and kissed her on the tip of her pointy nose. "I'll call you tomorrow, okay?"

"Sure." Her voice seemed unsteady. Was she stammering or slurring?

Dennis let go of her hand and opened the door. "Until tomorrow." He walked away. When he got inside his car, he saw Layla still standing at the open door. He blew her a kiss. "Bye."

"Bye," she waved and returned his air-blown kiss with one of her own.

***

Layla closed the door and leaned against it. She inhaled and exhaled deeply with her eyes closed with satisfaction and the thoughts of the night. The phone rang and brought her to reality.

"Hello," Layla spoke softly into the phone.

"Girl, what is wrong with you?" Kacie laughed into the phone.

"What do you mean? Nothing's wrong with me. I just had a funny thought before the phone rang," Layla told her. "What's up?"

"Nothing, not really. I'm folding some clothes. I remembered you said you had a date with Dennis."

"Yep. I did. We went for dinner. I had a fantastic time. He told me that he's in love with me." Layla said the words quickly.

"He said what?" Kacie asked again, sounding just as surprised as Layla did when he told her.

"He said he's in love with me." Layla sat on the edge of her bed and began fanning her face with her hand.

"Did you tell him that you love him too?" asked Kacie, curious to hear Layla's obvious response.

"No. That's it, Kacie." Layla was silent.

"What do you mean?"

"I mean, I couldn't tell him something I don't know. We haven't been seeing each other for that long. And I didn't feel right telling him that I love him. I want to be sure that he's sincere. Plus, I need to be sure of myself too."

"You know what, Layla? That's what makes me so mad at you sometimes. You make mountains out of molehills. The man confesses his love for you and you know good and well that you're in love with him too. For goodness sake, it's all you ever talk about. Me and Envy used to listen to you go on and on about this new gospel group, or a new gospel CD, or the songs that you were anxious to sing at church. Everything was about singing, the church, or about church and singing," Kacie said sarcastically. "Now you call me up to tell me that Dennis, not good for nothing Mike, but Dennis, whatever his last name is, admits that he's in love with you and all you can say is you want to be sure about how he feels. The man told you how he feels," Kacie yelled into the phone. "You are some kind of crazy."

"I don't see it like that. I'm thirty years old. I am not about to be played by some man I've barely known for three months," Layla explained in a loud voice and stood up from the bed. She began to pace back and forth at the edge of her king-sized bed. "I hope you don't take this the wrong way."

"Don't worry, I won't. I'm sure I already know what you're about to say," Kacie retorted.

"Every one of your children's daddies, I bet they told you the same thing. They came with that *I love you* line and you fell for it every time. Hook, line, and sinker. Now you have six, soon-to-be seven children and six baby daddies. I don't want to be like that. I want to be with a man who truly loves me, Kacie." Layla's voice sounded like she was struggling with her emotions. "Please don't be angry with me for coming to you like that."

"I'm not." Kacie's tone sounded saddened and maybe even hurt. Was it because everything that Layla said was true about her? Was it because she had yet believed in another man's love for her and now was again about to be left holding the bag, or maybe it would be better to say, holding the baby?

"I hear where you're coming from and I understand you. I don't want you to go through what I've gone through either. Don't get me wrong; I love my children. I love all of them. But I just keep getting things twisted. I keep wanting to believe that when I meet a guy and he begins to tell me he loves me, he's being for real. But it never happens because I fall for the lies and then jump in the sack with him and he hangs around long enough for me to get pregnant—then it's over. He goes ghost."

Suddenly, Kacie's tone went from sounding down to perking up like she'd been injected with a dose of B12.

"Honey, but that's aw'right, 'cause I take care of my children. As for Deacon, he's going to get what's coming to him. And from now on any man that steps to this sister better come correct because I'm not taking crap anymore. After I drop this load, it's on," she lashed out but Layla didn't take it personally.

"That's good. It's time out for letting men walk all over you, Kacie. That's why I have to be careful. I've seen the hurt on your face far too many times to get caught up in mind games with Dennis. *Shoots*, I don't have to look at you. I can look at myself. The way I allowed Mike to use me over and over again like a kitchen mop until he almost took my life. No more. I deserve more. I deserve to be treated better."

"I hear you, girl." Kacie chortled.

"I'm just telling you what God loves – the truth." She took a deep breath. "I'm going to have to learn how to love myself before I think about giving my love to someone else. I know it's going to take a lot of prayer and self-discipline, but I'm willing to do it. In the meantime, I'm going to continue to see Dennis. He's good to me and he's good for me. But the moment I detect any insincerity in him, he's out."

"Yeah, I hear you. Hold up a minute," Kacie said and started groaning.

"What's wrong with you?" Layla asked.

"I just had a contraction. Oh, that hurt."

"Do you need to call the ambulance?" Layla asked. "Goodness, it's times like these I wish I could drive."

"No, don't sweat it, girl. It's not time. Believe me, as many babies as I've dropped, I know when it's time to go to the hospital. Now what was I saying?"

Layla spoke up, "Girl, I don't know. You got me all scared and stuff."

"Oh, now I remember. I was about to tell you that you know how these men be doing. Did I tell you I wrote a letter to Deacon's wife?"

Layla yelped. "No, for real. Ohmigosh! What happened?"

"I just did it a couple of weeks ago. I wasn't going to tell you or Envy until I heard something, but so far I haven't heard a thing. I just knew she would have called by now. If nothing but for curiosity."

"And Deacon? What is he saying?"

"Nothing really. But he just don't know, I can go from sweet to insane in less than a second. If I come to church and I see him, it's no telling what I'll do. I might just stand up in front of the church and let everybody know about him. Tell all of his business."

"You know you wouldn't do anything like that," Layla snickered.

"Wanna bet? I heard about this first lady who got up one Sunday morning and told all about the pastor and his mistress. People said she put all her husband's business out before the church like she was spreading margarine on toasted bread. I think a lot of his members left the church after she did that. First Lady or no First Lady, she let him know she wasn't the one to be messing over. And that's exactly how I feel about Deacon. I'm tired of being walked on. Time for payback, baby."

"Vengeance is mine says the Lord. You know that, Kacie."

"Yeah I know that, but I'm sorry. I'm just going to have to plead for God to forgive me because I'm going to give God some help this time around."

"Okay, don't say I didn't warn you. Don't let the devil get you entangled in some mess. You've got your kids to think about," Layla told her.

"I hear you, but I'd be lying if I told you that I'm not going to do anything either. Well, look, let's change the subject. Get your butt together and jump on that man you have. He seems to love you a lot. Don't start shucking and jiving around and then lose him to some of these vipers out in the streets," Kacie candidly advised her friend.

"Look, I'll check you later. I've got more than an earful from you. I'm going to kick back and then see what's on television."

"All right. But don't forget everything I said. Don't let a good man slip through your fingers. I'll talk to you later. Bye."

The ladies hung up the phone.

Layla flipped the remote while she replayed the earlier night's events over and over in her head. *Dennis loves me. What if he's telling the truth? Supposed he really does love me?* Layla smiled at the thoughts pouring through her mind. For a moment, her thoughts remained on Dennis until she saw something on TV that looked like it might be good. She watched the movie until the commercial break.

"Father God, reveal to me the true intentions of Dennis. Show me too, Lord, how to love myself. Help me to be more disciplined with my eating and to take better care of me. Then show me how to love someone else, the way you love me; the way that Dennis says he loves me – unconditionally."

18

*"One man's justice is another's injustice; one man's
beauty another's ugliness; one man's wisdom another's
folly." Ralph Emerson*

Boom!

Kacie sprung up in the bed at the sound. Her heart felt
like it was about to pop out of her chest. The sound
roared again. Being awakened out of her sleep made her
mind somewhat confused. She shook her head like it
would help her to gather her thoughts.

"Open this darn door before I kick it in," Deacon
screamed.

Kacie threw the covers off and quickly peeped at the
clock. It was one thirty in the morning. "What the...." she
began to ask herself but instead, grabbed her robe off the
edge of the closet door and went to the door.

"What do you want?" she asked him without opening
the door. She was nobody's fool. She reasoned that he
finally heard about the letter or his wife maybe finally
had thrown him out.

"Open this door," he ranted. One cuss word after
another poured from his mouth.

"I am not opening the door with you cussing at me
like that. What do you want, Deacon? It's almost two
o'clock in the morning. Whatever you have to say will
just have to wait until daylight." She'd never heard the
rage in his voice that she was hearing tonight. She
carefully checked the two locks on the door to make sure
they were in place. They were. She did not want to find
herself in the same position as her dear friend Layla.

"You lying little witch. How dare you try to destroy
my life. Writing all those lies and sending it to my wife.
You'll pay for what you're doing. You listen to what I'm
telling you. You're going to be sorry, Kacie. Real sorry."

He beat against the door for a while and then started again with his threats. "You know that brat you're carrying isn't mine. You twisted, tiptoed foot, lying heifer. You need to go somewhere else and find your baby's daddy because it sure isn't me."

"Deacon, I'm warning you. If you don't get away from my door yelling and cussing, I'm calling the police. They'll lock your butt up and then I'll call the church and let them know what kind of trustee represents them."

If she was afraid of him, it was impossible to tell.

"You did this to yourself. Now get away from my door before you wake up my kids," she screamed from the inside and hit the door with her balled fist.

Furious, she swiftly turned around and almost lost her footing as her bent legs formed a scissor shape and caused her to fall. She narrowly escaped hitting her face on the linoleum floor. She sat on the cold floor for a few minutes and listened until she heard Deacon's voice trail off.

Kacie held her swelled belly. The belly that carried Deacon's child. Crocodile tears dropped to the floor and fell harder when the baby started kicking.

Kacie remained on the floor for a while until she gathered energy enough to get up and go back to her bedroom, where sleep evaded her.

The phone rang just when she had managed to fall asleep. She clumsily searched for it without opening her puffy red eyes.

"Hello," she answered slowly.

"I don't know why you're making all of this mess up about my husband. It's women like you that destroy marriages. You're a homewrecker. You'll burn in hell for coming between the marriage of me and my husband," the woman on the other end shouted into the phone.

The piercing words woke Kacie up and she quickly sat up and swung her legs on the side of the bed.

"Who is this?" Kacie asked as if she didn't already know it was Deacon's wife.

"You know darn well who this is. Unless you're trying to destroy more than me and Deacon's marriage. I wouldn't be surprised if you were," the woman snarled.

"Look, I don't know where you're coming from with this. But if this is Martha, then it's your husband you need to be going off on, if anybody. I didn't initiate anything with him. He's the one who lied to me. He's the one who never bothered telling me that he was a married man."

Kacie's anger was mounting. She wanted to sympathize with Deacon's wife, but at the moment, the way Martha was talking to her, Kacie lost all feelings of being sympathetic and understanding.

"I'm carrying your husband's child. As much as I hate that fact, there is nothing I can do to change it. As for your marriage, that's between you and Deacon. All I want out of this is his total support of his child. He can do it the easy way, or he can make this hard. Either way, it doesn't matter one way or the other to me. When I realized that he probably hadn't told you about us, then I wrote you a letter. Why it's taken you two weeks to respond, I don't know and I don't care. But you need to face the truth, lady," Kacie yelled into the phone.

"I got the letter; I sure did. I got it a while back, but unlike you, I sat on it. I had to think. I talked to my husband like a wife should rather than chasing you down. But the more I read that letter, the more I realized that you're one of those sluts who doesn't understand anything but a good butt-whipping and cussing out. And if it wasn't for your twisted up legs," Martha laughed, "You'd feel my size nines up your behind. That's how you trapped Deacon anyway, playing like you were a weak, helpless little handicapped woman who needed help."

"For your information, you have it twisted. As for me and my cerebral palsy, it has nothing to do with the fact that your husband still wanted me and chased me down." Kacie argued back.

"Deacon told me how many baby daddies you have. He told me how you went after him at church. You're a whoremonger and a hypocrite. Deacon cannot have children and your face is going to be cracked when that baby you're carrying turns out not to be my husband's. But DNA will reveal the truth. I believe in my husband, Miz Mayweather. He's never cheated on me before and then some Jezebel harlot like you throws yourself on him. Sending me that letter proves that you're a desperate, heartless woman. You want Deacon at any cost. But it isn't going to happen, sweetheart. Find yourself another man to destroy."

Before Kacie could retaliate with her outpour of words, she heard the dial tone in her ear.

She threw the phone on the floor. As she did often when she was mad, she got up and started issuing one order after another to her kids. Hollering at one to see about the Keshena and yelling at the others to do one chore after another. Her stance was more pronounced, revealing her anger. After she barked one order after another to the kids, she retreated into her bathroom, ran some water, and took a hot bath.

Afterward, she dressed in an outfit appropriate for the changing season. The baby kicked again. This time it was a sharp kick, causing Kacie to stop in her tracks and grab hold of her stomach. Eight months pregnant. She couldn't wait until she popped this baby, because afterward, she planned payback. Payback for everything Deacon had done, and things weren't going to be pretty, not pretty at all for him.

Kacie heard the kids scuffling, arguing, and yelling at one another. As long as they were doing what she'd ordered them to do, they could yell and scream all they wanted. She wasn't in the mood to break up fights and arguments. Too much about the past night and the morning's events to deal with. She made sure they made buttered toast, something quick, for their breakfast and then she rushed them to the car and carried them to school and Keshena to daycare. She had to work the morning shift at the store and dreaded it more than ever.

Kacie went to the back of the stockroom and called Envy.

"Miss Wilson's office, may I help you?" the administrative assistant said in the receiver.

"Yes, I need to speak to her please."

"May I tell her who's calling?"

No, you may not tell her who's calling. It's none of your business. "Yes, tell her it's Kacie," she spoke dryly to Envy's assistant.

"Thank you. Hold, please."

"Hey, girl. What's up?" Envy said when she picked up the phone seconds later.

"I don't know. I'm so pissed."

"About what?" asked Envy.

"Do you know Deacon had the nerve to pop up over my house about one o'clock this morning, bamming on the door like a maniac? I tell you, Envy, I'm so fired up I could go over to his place and burn it down."

"Hold up, don't do anything stupid, Kacie. Where are you?"

"I'm at work. I don't want to be in this place. I feel like walking off. And I might just do it too."

"Did you let him in?" Envy asked, momentarily ignoring Kacie's remarks about her job.

"No, I didn't let him in. If you heard all of what he was saying, it was like he wanted to do something bad to me. I only got him to leave after I threatened to call the police. I wasn't about to be another victim like Layla."

The words coming from Envy's mouth sounded full of anger too. "No, he didn't? You should have called the police anyway. He had no right coming to your house acting a fool like that. I know you were scared to death, and what about the kids? Did they hear him? You know they like Deacon. They seem to think he's such a good man. If they only knew what a fool he is."

"Thank God, the kids didn't wake up. If they did, they didn't get out of their beds or anything. But that's not all I have to tell you. I have to hurry up too. My break is just about over. After he left this morning, his wife called."

"His wife?" Envy asked with total surprise in her voice.

"Yes, Martha Riggs, his dumb wife. All she did was talk about her husband being honorable and they can't have children. She even had the nerve to make fun of my cerebral palsy." Kacie almost started to cry but didn't.

"Kacie," this is getting out of hand. "I don't want you or anyone getting hurt. You're almost about to drop that baby you're carrying. Being frustrated and irritable is not good for you or the baby. I tell you what, I'm going to call Deacon and let him know that he needs to chill. When the baby comes, y'all can do a DNA test since that's what he wants. When it turns out that the baby is his, then put him on child support and forget about his monkey butt. Calling himself a trustee of the church and all holy and stuff. Now you see why I don't deal seriously with these men out here? They're nothing but trouble and all they look out for is themselves. I say, use them before they use you. From now on, you better make that your motto. And for heaven's sake get your tubes tied this time," Envy blurted out in a sharp tone.

"I hear you." Kacie's tone suddenly shifted to an almost inaudible whisper. Then she released a long sigh. "I'll talk to you when I get off."

"Okay, I have a busy day today. Maybe later this evening me and Layla will come by and check on you. Will that be all right? I'll call her before I leave the office. "

"Sure. I guess that'll be okay. I could use a couple of shoulders to cry on." Kacie managed a slight chuckle.

"Then we'll see you this evening. And please, please, Kacie, watch out for yourself. If Deacon happens to come on your job or if you see him lurking around, call the police, and that goes for that lunatic wife of his too," Envy warned.

"I will. I gotta go," Kacie whispered. "My manager just came back here." Kacie closed her flip phone and zoomed past her manager like a speeding bullet. *He better not say anything to me, or so help me, I'm walking out of this place. I'll just have to tell DHS that I couldn't take it anymore and I quit. They better not penalize me either.*

The workday turned out busier than ever. By the time three o'clock rolled around, Kacie couldn't wait a minute longer. She punched her timecard and swished past everybody in sight without stopping. When she made it to her car, she jumped inside and sped off, disregarding the 35 miles per hour speed limit. She stopped by the daycare to pick up Keshena. The kids arrived home from school shortly thereafter. No time for Kacie to have a moment of solitude.

"Put your backpacks on the table so I can check them and then go change out of your uniforms," she ordered.

Kacie scanned through each child's backpack, checking to see what homework they had, if any, or if there was anything inside she needed to read or sign.

Keshena was walking and gained added support by holding onto Kacie's leg while Kacie sat down in the chair reviewing the contents of the backpacks.

"Kassandra, when you finish changing, come in here and get Keshena so I can cook," she said loud enough for her orders to reach Kassandra's ears.

Kacie leafed through Kassandra's backpack first. All she had for homework was a page of math problems and a list of spelling words.

Kassandra marched to the living room, picked up Keshena, and placed her on her hip.

"Give her a fruit cup or something to keep her out of my way, and then start on your homework," Kacie instructed.

Knowing the weekly routine, one by one the rest of the children came into the den while Kacie went over their assignments with them. She hardly ever attended any of their school functions, but when it came to school assignments and homework, she stuck to her kids like white on rice.

Y'all know what to do." She pointed a sharp fingernail at them. "I don't want to hear any arguing or fighting. Just do your homework while I fix dinner."

Kacie began dinner by making Mac 'n cheese hamburger helper. A pack of frozen green beans, to which Kacie added some Mrs. Dash seasoning and a piece of ham she had left in the freezer to give the beans added flavor.

The kids loved dinner rolls, so she placed two packages in the oven and set out a two-liter bottle of fruit punch soda.

Afterward, Kacie called Envy. "Y'all coming?" she asked.

"Yea. I am. I just left work. I called Layla. She's not coming." Envy told Kacie.

"Why? What's up with her?" Kacie's voice dropped.

"She said she already had plans. She and Dennis are going to a movie. I told her about what happened with Deacon and his wife. She said she was going to try to call you before she left. But I'll be over there around six."

"Fine, I'll see you later. Let me get back to fixing dinner."

"Whatcha cooking?" Envy asked.

"Mac'n cheese hamburger helper, green beans, and dinner rolls. Nothing fancy. Just quick and tasty."

"Sounds good. If you have any leftovers, set me a small plate aside."

"Will do." Both ladies ended their call. Kacie finished preparing dinner. When the children gathered at the table, she sat down and ate with them, something she rarely did. The kids seemed to enjoy having their mother eating dinner with them.

Afterward, the children cleared the table and started cleaning the kitchen according to the chore list Kacie had pinned on the refrigerator.

Kacie retired to the den and called Layla.

Layla answered on the first ring. "Hi, girl. Did Envy tell you I won't be able to come tonight?" Layla asked right away.

"Yea, she told me. I'm glad you and Dennis seem to be doing great together. Somebody between the three of us needs to be having some good luck."

"We're all blessed. Maybe things don't go the way we think they ought to all the time, but we're still blessed. Remember that God said he will never leave us or forsake us."

"Mmm," Kacie moaned in a sarcastic tone. "I sure feel forsaken. Envy told you about Deacon and his wife?"

"Yeah, she told me. But you were wrong for writing that letter. And before you get bent out of shape, I'm not taking sides. But that letter started up a bunch of unnecessary drama. You and I both know that. If you don't want to admit it to me, then at least admit it to yourself."

"I can't admit something that I don't believe. If I had not sent that letter, then Deacon's wife probably would still be walking around totally unaware that her dear trustee of a husband has a baby on the outside. As for drama, he's the one to blame. He should have told me in the first place that he was married. But naw, he had to act like he was so crazy about me. He's nothing but a lying dog, and he deserves everything that happens to him for getting me pregnant." Kacie started crying. "And you, of all people, should understand how it feels to be misused."

"I understand. Believe me; I'm not trying to come off like I'm judging you. All I'm trying to get through to you, Kacie, is that you have to learn to stop taking things into your own hands. You need to seek God's forgiveness for yourself instead of being vindictive. No matter what you say, sending that letter was vindictive. I'm sorry if what I'm saying hurts you, but it's the truth."

Followed by a moment of silence, Kacie spoke up. There was a slight bitterness resonating in her voice.

"Maybe you don't want to come across like you're judging me, but that's exactly how you sound. I bet you didn't hear me condemning you when you were messing off with Mike. I bet you didn't hear me condemning you when you were stuffing your face like you were eating your last supper. But now, here you are, just because you finally have a decent man in your life, playing the judgment card with me?" Kacie's voice sounded like she was choking and gasping for her next breath. "Don't you know that I'm hurt, or have you gotten so tied up with Dennis that you've forgotten what it means to be hurt by a man?" She paused long enough for Layla to respond.

"I'm sorry. I told you that was not my intent. But slinging hurtful words toward me is not going to solve anything. I never have professed to be perfect. I've never tried to come off as self-righteous or anything like that. You and Envy are my dearest friends. I never want to see you hurt, and I especially never want to be the one to cause either of you any hurt either." Layla's voice cracked. "I'm going to let you go. And again, I ask you to forgive me. I really wasn't judging or condemning you. Anyway, we'll talk later. Bye, Kacie."

Kacie heard the dial tone and laid down her phone. She kept crying while holding her head in both of her hands. She wiped her face and sniffled when Keshena came toddling into the den where she was. She went straight to Kacie and tried to pull herself up on Kacie's lap. Kacie eased her baby's struggle by picking her up and holding her in her lap.

Layla was right about everything she had said, whether Kacie admitted it to Layla or not. The truth was the truth and the truth could definitely hurt. But Kacie, holding on to Keshena and looking red-eyed as Kali, Kendra, Kenny, Kassandra, and Keith came into the den, was a reminder of her torrid past. Every day her past played itself out in the form of her precious, sweet innocent, illegitimate children. She rubbed her belly in a circular motion before she sat back in silence and watched as Kenny looked for her approval to turn on the television.

"You can turn it on," Kacie automatically responded in a tender voice like the true mother she was.

19

"I don't want to be bothered right now, Bill. Dang, can't you give a girl time to get home, relax and chill before you call?" There was no mistaking the tone of Envy's voice that she was peeved.

"Of course I want you to have time to chill. That's why I'm calling. I want to come over there, or you can come to my place. I'll fix you a strawberry martini, a light dinner, and salad. Then I'll run you a hot bubble bath. After I bathe you, I'll give you my signature aromatherapy massage."

The offer sounded enticing. There was no denying it. With every word that poured from her friend Bill's thin, sensual mouth, Envy wiggled in the car.

"I'm on my way to one of my girlfriends' house. As much as I'd like to take you up on your offer, I can't. She needs a shoulder to lean on. I can't let her down," she said seductively in a, *no I can't,* but *yes I sure want to* voice.

He apparently picked up on her reservation so he continued his over-the-phone seduction. "Envy, you know you keep me wanting you, girl. All I want is a little of your time. I'm leaving town tomorrow morning on business. I won't be back until late Friday night. I sure would like to spend tonight satisfying you."

Envy slowed her roll. She imagined his curly, light golden hair, arresting good looks, and his simple style of dress. A pair of hands so powerful yet light as a feather could remove every tensed muscle in her body. She smiled in the car while he continued his style of drawing her more toward his way of thinking. Envy mixed her pleasurable thoughts with each word that poured from his mouth. His air of authority was a perfect mix with his self-confident demeanor.

"Your place. Seven-thirty," Envy said.

"That's my girl. You know I'll make it more than worth your time."

"You always do," Envy responded and closed the flip phone. It was almost five o'clock. She could still stop by Kacie's house now, console her and then have time to make it to Cordova where Bill lived in a private, gated community with sprawling houses that left no doubt of the success and wealth of the people who lived behind the gate.

Envy said hello to Kacie and the kids when she walked inside the house and went straight away to prepare a miniature-sized portion of the leftover dinner Kacie had prepared for the kids. They talked more about her situation with Deacon and what she was going to do about the baby constantly growing inside her. Envy felt sorry for Kacie, but there was really nothing she could say or do that would

"Kacie, believe me, I'm glad I'm not walking in your shoes because I don't know what I would do in your situation," commented Envy.

"I appreciate you for admitting that. I'm glad you didn't come off like Layla did when I talked to her."

"What do you mean? What did Layla say?" Envy asked and sat her plate on the end table next to the sofa.

Kacie pursed her lips together and shook her head in discontent. "Only how wrong I was for sending that letter to Deacon's wife. You know, maybe I was wrong. I'll admit that, but like I told her, she had no right to come down on me like she's all of a sudden pure as the driven snow." Kacie's sad countenance and disappointment were clear as she hung her head.

"Kacie, Layla didn't mean to be judgmental, I'm sure. She's just concerned about you, that's all. I am too. All of us were shocked to learn at his ordination services that he had a wife. I feel for you, girl." Envy sat on the sofa next to Kacie and placed her hand over hers in a show of support and friendship. "We all react differently when we're faced with disappointments or trials and tribulations. I can't tell you how many times the mistakes I've made throughout my life play over and over in my mind like a song on loop. I'm living my life like it's golden when it's a tarnished mess. So I am the last person to judge anyone." Envy's face reddened.

"Thanks for that. You're such a good friend." Kacie leaned over on Envy's shoulder and the two friends sat in silence until Envy broke the seal.

"I've messed up so much in my life. I've done some things that I'm so ashamed of, Kacie. Just because it looks like I've got it all together on the outside, doesn't make it so. If God can't make it right for me after all of this time, I don't know if I'll ever escape the troubles of my past."

Kacie lifted her head and transferred her eyes to Envy's solemn-looking face. "What are you talking about?" Kacie asked, looking bewildered.

Envy avoided her by ignoring the question.

Envy reached for her empty plate, got up from the couch, and walked quickly toward the kitchen with Kacie following behind.

"It's not going to be that easy. I am not going to let you get by without telling me what's going on with you. I've been so busy worried about myself and my situation that I've failed to make sure my friends are okay. And for that, I'm asking for your forgiveness."

"Kacie, there's no need to apologize. I'm doing fine. I was merely saying that I have stuff I've done that I'm sorry about. That's all." Envy washed her plate while Kacie sat at the kitchen table.

"I don't know what you've done but I do know what I've done. I know the mistakes I've made and I have a lot for God to forgive me for. All I have to do is look at every one of my children and I'm reminded of how I've laid with man after man. Every time this baby kicks, I'm reminded that I'm carrying the child of a married man. I don't know if I will ever measure up to being a Christian, or to becoming all that I'm supposed to be if I say that I'm a Christian." Kacie flung her hands out toward the sky in a fit of desperation. She pushed herself from the kitchen table. "I've screwed up my life so badly, Envy. So nothing can compare to what I've done. Nothing."

Slowly, as if being cautious Envy said, "I wouldn't bet on that." It was her turn to push away from the conversation they were about to embark on. "Look, I have to leave. I wanted to stay longer but I have a business partner I'm meeting at seven-thirty."

"Sure. Thanks for coming by and for a listening ear," replied Kacie.

"Somehow, this is all going to work out. You'll see," responded Envy as she walked toward the door.

"Aww." Kacie bent over, clutching her stomach tightly, and leaned against the kitchen wall to keep from falling. "Aww," she cried out again.

Envy rushed to her and saw the drained look on Kacie's face. She was pale.

"What's wrong? Do I need to call 911?" asked Envy nervously. She placed both hands to the side of her head and clumsily stumbled in place.

"No," Kacie managed to tell her. Her teeth clenched like she was trying to ward off the sharp pains.

"Ahhh," she said in a different tone that may have indicated that the pains were subsiding.

"I'm calling 911," Envy insisted.

"No, I told you," demanded Kacie. "The pain is gone." Kacie sat down again in the nearby kitchen chair. "The pains are just letting me know that my baby is getting in position. I'm not going into labor. I have a full three weeks to go. I went to the doctor last week. I had dilated just one centimeter. Sometimes sharp pains will come and go like that."

"You are still making me leery about leaving you here in pain."

"Envy," Kacie waved her hand off in the direction of the door, "will you get on out of here? Believe me, don't you think that after six kids I know when I'm in labor?" Kacie managed to laugh and some of the color returned to her ashen face. "I'm fine. Really. If anything changes, I'll call you, now shoo. I'm going to go and lay down until this passes." Kacie waved Envy away again.

"Okay, but you better call if anything changes. I do know that babies come when they're good and ready, so I don't care what the doctor told you last week. Things can change without notice when it comes to a baby," Envy stated like she was sure of her statement.

Kacie smiled lightly. "And just when did you become a baby pro? You've never been pregnant. Leave the expert advice to one who knows." This time, Kacie giggled but Envy's face turned a shade of deep crimson.

"I'll check on you later," Envy said and hurried out the door before Kacie struck up a conversation about pregnancy and what women experience.

For a few minutes, Envy sat outside in her car to regain her self-composure. She was shaken by Kacie's pains and also reminded of her past like what had happened was just yesterday. She sighed heavily and turned the ignition. When the car started, she sped off toward Bill's. Bill would be just the one to relieve her tension and stress that had built up during the week. Out of all of her bedmates, Bill was the one with the magic touch; and magic was the only thing that could clear her mind of thoughts she didn't want to think about.

Thirty-two minutes after leaving Kacie's house, Envy pulled up to the security guard stationed outside of Bill's gated community. "I'm here to see Bill Martin. He's expecting me."

The guard called Bill and the gate opened to allow her access. She made several turns until she arrived in front of Bill's 4,500-square-foot house. Every time she pulled up in the circular drive, she imagined how it would be so easy to let Bill love and take care of her. He had the means and he ravished over her every time she was with him. He was a great businessman who was skilled in and out of bed. His need to give affection also made Envy think that Bill was a good father. He'd been married before and he and his ex-wife had two children, eight and ten years old. He adored his kids and pictures of them were spread throughout the huge house.

She walked up to the door, and before knocking, he opened it and met her with the promised strawberry martini in his hand. He passed it to her, encircled his hand around her waist, and led her inside.

True to his word, Bill delivered on every one of his promises. Caesar salad, succulent pork loin with marinated vegetables. Envy's appetite awakened when she saw the presentation of the food on her dinner plate. After dinner, Bill made her another martini and insisted that she relax until he prepared her bubble bath.

The warm bath was heavenly. She laid her head against the bath pillow, closed her eyes, and moaned with pleasure as Bill gingerly washed her. His words were none. His touch was magnetic. Out of all the men she'd given her body to, Bill was the one that knew everything she liked and didn't like. He made sure he always came through, which is why he was at the top of her list of partners.

At the end of her bath, he reached for her hand and helped her step out of the tub. Smiles and looks of desire were shared between them in the place of words. Using a lush, thick towel from the towel warmer rack, he wrapped the floor-length towel around her shoulders and led her to the back of his house, into a room that he called his relaxation room. Inside the room, there was everything needed and set up for a professional massage. Bill had admitted to her not long after they met a year before, that he was a licensed massage therapist. Being a massage therapist, however, was not how he had amassed his fortune. His involvement in software engineering for some of the world's largest corporations assured him a seven-figure salary.

Envy smiled as he led her to the massage table. *I sure know how to pick 'em. Look at him. Fine, attentive, rich, and a great lover. I could see myself as Mrs....* She shook her head to dispel the thought.

"You all right?" he asked tenderly.

"Yes, I'm wonderful." Envy laid belly down and placed her head on the face pillow. Removing oil from the double holster, Bill began to knead her tight, tensed muscles. His hands were perfect and every touch sent chills coursing up and down her spine. She gasped when he hit the small of her back.

"You're especially tense tonight. What is it?" he asked sincerely. "I've never known you to be this stressed."

She answered him with a light moan.

He moved down and used his hands to roll in a curvature motion over her butt, slowly moving along her thighs on down to the tips of her feet. She became quiet as a mouse. Against her will, her eyes closed and her body began to relax.

Next, Bill reached for the bottle of warm aromatherapy oil and performed the same massage again starting at her neck, moving to her shoulders, lower back, buttocks, and down the remainder of her body. With the aid of the warm oil, Bill's touch set her on fire as he massaged her front. No doubt, by the time Bill finished, Envy was ready. Ready for him to do whatever he wanted to do to her.

He lifted her in his arms and carried her almost limp body up the hall and into his master suite. There he kissed her cheeks, her eyelids, all around her lips knowing that for Envy, kissing was off bounds. But he more than made up for not being able to kiss her lips because he used his magic touch to bring her to heights of excitement and passion that only Bill was capable of doing.

Spent, the two of them lay in his massive bed and he held her in the circle of his muscled biceps. In a matter of seconds, Envy was asleep.

***

Layla screamed when the man came up behind the woman and placed his dirty, claw-like hands over her surprised mouth. She fought hard against the monstrous man, but she was no match for his power. He dragged her kicking and screaming into a darkened warehouse and locked her inside a cage. The woman screamed, cried, and pleaded for him to release her. Grabbing her head in her hands, she screamed over and over again when she saw his toothless mouth walking toward her with a chainsaw. Layla gripped Dennis's arm and held on to it tightly.

He chuckled before he whispered. "It's only a movie, baby. Don't be scared." He chuckled again.

"I can't help it. It's scary." She took a handful of the buttery bucket of popcorn, tilted her head back slightly, and placed the delicious popcorn in her mouth. Picking up the soda from its holder, Layla gulped a couple of swallows to wash the popcorn down. She did this several times while she and Dennis whispered about the horror flick playing on the big screen.

On their way home, Dennis invited her to his house. He'd extended the invitation several times during the time they had been dating, but Layla usually refused. But tonight, she didn't know why, but she readily took him up on his invitation and accepted it willingly.

Dennis was a man she trusted. When she was with him, she felt a connection of their spirits. Dennis brought out confidence and high esteem in her. He treated her like she was the most beautiful girl in the world and that he only had eyes for her. His confession of love for her was the ultimate icing on the cake. Now she had to sit down with herself and look within her spirit and heart to see if what she felt for him was love too. Or was she smitten by him because of how he treated her?

"You okay," asked Dennis and he quickly looked her way.

"I'm more than okay. I'm fantastic." Layla grinned.

Dennis reached over his head and flipped down the sun blocker. He pulled a CD from the CD holder and flipped it into the player. "I want you to lie back, and listen closely to every word. It's how I feel about you. Seriously," he said and looked at her again.

Layla laid her head back against the headrest, closed her eyes, and listened to the song. She wasn't familiar with it because listening to gospel was her thing. *"Lost without you ...How does it feel to know that I love you, baby..."*

The lyrics of the song brought tears to Layla's eyes. She felt every word. The smoothness of the man's voice reminded her of Dennis. Every word pouring through the speaker touched her mind, her heart, and her spirit. Yes, she did love him. *Thank you, God. I know for myself what being in love is. I do love this man. I love him and thank you, Lord, for bringing Dennis into my life.*

She listened and this time she reached across the seat and held onto Dennis's hand while the remainder of the Robin Thicke song played. The song came to an end just as they turned into Dennis's driveway. Another tear rolled down Layla's face. Dennis was moved by her emotions.

Before getting out of the car, he lightly took hold of her hand. In silence, she stared at him. He smoothed back a strand of loose hair from her round face, and then placed his hand around the back of her neck, pulling her toward him. He cupped her chin tenderly and kissed her long and hard. Layla breathed lightly.

"Come on, let's go inside," he said when their lips parted.

Layla liked the laid-back style of Dennis's house. Traditional, open-spaced, hardwood floors, and color. His taste was impeccable.

"Help yourself. Look around. This is home. I'll fix us something to drink." he told her when he saw her looking somewhat like a frightened child, unsure if she could freely move about or should she stand still. Layla was glad that he'd given her the okay to walk through the house.

Each room had its own traditional flavor. The open living area and family room was an eclectic, yellow-gold color palette mixed with lush reds and browns.

Layla moved cautiously like a cat on the prowl for its prey. The first two bedrooms were traditionally decorated as was the bathroom. She was startled by Dennis when he eased behind her and stole a kiss on her neck.

Layla turned and Dennis gave her a glass of sparkling cider.

"How do you like everything so far?"

"It's…It's gorgeous," Layla complimented and took a sip of her cider.

"I wish I could take all of the credit, but I can't."

"What do you mean?"

"I have two sisters who are interior designers. I told them what I liked and they took over and made it happen." He spoke proudly and had an upward turn of his mouth in a smile when he spoke about his sisters. "Let me show you my room. It's on the other side of the house."

Dennis walked and turned to the right and followed another hallway until they reached another entrance. Dennis's room was exuberant. A tranquil, soft color palette ran throughout the room.

"God has blessed you, Dennis." Layla turned, sipped on her cider again, and watched him without blinking an eye. "I hope you don't take it for granted."

"I don't. Let me show you one more thing." He tugged her gently by the bend of her elbow and led her to another entrance that showcased a sitting area like that out of *Home and Garden* until they reached another door inside the sitting room. He opened the door and Layla's eyes widened in surprise. Fragrant candles, a Bible she saw was opened to Deuteronomy Chapter 28, and a patterned pillow with Bible inscriptions was on the floor for kneeling. There was a small cherry wood table with a booklight and a padded chair. On the walls were plaques and pictures, all of a scriptural nature.

"This is where I come for solitude and alone time with God. I attend church because I like to fellowship with other individuals who worship the same God I do. But this is where I spend my one on one time with Him—my prayer closet."

Layla remained speechless. Her eyes remained focused on the prayer closet until she could contain herself no longer. "May I?" asked Layla.

"You may," he replied and extended his hand outward.

Layla walked inside the prayer closet. Instantly, a feeling of peace consumed her like never before. Her spirit seemed to become enlightened. Indeed it was a sanctuary, sacred ground. She sensed the presence of God.

"I've heard of prayer closets but I've never seen one." She admired the closet for a while and then walked back into the sitting room.

"I'm glad you approve." His infectious laughter brought even more joy into her spirit. "Hey, where is your cider?" he asked.

"Oops, I think I left it in your bedroom. I'm sorry. I don't want to mess up your house. You may not invite me back," she said teasingly, though she was serious. She would love to spend time here if Dennis wanted her to.

"No problem. I'll let you pass this time," he joked. He saw the half glass of cider setting on the table in the bedroom. He picked it up and carried it back to the kitchen with Layla following. "Since we've seen a movie already, what do you think about dancing?" He took hold of her hand and led her into the family room.

Surprise washed over her face. "I don't think so. The only dance I know how to do is the electric slide."

"All right, the electric slide it is. Then it's going to be my turn to choose a dance."

"Dennis, I wasn't serious." Layla tried to explain.

"Too late. You can't renege on me now." Dennis turned on the music system and chose a CD that was perfect for doing the electric slide. He took four or five more CDs and placed them in the CD changer. The first song came on and Dennis swiftly moved over to where Layla stood. "Let's go," he instructed and laughed. He began doing the electric slide.

When Layla remained in the same spot, he took hold of her hand, insisting that she dance along with him. Reluctantly she did.

After a few minutes, they were laughing until Layla almost started crying from laughing so hard. When the song ended, she inhaled and then deeply exhaled.

The next song was a slow jam. Dennis pulled her into the curve of his chiseled body. His hands traveled slowly down the length of her back while they slow danced. Layla's heart pounded like it was about to jump out of her chest. The feel of her body next to his made her emotions swirl and her mind cloudy with desire.

His mouth covered Layla's; his tongue explored hers and they both breathed heavily in a full state of willful desire.

When the song ended, they remained in the center of the den floor.

Dennis caressed her thickness and buried his face against her throat.

Layla trembled as the mere touch of his roving hands sparked warm shivers in her body.

"I want you, girl. Do you want me?" he asked.

Layla didn't miss a beat. She immediately responded, "Yes."

Dennis led her to his bedroom and pulled the covers back. When she appeared to be getting nervous, Dennis smothered her with kisses and whispered warmly in her ear, "Don't be afraid of me. I won't hurt the one I love."

He pushed Layla back on the bed and slowly began to peel away from her anything that posed a barrier. He did the same to himself, and looking at him, her defenses weakened and then disappeared altogether.

Layla gasped while they explored each other's bodies. He was intoxicating. There was no turning back. Layla didn't want to turn back. The flames of passion were searing and overrode everything, even her Christian values.

20

"It is foolish to wish for beauty. Sensible people never either desire it for themselves or care about it in others. If the mind be but well cultivated, and the heart well disposed, no one ever cares for the exterior." Bronte

Envy stepped outside on her porch and immediately felt a strangeness within. She looked at Mrs. Rawlings' porch. Envy knocked on the elderly woman's door with Fischer yelping beside her.

It wasn't like Mrs. Rawlings not to be peering through the curtains or outside in her garden. "Fischer, where is she?" she asked the dog, and he barked in return.

The daily newspaper laid in front of Mrs. Rawlings' door untouched, which heightened Envy's concern. She pushed back her glasses, pulled out her cell phone, and called Mrs. Rawlings' home phone again. She could hear it ringing through Mrs. Rawlings' door. When her voicemail came on again, Envy started walking around the duplex to see if she could see anything through Mrs. Rawlings' windows. She should have been glad that Mrs. Rawlings had kept out of her business for a change. She was one nosy neighbor, but as much as she may have hated to admit it, she sometimes enjoyed the fact that there was someone who was concerned about her. It surely wasn't her sister whom she'd only spoken to once since their mother's death. She hadn't heard anything from her father either, not that she expected to.

Mrs. Rawlings, on the other hand, was sometimes overbearing, always nosy, and acted like she was clairvoyant at times, but some attention was better than no attention. She and Fischer walked back around to the front of the duplex.

"Fischer, we're going to have to call 911. I don't like what's going on, or should I say what's not going on."

Fischer wagged his tail and barked up and down, rubbing his paws against Mrs. Rawlings' door.

"Shush, Fischer." Envy paused when she saw the knob slowly turn and heard the creaking sound of Mrs. Rawlings' door open.

Looking white as a ghost and like she'd lost 10 pounds of her already frail 100-pound frame, Envy gasped at the sight of Mrs. Rawlings.

Fischer started barking again.

"Mrs. Rawlings, what's wrong?" Without waiting on an invitation to enter the apartment, Envy forced herself to pass Mrs. Rawlings. The putrid smell inside the house almost made Envy vomit.

Mrs. Rawlings always kept a clean house. As long as she'd known her elderly neighbor, there was never a time that Envy smelled anything like she did today. It was a smell of urine and feces. Totally out of character for the old woman.

Envy held Mrs. Rawlings up by encircling her hand around her waist and using the other hand to brace her body. The smell was on Mrs. Rawlings too.

She helped the old lady to the sofa and Envy proceeded to call 911. Afterward, she went into the bathroom. It was clean, except for the toilet which hadn't been flushed.

Envy flushed the toilet and searched through the bathroom closet and found a wash pail, ran hot water in it, and grabbed a bar of soap. She hurried back to Mrs. Rawlings.

Next, she went into her bedroom. The smell of soiled sheets made Envy cover her nose and mouth. She searched through the drawers until she found a clean pair of underwear and a clean robe. She didn't want Mrs. Rawlings to be embarrassed and humiliated when the ambulance arrived.

Envy moved with breakneck speed, and though she'd never done such a thing before, she held her breath and washed and cleaned Mrs. Rawlings until the smell was gone. She put on her clean underwear and house dress, finishing just in time as she heard the sound of the ambulance siren and Fischer's wild barking.

Envy ran and opened the door as quickly as she could to let Fischer in the house. The ambulance pulled into the driveway and Envy directed them to Mrs. Rawlings' apartment. They immediately checked her vitals and asked Envy several questions about Mrs. Rawlings' health.

"Appears as if she might have had a stroke," one of the paramedics said. They called in the vital signs while they carried her into the ambulance. "What hospital, ma'am?" Envy remained quiet. The EMT repeated the question, this time more forcefully like he was telling her to hurry up.

"Uhh, Methodist Healthcare University Central," Envy told them.

"You riding with her?" the same EMT asked.

"No, I'll follow in my car. Just get her to the hospital. I'll be right there. Is she going to be all right?"

"Ma'am, we need to get her to a hospital right away." He jumped inside the back of the ambulance with Mrs. Rawlings and another EMT who was placing oxygen over her mouth, and an IV in Mrs. Rawlings' scaly arms. The heavy doors closed on the ambulance and whisked off down the street.

Envy returned to Mrs. Rawlings' house and removed the soiled items. At first thought, she was going to wash them, but then she changed her mind and placed them in a plastic trash bag. She found a can of Lysol and sprayed it around the house. She'd call Merry Maids to come over and give the house a thorough cleaning once she found out how Mrs. Rawlings was doing. She scrubbed her hands until they became wrinkled and then used a Clorox rag to wipe down the doorknob that Mrs. Rawlings had touched when she opened the door for Envy. She grabbed the keys off the key hook, locked the woman's door, and then hurried to her apartment to change into a pair of jeans and a shirt.

"Fischer, I have to go check on Mrs. Rawlings. Be a good boy." She patted his head and dashed out of the door and jumped into her car. By the time she made it to the hospital, Mrs. Rawlings was in the emergency room. They were running a battery of tests on her. She was barely conscious and unable to move when they allowed Envy into the room with Mrs. Rawlings.

The doctor came in and explained to Envy that they were going to admit Mrs. Rawlings into the hospital.

"She's suffered a stroke and now she's in a diabetic coma. This is pretty serious, ma'am," he said with sorrow.

She twirled around, unsure of what to say or do. "But is she going to be all right?" Envy turned and focused her attention back on the doctor.

"We're doing all we can. She's being admitted to CCU where she can be watched 24/7. How long has she been like this?" the doctor asked with raised eyebrows.

"I don't know. I hadn't seen her in a couple of days so I knocked on her door. We live in a duplex next door to each other. She's always peeping out of her window, or outside in her yard. When I realized I hadn't seen her, I knocked on her door but she didn't answer. I saw her morning newspaper in front of her door and that made me really frightened. I was getting ready to call 911 when she opened the door. That's when I saw that something was wrong with her. She didn't speak to me or say anything. She had soiled her clothes and bed. I managed to clean her up before the EMTs arrived. That's all I can tell you."

The doctor turned to leave. "We'll call you when we get her settled into CCU. It shouldn't be much longer. There are two more tests we need to run."

"Thank you, doctor." Envy sat in the waiting room area and waited for another hour until she heard them call her name. The receptionist directed her to the CCU waiting room and nurses' station. "How is Mrs. Rawlings? She was just admitted to CCU." The nurse scanned the patient list. "Are you related to her?"

"Yes," Envy lied. "I'm her granddaughter. She has no family other than me." That much about having no other family was true as far as Envy knew. Mrs. Rawlings had no living relatives who were able to see about her. If she did, they must be just as old or sickly as she was because no one ever came to visit, except for church members.

Envy would call Mrs. Rawlings' church tomorrow during office hours so they could place her on the sick and shut-in list.

"Ma'am, if you want to go home, you can. You can leave your contact information and we'll let you know if there's any change in Mrs. Rawlings' condition. Right now, we're working to get her sugar level stabilized and testing to see the extent of her stroke. It's not likely that you'll be able to see her again until tomorrow morning." The nurse was kind and her voice sounded compassionate.

"Thank you. I just want to make sure she's going to be all right." Envy tried to hold back tears.

The nurse walked over to where Envy sat. She reached out and hugged Envy. "She'll be fine. We're going to take good care of her. I promise. I'll be here all night. And there's going to be someone monitoring her

around the clock, okay?" She patted Envy on the
shoulder.

"Okay, I appreciate your concern."

"That's what we're here for. We'll do all we can for
her."

Envy turned and slowly walked away. A flurry of
thoughts from her past spilled over in her mind as she
sped on the interstate and toward home. So much had
happened in her life that she didn't know where to start.
Mistake after mistake she'd made. She pulled up in the
driveway hurriedly, locked the car door, and ran up the
walk and inside her apartment.

Fischer jumped up and down, begging for attention,
but this was one of those nights she didn't want to be
bothered by anyone.

"Go away, Fischer. I don't feel like petting you right
now. I need a break." She huffed past him and he plopped
down and whined as she went to her bedroom and
slammed the door.

She continued to survey her life. She thought of her
mother and the name she'd given her. It was her mother's
fault that so much bad luck had crossed her path. Her
father couldn't care less about her. He had a new family,
kids, the whole shebang.

Then there was Nikkei. The only sister she had, other
than the new set of siblings her father had, but who was
counting them? Nikkei was busy living her life with a
great husband and two kids. The perfect all-American
dream. No financial worries or anything hard ever came
across Nikkei's path.

The small insurance policy mother had was enough to
give her a nice funeral, and the remaining money was
split between the two of them. It turned out to be a little
less than ten thousand dollars for each of them. But that
was no money. Envy had more than that amount of

money put away in her 401K and she placed her mother's inheritance in it too. So money wasn't her problem and money couldn't solve her problem. It was her life. The numerous men she'd bedded; some with names she remembered and others who got up from her bed and disappeared like a wisp of wind. None of them could make her forget the hurt, the anguish of her troubled life.

She wouldn't admit it, but she didn't miss her own mother. Her own dead mother and she barely felt anything when she died. The only people who meant anything to her were Layla, Kacie, and Mrs. Rawlings.

Too distracted to do anything but mope, Envy went and lay on her sofa, crossed her legs and arms, and flicked on the television. One channel after another, but nothing piqued her interest.

Next, she pulled one of her novels off the table that she hadn't finished reading. As much as she loved reading, even the novel couldn't keep her mind from wandering. She tossed and turned on the sofa, but there was nothing that would rest her mind. Fischer lay down on the rug in front of her.

"Fischer, come on boy. You wanna go on a walk?" Fischer jumped up and wagged his tail.

Envy got up, went into the bedroom to get her cell phone from her purse, and then took Fischer out on a walk.

The weather was perfect. She inhaled the scent of flowers that the breeze sent her way. Lifting her head toward the sky, she surveyed the beauty of all God's creation.

"Lord, why did you make me? You said I'm fearfully and wonderfully made but look at me. I don't know what direction my life is going. I feel like such a fake. I can't carry this burden around my neck like a noose anymore. I can't keep hiding and running from what I've done. I need a way of escape. God, I need you so badly. Will you please help me to…."

Envy looked at her phone. It was Kacie. "Dang, I don't feel like talking to anyone tonight," she shouted out in the night. When she remembered the pains Kacie had, she thought she'd better answer to make sure Kacie was fine.

Dryly she answered the phone. "What is it, Kacie?"

"I'm at the hospital." Kacie cried. "I'm in labor. Can you check, ahhh," she screamed out in pain as a contraction wracked her body. "The kids are home alone."

"Why didn't the paramedics take the kids or call for CPS to come and get them? Why didn't they call me?" Envy said frantically.

"Because….ahhh. I drove myself. I've got to go." Kacie hung up the phone.

"Hold up, which hospital?"

"The Med…Labor and Delivery."

Envy immediately called Layla and prayed that she was back at home from her date, but she didn't answer.

Envy hurriedly ended what was supposed to be a long, casual walk with Fischer. He took care of his business and she was glad about it. She rushed to the apartment, put Fischer inside, and got her keys and purse. On the way to the car, she called Layla again. No answer. She called again. No answer.

"Dang," Envy ended the call. "Now what do I do?" She drove in the direction of Kacie's house as she remembered that Kacie had been through this several times, so the most important thing now would be to go and be with the children. She would call Layla again when she got to Kacie's house. Envy's concern was that the baby, however, was arriving early.

Kassandra barely pulled back the curtain and opened the door when she saw that it was Aunt Envy.

"Hi, Kassandra. Are you kids okay?" Envy went through the room checking each one of them like they'd just been injured in an accident of some sort. She was nervous as all get out.

"We're fine, Aunt Envy. Momma's gone to the hospital to have the baby."

"She drove her car."

Envy smiled.

"I want a sister," Kendra said. "I don't want another brother."

"I do," yelled Kenny. "Girls are too bossy."

"Okay, that's enough. We're going to be thankful to God whether it's a boy or a girl, all right?" remarked Envy. She got all the kids' night clothes together and made sure they took their baths. Afterward, she let them have a snack and watch a movie. At nine o'clock, she had them in bed.

Exhausted, Envy lay on the sofa and called the hospital to check on Mrs. Rawlings. The nurse she talked to at the hospital earlier answered.

"We're keeping her comfortable, Miss Wilson, but she's still not out of the woods. But, rest assured, I have your number and I promise to call you if there are any changes."

"Thank you so much. You're a godsend."

The phone rang as quickly as Envy ended the call. This time it was Kacie.

"How are you? How many centimeters are you?"

"I'm...I'm about eight and a half. They might have to do a c-section. I'll know when the doctor gets in here. The nurse just went and called him. Looks like the baby wants to come out feet first."

"Oh no, that's not good," Envy replied in a fit.

"I'll be all right. Will you do me a favor and call Deacon to let him know I'm in labor."

Envy couldn't believe what she was hearing. After the way he'd been treating her, she still wanted him to know that she was in labor.

"I don't think that's a good idea, Kacie. That's only adding stress to your situation. Forget him. He hasn't bothered to try to call you, come by to check on you, or anything. All you need to do now is follow the doctor's orders and bring a healthy baby into this world. You can handle Deacon after all of this is over," retorted Envy.

Kacie hollered. Envy didn't know if it was because of a labor contraction or anger.

"Look, I want you to call him. If you won't, I'm going to call his house and tell his wife that she needs to get her husband out here to this hospital right away."

This time it was Envy's turn to get mad. "Look, I'm not going to do your dirty work. It's stupid and you're only bringing trouble on yourself. So if you want to lay up there and call that man's house, do it. I'm not going to be your send-out on this one. So, change the subject. Layla must be still on her date with Dennis because she didn't answer her phone. I don't know how many times I've tried to convince her to get a cell phone."

Kacie ignored Envy's remarks about Layla. "Are you going to call him, Envy? Please, do this one thing for me. And I swear I won't ask you to do anything else like this."

"First of all, swearing is not necessary." Envy sighed. "What's the fool's cell phone number? Envy said furiously.

"Thank you, oh thank you so much. Aww," another contraction hit Kacie. After another contraction, she gave the cell phone number to Envy. "I'll try to call you back if I can. But tell him where I am and that the baby is coming early. Tell him I need him and that there's no one at the hospital with me."

"You are so pitiful," Envy said and ended the call without saying goodbye.

Envy dialed the number Kacie had given her. The phone rang.

To her surprise, Deacon answered.

"Hello, Deacon."

"Yeah, this is Deacon. Who is this?" He didn't sound welcoming at all.

"This is Envy. You know, Kacie's friend. And please, don't hang up. She wanted me to call to tell you that she's in early labor. She drove herself," Envy said with prominence. "I'm here with the kids. I know how you feel about Kacie being pregnant, but if there is the slightest chance that this is your child, you should at least go check on her and the baby."

"Look, I don't care who you are to Kacie. I don't appreciate you calling me and trying to tell me what to do. She's probably not having the baby early. It just proves that she was lying, telling me she was pregnant by me when it's some other unfortunate guy's brat." His voice was cold and emotionless.

"Look, I don't like having to call you like you don't care for talking to me. But this is not about you or me, and it's not about Kacie. It's about a baby that's about to come into the world. Now, like I said if you have an ounce of compassion, you'll at least go to check on her condition. As soon as I can find someone to watch these kids, I'll come out there."

"Where is she?" he asked reluctantly.

Envy exhaled.

"Regional Med Labor and Delivery. And thanks, Deacon. I mean that."

"Whatever." He hung up abruptly. Envy could care less that he hung up on her. He was the fool, the one who got caught cheating. He deserved whatever he got. She saw a blanket on the chair, picked it up, and curled up on Kacie's den sofa.

Envy opened her eyes and quickly remembered where she was and why. She ran to the back to check on the children. Kassandra and Kali were in their room; Kali was asleep and Kassandra reading a chapter book.

"It's time to go to sleep, baby." Envy walked to Kassandra's bed. She spoke in a soothing voice, removed the book from Kassandra's hands, and tucked her in.

"Has momma had the baby yet?" asked Kassandra.

"No, sweetie. Not yet. But she's doing just fine. You get some sleep, okay?" Envy kissed the little girl on her forehead then turned to pull the cover up to Kali's neck before leaving the room to go check on the rest of the children. Everyone else was asleep.

Keshena was in the bed with Kendra, not her own. She had one foot rested across Kendra's tummy and looked like the picture of perfect peace as she slept sideways in the twin bed.

Heading back to the front of the house, she heard her cell phone ringing. She picked up her pace and grabbed it in time to hear Layla on the other end. "Layla, hey. You at home?"

"No, is anything wrong? I checked my messages. You called several times."

It was well past midnight. Envy smiled. "I had called to see if I could bring Kacie's kids over there while I went to check on her. She's in labor and I was going to go to the hospital to be with her," explained Envy. "Can you believe she drove herself to the hospital?" Envy said.

"That girl has gall. Is she all right? There's nothing wrong with the baby is there?" Concern was evident in the tone of Layla's voice.

"I don't think so. She might have to have a c-section because the baby is trying to come out feet first. When will you be home?" Envy asked more out of curiosity than for Kacie and her kids' sake.

Layla was quiet. She closed the silence by answering, "Tomorrow, early."

"Umm, well you and Dennis have fun." Envy giggled into the receiver. She was happy that Layla sounded happy.

So far, Dennis seemed like a decent guy. He was always asking Layla to do things with him. He'd been to Bible study a couple of times with her and was at her house almost every day having lunch with Layla during his lunch break.

"Somebody deserves to have some fun," Envy said.

"Thanks and bye, girl. I'll talk to you in the morning." Layla chuckled and then ended her call.

***

Early the next morning, Dennis dropped Layla off at her apartment and went to work. She went inside and took a shower, washing last night's and this morning's scent of love from her body, followed by dressing into a pair of capris and a quarter-length pullover U-neck shirt.

Dialing Envy, she listened to the ringtone until Envy picked up the phone. "Good morning."

Sleepy from having tossed and turned most of the night, Envy answered in a rough voice. "What time is it?"

"Six forty. You sound like you're still asleep."

"I was, but I don't need to be." Envy sat up. "I hear the kids in the back. I need to get up and fix them something to eat and then get them off to school. Shoots, they're going to be late already. I'll call you back." This time her voice sounded hurried.

"Okay. Bye."

"Kids, get ready for school," Envy called out and rushed along the hallway to check on them. Much to her surprise, they were already dressed, including little Keshena. *Dang, Kacie has them trained.* "My, my, aren't y'all a bunch of smart kids? You're already up and dressed? That's great. What time are you all supposed to leave for school," she asked no one in particular."

"Seven fifteen," answered Kendra.

"Oh, my that's not going to leave much time for me to get your breakfast ready. Come on, I'll stop and get y'all some sausage and biscuits on the way to school."

"We can eat at school if we get there by seven thirty," Kendra told her.

"No, you'll still be rushing. I don't mind stopping by Mickey D's. It's on the way to your school anyway. Now, come on, let's get ready to get out of here. I have to go home and let Fischer out to use the bathroom after I drop you guys off at school."

On the way home after dropping off the children, Envy called Kacie's room but there was no answer. She arrived home, fed and walked Fischer, then took a shower and dressed. She called the office and informed her assistant, Felicia that she wouldn't be in until later.

"Felicia, I don't show that I have any urgent meetings or projects today," Envy told her and continued to browse through her phone calendar.

"No, everything is pretty clear, so take your time. I'll call you if anything comes up," Felicia assured her.

"Sounds good to me. Have a good day. I'll see you later."

Envy changed into a casual two-piece chartreuse pantsuit and a pair of mules; out the door she went to visit Kacie.

When she made it downtown, the hospital parking lot and side streets were packed. She drove around the block several times, for nearly twenty minutes before she gave up and parked in the hospital garage.

The walk to Labor and Delivery took just as long. Envy was almost out of breath when she stepped off the last elevator. "I'm looking for Kacie Mayweather's room, please."

The nurse checked the chart and pointed Envy to the corridor that led to Kacie's room. She knocked and went inside the room. Kacie was lying in bed asleep. A small portable crib was sitting beside her.

Tip-toeing so as not to disturb them, Envy smiled when she peered into the crib; Kacie had given birth. There laid a creamy brown-skinned baby dressed in blue with a sky blue covering on his head, sound asleep.

"Oh, you're so precious. Such a precious little thing," she whispered and ever so lightly lifted his tiny cap and touched his head, which was covered with sprinkles of brown hair. She then replaced it back over his round moon pie-shaped head.

Envy whirled around startled when she heard the toilet in Kacie's room flush. She faced Deacon head-on.

"What are you doing here?" She placed one hand on her hip and placed her weight on the right side.

"Since when did I have to start answering to you? I have a wife." Deacon snarled and brushed past her to glimpse at the sleeping baby. He didn't appear to look at Kacie, not once.

"Since I called and told you to come out here to see about Kacie. I guess looking at this beautiful baby boy, you're satisfied now that he's yours." Envy huffed and intertwined her arms.

"He is a handsome little fella. But only DNA will tell if he's mine or not. Maybe miracles do happen. Maybe you don't care to admit it, but I don't have a problem reminding you that your friend over there has six children already and every one of them has a different daddy. I don't know if they took DNA or not, but I'm not like them. I'm having a DNA test because like I keep telling Kacie, I'm sterile." Deacon's body stiffened and his jawline twitched.

"Sterile? Please." Envy flung her arms. "You know what? Men like you make me sick to my stomach," she said louder than she intended.

"Hey, what's going on?" Kacie asked when she opened her eyes, obviously awakened by the banter being exchanged between Deacon and Envy.

Envy went and stood next to Kacie's bed, and gently rubbed her hair. "The baby is adorable, Kacie. He's a big boy too."

Kacie turned her head toward him. "He weighed nine pounds, seven ounces and he's twenty-three inches long."

"Wow, no wonder he looks like he's two or three months old already," Envy remarked and chuckled while Deacon stood in silence near the sleeping infant.

Kacie shifted her eyes in Deacon's direction. "Deacon, you're still here?" Kacie asked more with surprise edged in her voice rather than interrogation.

"I was just about to leave. Suddenly, the room became stuffy. I'll call you later. Remember, what we talked about," he said with attitude. He rolled his eyes at Envy and swiftly left the room.

Kacie made no effort to respond and instead watched Deacon take one last look at their child and exited the room.

"I wish I could really tell you what I think of him." Envy fumed.

"Don't bother. I think I already know because I feel the same. He wants a DNA test right away. They're going to do it while I'm in the hospital. He's supposed to be back here in the morning for the test." Kacie's lips stuck out and her eyes began to shine like stars, only they were tears.

Envy rubbed up and down Kacie's arms in a comforting act. "Girl, don't worry. Do what you have to do. All he's going to do is pay child support and get visitation."

"I know, but I don't know if I can take it. I still love him. If I have to see him every time he comes to visit Kyland, I don't know what I'll do."

"Kyland? Is that the baby's name?"

"Yea, Kyland Dyson Mayweather; until the DNA results come back, and then he'll take on Deacon's last name, Riggs.

"I guess worse things can happen." Kyland began to stir and stretch. His mouth opened and before he could be picked up, he started bellowing. "Boy, do you have a strong set of lungs on you. Let me hurry up and get you to your momma," Envy said. She quickly went over to the sink and washed her hands then returned to pick up the fussing baby. She held him and made cooing sounds before passing him to Kacie to breastfeed. He shushed as soon as his mouth latched on to her nipple.

"I don't know how in the world you can do that. Doesn't it hurt?" Envy frowned in disgust.

Kacie laughed. "Does it hurt when a man is feeding on yours?"

"Oooh, you're wrong for that. You got me on that one."

They kept talking until a nurse came in and interrupted their chatter.

"Excuse me. I won't be in here but a minute. Do you need anything Mrs. Mayweather?" the nurse asked.

"No, I'm fine."

"I see the little one is fine too. Has he had a bowel movement today?"

"Yes, he had one early this morning," replied Kacie.

"Good. And how about you? Have you been doing your coughing and breathing exercises?"

"Yes, but it hurts really bad."

"I know, hon, but you have to do them. It'll help the soreness in your belly." The nurse proceeded to take her vitals while Kyland continued suckling without so much as stopping to take a breath. The nurse turned to leave. "I'll come back to check on you and the baby a little later. Until then, call if you need us."

"I will. Thank you," replied Kacie. Envy, will you please pass me a pamper? He's going to need to be changed when he finishes nursing."

A slight tap on the door, and in walked Layla. "Hi, girl. You've had the baby? Why didn't anyone call and tell me?" she asked and walked to the other side of Kacie's bed.

"I didn't know she'd had it either. Not until I came up here," Envy stated.

Kacie spoke and explained, "I was going to call both of you, but like you saw when you got here, Envy; Deacon was here. Things happened so fast, and then I fell asleep. When I woke up, Envy was already here with Deacon." Kacie looked directly at Layla. "I'm sure you can imagine that scene," laughed Kacie.

"What was he doing here? Checking to see if the baby has his ears, or his nose like he's on an episode of Maury or something?" Layla asked sarcastically.

"And that dog, he's getting a DNA test first thing in the morning," Envy told her.

"Are you going to let me talk anytime soon?" Kacie inquired of Envy.

Envy shrugged her shoulders. "Go right ahead. The floor is yours."

"It's true; we are doing a DNA test in the morning. And like I told, Envy, I'm glad. That way he won't be going around like I was just somebody he had a one-night stand or two with. I wonder how he's going to explain that to little Miss Wifey? I wish I could be a fly on the wall for that conversation." Kacie laughed. "By the way, how did you get up here?"

"Dennis, who else?" she said and smiled.

"I'm scared of you, girl," remarked Kacie and laughed.

"But getting back to Miss Wifey," said Layla, "I think all three of us wish we could be flies on the wall." Layla tilted her head slightly to the side and giggled. She looked at the baby sleeping soundly and suckling every now and then on Kacie's breast. "What's this handsome boy's name?"

"Kyland. Kyland Dyson Mayweather."

Kyland pulled away from Kacie's breast. She burped him and then changed his diaper and he fell right back to sleep. She turned and placed him in his bassinet, and for the next minute or two, the three friends watched Kyland sleeping, his tiny chest and tummy going up and down.

"Where were you last night?" Laughed Kacie, followed by a stare of amusement from Envy. "How did things go with you and Dennis?" urged Kacie.

"What?" Layla stretched forth her hands. "I don't know what y'all are talking about." Her voice rose with a measure of surprise at their forthrightness.

254

"Oh, please, give us the low down. I know if you stayed out all night long, you just weren't sleeping, and you said he brought you to the hospital," Envy said and flapped a hand in her direction.

"I'm a Christian woman and you know that; and so do you, Kacie," Layla explained.

"Tell us something we don't know already. Being a Christian doesn't mean you're perfect, not by a long shot. I think we all can testify to that. All we have to do is look at that little beautiful boy sleeping. Now, did you, or did y'all not?" Envy sounded insistent.

"Did." Layla's face turned three shades of crimson.

"Ohmigosh. How was it?" Kacie came right out and asked.

"No, that's all I'm telling y'all. Everything else is between me and Dennis. Except the part when he told me he was in love with me." Layla jumped lightly on her tiptoes and placed her hands over her mouth.

"Layla," Envy said first. "That's wonderful." She moseyed to the side of the bed where Layla stood and hugged her tightly. "I'm so happy for you."

"Thank you, Envy." Layla was all smiles.

"Me too," Kacie added. "It's about time things start changing for us. When I get out of here, we're going to celebrate. Hug me too," she said.

Layla walked toward her and hugged Kacie. "Thanks, Kacie."

"I'm sorry to break up this celebration, but I need to leave. I have to stop by Methodist and check on Mrs. Rawlings. She's in CCU. If I'm going to make it back to get your kids before they get out of school, then I need to be out of here," explained Envy.

"Don't worry about the kids." Layla turned her eyes toward Kacie. "Dennis is going to pick me up from here in an hour. He said he would drop me off at your house,

Kacie or he'll take me to pick up the kids so they won't have to stop by the daycare to pick up Keshena. I'll hang out over at your house tonight, Kacie. Envy, that way you can take your time doing what you have to do. Are you going back to work?"

"No, because I planned on getting the kids. But are you sure about the kids? I don't mind picking them up and watching them."

"Hey, wait you two. I am the mother." Kacie laughed while holding on to her tender belly. "What would I do without the two of you? Here you are, arguing over who's going to care for my children. I love you guys so much."

"We love you too, Kacie," Layla replied.

"Layla, it'd be good if you could get the kids for me today. I'll give you my extra key. Envy, you go see about your neighbor and go on to work"

"Layla, call me if your plans change," added Envy.

"Okay, I will. So everything is settled, Kacie. No need to worry," Layla told her.

Envy eyed Kacie. "I'm outta here." She kissed Kacie on the forehead, patted the baby on the back, and hugged Layla. "See y'all."

21

"In an ugly and unhappy world, the richest man can only purchase ugliness and unhappiness." George Shaw

Envy's face revealed total shock when she saw how frail and ghastly Mrs. Rawlings looked. Her eyes were closed and the thin skin of wrinkles that covered her face and arms brought tears to Envy's eyes. She walked to Mrs. Rawlings' bedside and stared at the tubes running from her nose and her throat. She looked at the IV needle taped to her thin, bony hand.

Envy watched as the sheet that covered her barely moved up and down. A strange odor was in the room. *Could it be the smell of death? Was her dear neighbor and friend going to leave her too?*

Envy turned around when she heard the door opening to Mrs. Rawlings' room.

"Hello, ma'am. Are you Mrs. Rawlings' granddaughter?"

"Yes," Envy told the nurse, knowing if they suspected she wasn't any relation to Mrs. Rawlings, she would be unable to get any information concerning her health. "How is she?" Envy asked and laid her hand on top of Mrs. Rawlings'.

"We're keeping her comfortable. But honestly, honey, she's in extremely critical condition. The doctor should be here later this afternoon. If you're still here, you can talk to him and ask him all of the questions you want," the nurse offered.

"Can she hear us?"

"I don't know, but it surely won't hurt to talk to her." The nurse checked her tubes and IV.

"Nurse, I think I'm going to go to work. I plan to be back in a couple of hours so I can catch the doctor.

Here's my number if anything, and I mean, anything changes." Envy passed a business card to the nurse.

"I'll be sure to call you. I'm going to make sure we have your information in her chart too."

"Thank you so much."

"You're welcome. It's good to see that she has someone who loves her enough to come and check on her," the nurse told her. "You have no idea how many senior people are brought to this hospital and no one comes to see them. I tell you, it breaks my heart."

Envy could barely look at the nurse. Her eyes were getting misty. She began to understand that she'd taken Mrs. Rawlings' care and concern for granted. Now she was on the verge of losing her.

"I'm here, I'm right here with you," Envy whispered and the nurse left out. "I'm going to run to work and I promise to be back shortly, okay?" Mrs. Rawlings said nothing. "Mrs. Rawlings, if you can hear me, try to squeeze my hand. Come on; squeeze my hand, Mrs. Rawlings."

Envy felt an ever so slight movement in Mrs. Rawlings' hand. "That's it. I knew you were in there somewhere. I knew it. You're going to be just fine, you hear me?"

Again, Mrs. Rawlings barely flinched her hand. It was good enough for Envy. She smiled and said out loud, "Thank you, God. Thank you for Mrs. Rawlings, Lord. Take care of her and heal her, dear God. Don't let her be in pain. Don't let her suffer, Father. Let her know how much I love her, dear God." This time Envy couldn't control the river of tears that poured from her eyes.

Mrs. Rawlings moved her hand again. "I love you, Mrs. Rawlings. But God does love you more. You do know that, don't you, Mrs. Rawlings?"

It took a second but Mrs. Rawlings moved her fingers slowly.

Envy kissed Mrs. Rawlings on the cheek and told her again, "I'll be back later. I promise."

Envy cried all the way to her car. She sat in the car for a while before she finally started it and went to work. It took about twenty minutes for her to make it to the office. She barely stepped off the elevator and headed in the direction of her office when she heard her assistant.

"Miss Wilson, hello. You made it just in time. Mr. Peace just called a special meeting for all of his direct reports. I was just getting ready to call his executive assistant to tell him you wouldn't be in today."

"I told you I was coming in. Where is the meeting? In his office or the executive suite?" she asked in a somber tone.

"The executive suite," answered Envy's administrative assistant.

"Okay, get my laptop and my legal pad please."

"Done already," the assistant responded.

"Thank you. I don't know what I'd do without you. While I'm in the meeting, forward my calls to my voicemail, unless it's from The Med or Methodist Hospital. I have two friends, one at each hospital. If either of them calls, please text me. I'm stressing so bad, that my mind is not on this place. But I'm going to go up here and do my best to concentrate on what our Executive VP has to say."

"You'll be just fine," the assistant reassured her.

"I hope you know what you're talking about." Envy laughed slightly before heading to her meeting.

An hour and forty-five minutes later, Envy returned to her office; washed out from listening to Mr. Peace ramble about implementing new changes and restructuring the company departments. She searched through her phone for messages and texts while she rode the elevator to her floor. There had been no calls or texts from Layla or either of the hospitals.

Stepping off the elevator, her phone rang. It was Leonard. Her lips curled upward until they formed into a noticeable smile, but she didn't answer the call. There was too much left for her to do if she planned on getting out of the office by three; it was already two fifteen.

Envy waved a hurried hello to her assistant, went inside her office, and closed the door behind her. She scanned and answered several email messages, read desk mail, and listened to her voice messages. Fifteen minutes past her self-set deadline, she came out of the office, left some instructions for her assistant, and called it a day.

Envy eased her black framed designer glasses up on the bridge of her nose and strolled confidently toward the direction of her parked car. Her black heels click-clacked against the pavement. With each movement, her vintage style, high waist skirt, and crisp floral watercolor print shell signaled beauty and brains.

Sitting in her car, Envy thought about returning Leonard's call, but again, she told herself she must exercise self-control. As much as she wanted to talk to him, she chose to call Kacie instead.

"Kacie? Are you asleep?" Envy asked when she heard Kacie's sluggish voice.

"No. I was just laying here thinking about my life and what a mess I've made. You must have heard the sadness and shame I feel."

"Don't do this to yourself," Envy pleaded and started the engine, and zoomed off the parking lot. "Everything will be fine. Maybe you're going through that, uh, that thingamajig. You know, postpartum depression." Envy turned right at the first light and continued toward the expressway.

"It's not postpartum. It's called, facing the truth. I made a fool of myself again. Or should I say, I let another smooth-talking man make a fool out of me."

"Most of us at one time or another in life have been made a fool of, Kacie. Some more than others. But a fool is a fool. The thing about it is," Envy changed lanes and accelerated onto the expressway, "learn from your mistakes. Don't keep making the same ones. You have your tubes tied now, and you can go on with your life. When the baby turns out to be his, put Deacon on child support, and concentrate on making something of your life for you and your children."

"What are you talking about? I didn't get my tubes tied. I couldn't do it. It means closure. A type of closure I don't want to go through right now. Somewhere out there is a man for me, and he might want children with me."

Envy's mouth fell open. When she spoke it was with noted cynicism and total disbelief. "You know what; I do not believe the words that just came out of your mouth. Baby, let me stop holding back on you. It's time you hear the truth." She gunned the motor and the speedometer needle moved to 90. She was so hot with Kacie, she couldn't wait to let loose like she wanted to.

"Don't even go there. I'm no child, so don't step to me like I'm one," Kacie spat.

Envy exited the expressway and turned on Hacks Cross. Within minutes she was turning onto her street. As soon as she pulled into her driveway, she turned off the car but didn't bother to get out.

"Oh, I'm going there all right. I don't care if you meet the richest man on earth, you don't need to bring another child into this world. In case no one's reminded you lately, my dear," Envy spoke with dripping sarcasm and ridicule, "you have seven, seven children," Envy yelled. "And you're not exactly mother of the year, sweetheart."

261

"What do you mean by that?" Her deep inhales and exhales were heard loudly over the phone waves.

There was no mistaking to Envy that she'd struck a chord with Kacie. But she didn't give a darn. She was going to tell her everything she should have told her three or four babies ago.

"What I mean is you won't get any awards for being a good mother. You may feed them and keep them clothed but you rarely spend quality time with them. When was the last time you took them anywhere? You have so many of them, that if you wanted to take 'em somewhere you can't even get them all in the car. You'll be getting a ticket every time a police pulled up behind your stupid tail. And you're laying up there in the hospital like they removed part of your brain instead of a baby. You shoulda been telling them to snatch everything out of you that they could to make sure you wouldn't have another baby. You're sickening," Envy screamed into the phone.

"I don't have to listen to you. You're not exactly Miss America yourself. Do you think I don't know that there's a reason you moved way out there in the county? It's so me and Layla won't pop up over your house and catch one of your men laying up over there."

This time Envy listened to the harshness of Kacie's voice.

"What you got to say now? Cat got your tongue, huh? Yeah, I thought so. The only difference between me and you is that I don't kill my babies but you—God only knows how many you've probably gotten rid of."

Kacie's accusations were all wrong. She was going too far and Envy didn't want to hear any more of her lies.

"Shut up," yelled Envy. "You're the one who's a whore. You're nasty and filthy. You probably have more than babies coming out of your…Well let me put it this way; you need to have yourself checked for every STD in the book. Anytime you have seven children and just as many baby daddies that proves you're nasty. You run your fake butt up in the church pretending you're going to church to worship God when all you're looking for is the next man to lie up with. Who wants a slut? Haven't you heard, you can't turn a slut into a housewife? Well, you need to look in the mirror, Kacie. You need to take a long, hard look at yourself. Does Layla know you didn't get your tubes tied?"

"Layla isn't my momma, and neither are you. Either of y'all can take it or leave it. I don't need y'all and I don't need you to tell me what to do with my life or my children!"

Envy opened the car door and got out.

Fischer barked as soon as he heard the key turning in the door.

"Look, I don't want to hear any more of your excuses. Your mind is warped in more ways than one. I guess because you're handicapped, you feel like you have to take anything from these men out here. Or maybe you think having all of these babies will take the place of love."

"Oh, so now you're a psychologist? Look, I'm hanging up. My baby needs me." The phone went dead.

Envy patted Fischer, ran to the back to change into a light jogging suit, and then took Fischer on his afternoon walk before going back to sit with Mrs. Rawlings. Maybe the walk would ease some of her aggravation and tension. But looking up at the sky, Envy saw the sky growing dark, the same way her heart felt. How could she have been so judgmental toward Kacie when she had a hideous past she'd kept a secret for fifteen years? Walking along the familiar trail, Fischer led the way. Storm clouds formed above, and Envy's heart was turning just the same.

22

"Ugliness is better than beauty. It lasts longer and in the end, gravity will get us all." Johnny Depp

Three days after giving birth to Kyland, Kacie was discharged from the hospital. She didn't bother calling Envy. She called and told Layla that she was leaving the hospital.

"I know you aren't going to drive home, are you?" asked Layla like she knew already what Kacie's answer would be.

"I'm leaving the same way I got here; in my car," Kacie answered adamantly. "So, you don't have to worry about being there to wait on the kids to get home because I'll be there in plenty of time."

"I know they can walk home, but Envy was still picking them up from school and Keshena from daycare," Layla reminded her.

"Well, she won't have to ever worry about doing anything else for my kids. I'll call the school and let them know they're walking home. They get out a little early when they have to walk home."

Kacie had already called Envy but she didn't answer her cell phone or her home phone. Envy's assistant told Kacie that Envy had left for the day. Kacie could care less, she still left messages for Envy at every number she called, telling her not to pick up her kids.

"What are you talking about?" Layla asked innocently. "It's just one more day. And the kids love riding home instead of walking," responded Layla. "I don't know what's going on and why you're sounding so upset."

"Stop flogging, Layla, because you know darn well what's going on with that judgmental broad. I know Envy couldn't wait to tell you about our conversation the other night. Don't even let the lie drip from your lips. You're not like her, Layla, so don't even try to be."

Kacie was right. Layla had learned from Envy about the big blowout between the two friends. It was the reason she'd been having Dennis drop her off every afternoon at Kacie's house to wait on Envy to bring them home.

"We've been friends far too long to let it end over some disagreements. All three of us are imperfect. Shoot, everybody, for that matter has flaws and shortcomings. As much as I love God, look at what I'm doing. I've been sleeping with Dennis; I've slept with Mike before that, and I'm a glutton. All of it is sin in the eyes of God. We are all mixed up and messed up. That's why I'm glad God sent Jesus to die for me, and you and anyone who will believe in Him and accept Him as the sovereign one."

"I'll talk to you when I get home," Kacie stopped Layla's conversation. "The orderly just came in to get me and the baby. I'll call you when I get home."

"Okay, but we're going to talk this thing out when you get here. I know the kids are going to be happy to see you and their new baby brother."

"Yeah, probably. Look, I have to hang up. I'm about to go downstairs to the pathology lab," Kacie said insistently. "Bye now. Deacon is supposed to be meeting me there to do the DNA test before we leave the hospital."

She looked down at the baby she held in her arms and said in a baby voice, "You're not going to walk out on me or your son, Deacon Riggs." The orderly pushed her to Pathology and parked her wheelchair out of the way of others who were coming and going. Kacie waited while Kyland slept peacefully.

Moments later, Deacon walked into Pathology. The three of them sat in the waiting area until Kacie and Deacon's names were called. The test took less than seven minutes. Immediately afterward, Deacon looked at Kacie with fire in his eyes, before he turned away and walked out of the lab.

Kacie and Kyland were picked back up by another orderly and wheeled to the hospital exit. She conned the orderly into believing that a car that she saw about to pull up to the patient loading and unloading area was her ride and that there was no need to wait.

She got out of the wheelchair, and with Kyland in his carrier, she walked slowly to the patient parking lot, got in her car, and drove home with a huge smile on her face.

Layla had called Dennis as soon as she finished talking to Kacie. "Hi, Dennis. Kacie just called and told me that she's on her way home from the hospital, so she'll be here when the kids get home. When you finish your route, will you come get me?"

"Sure, I'm headed your way now."

Taking care of six children was tough. Layla couldn't understand how Kacie did it and worked a part-time job too. She certainly couldn't understand why she got pregnant again either.

When Envy told her that Kacie didn't get her tubes tied after she gave birth to Kyland, Layla was just as flabbergasted as Envy. Layla had no idea where Kacie's mindset could be.

Layla talked to Dennis until she heard the sound of a blaring horn. Layla looked out the window and saw Kacie's car pulling up in the driveway.

"Baby, I'll see you when you get here. Kacie just drove up. I'm going to go out and help her with the baby. I love you, bye," Layla said happily and hung up the phone.

Layla oohed and ahhed over Kyland and helped Kacie unpack the few items she brought home from the hospital. She put the baby carrier the hospital had given her next to Keshena's old crib that she'd set up in Kacie's bedroom.

The two ladies talked for a while and Layla prepared the kids and Kacie some dinner before Dennis arrived.

Kacie called Deacon as soon as Dennis came to pick up Layla, and before her other kids made it home from school.

Deacon didn't answer his phone.

"Kyland, mommy's going to get what's due to you. Believe that." She sat on the bed and bent over to kiss the soft spot on his head. She scrolled through her cell phone and found Deacon's home number. She was too tough for words to describe. She dialed the code on her phone so whoever answered on the other end wouldn't be able to see the number she was calling from.

A woman answered. "Hello."

"Martha? Martha, girl is this you?" Kacie fronted before she almost burst open with laughter, but managed to hold it back.

"Who is this?" the woman's voice sounded irritable.

Kacie responded with silence then answered the confused sounding woman with, "Martha, this is Kacie Mayweather." Kacie spoke in a calm, mild voice. "I called to tell Deacon that his son and I are home from the hospital. I know Deacon told you that I gave birth to his son, Kyland, didn't he? The paternity test has also been done, so you'll officially be Kyland's stepmother real soon."

"How dare you call this house with your lies. You're sick, you know that. When the paternity test comes back, you're going to really look stupid because it'll prove that baby isn't my husband's."

267

Martha shouted through the phone so loud that Kacie couldn't help laughing. She was doing exactly what she wanted; getting underneath Martha's skin.

"I'm not crazy. I know Deacon wants you to think that I'm a tramp just because I have other children. I am not a liar. I know the father of every one of my children, just like I know that Deacon is Kyland's father. You may not want to face the truth, but it is what it is, Martha. And you need to accept it because you're going to be seeing a lot more of me and Deacon's child. I'm not like some of these other baby mammas. I wouldn't dare keep Deacon from seeing his one and only son. Since the two of you don't have children, I know Kyland is going to mean the world to Deacon. But do me a favor, Martha." Kacie finally stopped talking, waiting to hear what Martha would say in response.

Silence.

"Okay, be like that. You don't have to say anything. But, I'm asking you, pleading with you and Deacon not to spoil Kyland too much when he's with y'all. Girl, Kyland," Kacie continued to harass Martha, "wait until you see him. He is so handsome and looks just like his daddy, but I don't need any spoiled child. Ummm," Kacie pretended to yawn. "I'm tired. Remember to tell Deacon we're home, and he can come by whenever he wants to. Bye, Martha. Nice talking to you, girl." Kacie ended the call.

***

The paternity test results were to be announced at Memphis Juvenile Court today, exactly two weeks after the test. Kacie carried baby Kyland in his carrier. She was glad that Layla had agreed to come along with her.

When Kacie walked into the overcrowded main lobby of Juvenile Court, she couldn't tell if Deacon had made it before she had. She looked at her cell phone. It was less than twenty minutes before the hearing. She walked down the hall and stopped at the wall where the court dockets were listed. After finding her name and the division she was supposed to be in, she turned and headed toward the area where the paternity tests were done. Then she saw them. Deacon and Martha were sitting in the waiting area. Kacie suddenly became enraged. She hoped that Deacon would have come by himself. She didn't want Martha to have anything to say about her, especially after Kacie saw how Martha seemed to be staring at her deformed legs. She switched her eyes away from the classily dressed woman and walked to the receptionist.

"I'm here to get the results of a paternity test," Kacie said so loud that everyone in the waiting area could probably hear her. My name is Kacie Mayweather. My baby's name is Kyland Mayweather – for now. His father is right over there." Kacie pointed and gloated this time. Kacie heard someone in the waiting room giggle.

"Ma'am, have a seat," the receptionist stated. "Someone will be calling you and the petitioner in just a few minutes."

"Thank you."

Kacie and Layla sat in front of Deacon and Martha on the other side of the waiting area. She turned Kyland's carrier around so that it faced Deacon and his wife. She wanted to make sure that Deacon and Martha got a good look at the beautiful little boy, who was a tiny replica of Deacon. Kacie folded her arms and started people-watching.

Today was the first time she'd seen or heard from him since he came to the hospital.

She was sure that Martha would have told Deacon that Kacie had called his house the day they were discharged from the hospital. If she did, he still hadn't bothered calling or coming by. Kacie had taken Kyland and the other kids to church the same week she got out of the hospital. She hoped that she would see Deacon but he wasn't at church, which was completely out of character for Deacon.

Layla said one of the choir members told her that after the gossip spread about him having an affair with her, Deacon transferred his church membership to his wife's church.

"Miss Mayweather. Mr. Riggs." The receptionist sounded like she'd been doing this for years. Her voice was lifeless.

Kyland began to stretch and twist in his carrier. It was time for his feeding. Deacon looked at the infant and then at Kacie before he turned and walked off without uttering a word. Placing a pacifier in his mouth to soothe him until she got inside the courtroom, Kacie glanced around the waiting area for him but they were already gone inside. Deacon hadn't bothered to offer his help at all. He could have asked to see him or hold him.

Kacie pushed the door open and caught a glimpse of Deacon and Martha sitting toward the front of the courtroom.

Kacie sat on the other side of the courtroom with Layla and popped a bottle full of her breast milk into Kyland's mouth. Stunned when she saw Deacon and Martha come over to where she sat, Kacie's mouth flew open.

"Oh, you want to see your baby? Don't worry, I'm not going to be the type of mother who keeps a father from his child," she said smugly.

"If by some miracle that baby is mine," Deacon pointed at Kyland and said to Kacie in a harsh voice, "I'm petitioning for sole custody. Your reputation pitted against mine will prove that you're an unfit mother." He placed his arm around Martha as she stood right next to him. "We're going to raise him the way he deserves to be raised. He's going to know what it is to have a real mother and father. If he's my son, he's going to be raised in the fear and knowledge of God.' He squeezed Martha closer to him and kissed her on the cheek.

For the first time since she'd had the baby, Kacie looked stunned. She never thought Deacon would fight for custody of little Kyland.

"You should see your face now," he mocked. "You look like you just got your hand caught in a car door." Martha walked hand in hand with him back to their seats, and then turned and looked back over her shoulder at Kacie with a revengeful smile.

Kacie remained silent and numb, while Layla whispered, "Don't let him get you upset. He's just trying to bully you."

The calling of their names by the bailiff to come stand in front of the judge was the only thing that brought Kacie's mind back to the reason they were there. She stood and grabbed Kyland's carrier while Layla and Martha remained seated. Following so close behind Deacon, Kacie tripped but managed not to let go of Kyland's carrier. She felt like her entire body had gone numb. The possibility of Deacon and his wife raising Kyland was too much for her to think about. Kacie was prepared for whatever Deacon might try to throw her way. Since yesterday's church service, she believed nothing was going to come against her, not even Deacon and his resources. She would allow him to be a father in Kyland's life and spend as much time with him as he wanted, but no way would she hand Kyland over without a fight.

"Miss Kacie Mayweather?" The counselor looked over her glasses and her striking sea-green eyes looked in

Kacie's direction. "Mr. Deacon Riggs?" she repeated the same gesture with him. The test performed on the two of you and the child whose name is Kyland Dyson Mayweather reveals that you, Mr. Deacon Riggs…are not the baby's father.

Kacie almost fell. Her head went straight into her hands as she sat Kyland's carrier on the floor next to her. Her screams could be heard along the hallway outside of the counselor's office. Deacon's inflammatory remarks pounded in her ears and he used his hands to emphasize one vial word after another by pointing at her.

The bailiff's ability to calm the couple down was unsuccessful. Kyland began to scream. Ignoring the bailiff's words, she called another bailiff to settle the courtroom controversy.

"No, no, Deacon you are Kyland's father. I swear. There's been some mistake," Kacie cried. Her teary eyes pleaded with someone, anyone to listen to her. "Ma'am," she told the judge. "We have to take another test. This is his baby, I tell you," she said uncontrollably. She lost her balance and fell to the floor next to the baby she wanted so badly to believe Deacon fathered.

Layla rushed up as fast as she could when she saw the unpleasant look on the bailiff's face, as she tried to help Kacie get up. The sight before her caused Layla to burst into tears.

"May we leave now?" Deacon said to one of the bailiffs, while Martha looked on with a disgusted look at Kacie. The look appeared to be one of victory mixed with disgust as Deacon watched Kacie's unrelenting outburst.

"I told you that baby wasn't mine. I told you." He pointed an accusatory finger at her. "Now look at yourself, you're a disgrace. While you down there on your knees hollering, you need to be praying and asking God to forgive you."

"Move on, sir," the bailiff ordered Deacon. Martha stood on the outside of the door with a triumphant look plastered on her face.

Kacie watched as Deacon and his wife marched down the hall like they'd just won the lottery.

Layla and the bailiff helped Kacie to her feet. "Come on, calm down, Kacie," Layla told her as she wiped her tears away. She picked up the baby carrier and with her other hand she held on to Kacie.

In the car, Kacie sobbed all the way home.

Layla pulled out the pacifier for Kyland and picked him up in her arms to soothe him before they left court. While he pulled on his pacifier, Layla called and told Envy the news. She promised to meet them at Kacie's house in an hour.

Stumbling into the house, Kacie didn't stop until she collapsed on the living room couch. "Oh, Layla how could this have happened?" Kacie cried.

When Envy arrived an hour later, Kyland was asleep but Kacie was still in the den, crying and bashing herself for what the tests revealed.

Envy rushed to Kacie's house. When she entered inside, she knelt and embraced her dear friend. She felt Kacie's hurt as she relived in her mind the way she felt when she left her baby in a school lavatory some fifteen years ago. She cried with Kacie, remembering the terrible things people were saying about the mother who deserted her newborn baby in a cold, nasty toilet.

Envy cried because she understood what it meant to be hurt. She understood what it meant to feel humiliated, to feel hopeless, and be thought of as less than everyone else.

Unlike Kacie, no one ever detected that Envy was nine months pregnant and only fifteen. She covered her small pregnant belly with shirts she wore outside of her skirts and pants. Not even her mother acted like she noticed a change in Envy during that time.

To Envy, Kacie was the bigger woman because Kacie never thought about giving up her children, having an abortion, or leaving them alone in a bathroom to die."

"Envy, Layla; I'm so ashamed. I just knew it was Deacon's baby. I just knew it was. I only slept with one other person during the time I was with Deacon. I didn't think it mattered because it was just that one time and, oh God, I've ruined everything. I've made a fool of myself."

Layla stood near the two women and analyzed her own life. Maybe she didn't have seven children and seven baby daddies. Maybe she hadn't slept with only three men in her thirty years. Maybe she was practicing celibacy, now. But what about her own past? She wasn't perfect, never had been, and never would be. She admitted to herself that she should grasp and take hold of today. She had someone who loved her, while she was fat and while she was a glutton.

Dennis loved her, and for that, she should have been thanking God instead of acting like she didn't feel the same about him. She continued to watch Kacie and Envy, and for the first time in a long time, she was reminded that life is short and each of God's children has their lives recorded with a date stamp for meeting their maker. It was time for a change. It was time to stop feeling sorry for herself and start loving herself the way Dennis loved her and the way God adored her. It was time.

After an hour or so, Kacie finally fell asleep.

"I'll stay here and wait for the kids to get home," Layla told Envy. "I know you need to get back to work."

"I wanted to make sure she was going to be all right first," said Envy and wiped the tears from her eyes. "I'll be back as soon as I can."

"Take your time. I'm not going anywhere."

The two friends clung to one another before Envy left to return to work, each with their own secrets and shame.

Layla grew up with a wonderful family who loved and cared for her, and who stood by her side, yet she still grew up feeling less than what God had created her to be.

Envy, with the harsh reality of a family that struggled to remain civil toward one another, lived a life of promiscuity, hoping somehow it would be payback for the shame she tucked safely away but seen by God himself.

***

Kacie awoke hours later. The house was quiet. She raised her head and saw Layla standing near the kitchen window talking on the phone, no doubt to Dennis.

"Layla," Kacie said.

Layla turned around. "Dennis, I'll call you back. Kacie just woke up," she said.

"You didn't have to get off the phone. Where are the kids?"

"They're asleep. It's almost nine o'clock."

"At night?" Kacie asked with her eyebrows drawn together and creating a frown.

"Yes, at night."

"I'm sorry, Layla. Why didn't you go home? You should have woke me up."

"No, you needed the rest. You need this time to yourself. So, I'm here. Envy came back over here after she left work but you were asleep. She left about an hour ago because she wanted to go to see Mrs. Rawlings. She said she would call back later and check on you."

"That's fine. I don't know what to do now, Layla. All I know is that I can't do it without you and Envy."

"And you won't have to do it without us. We're friends. All three of us, Kacie. Now do you want something to eat? I made the kids some spaghetti and garlic bread. Would you like some?"

"No, I'm not hungry."

Listen, to me, Kacie and then I'm through with it. "No amount of feeling bad can justify what's happened. You can't change what's happened. Your responsibility is to take care of those seven beautiful children you have. No kind of self-condemnation or self-inflicted pity parties, or wallowing over what you've done wrong will make what happened go away. God is the one who justifies. He's the one who promises to forgive us of our sins if we confess them to him. He is the one who says he is faithful and just. Not forgiving yourself is not earning you brownie points with God. If anything, it shows that you don't trust and believe in Him like you say that you do. Chew on that," Layla said, threw down the dish towel, and went into the den.

Kacie got up and followed behind Layla. "Maybe you're right. But you still haven't walked in my shoes. You've never experienced the teasing, pointing, and taunting from other children like I did when I was a child. You've never had one person after another stare at you like you were a freak in a circus sideshow."

Layla bit back. "How do you know what I went through? How can you say that I was never teased and made fun of? Well, let's set the record straight. I've always battled with my weight. I have been teased too. So come off the pity trip. Get over it, won't you?" Layla bellowed.

"How do I get over it? Do you think it's easy living with a physical disability? Do you think the good men just flock after me? Well, they don't, Layla. Maybe a person or two has said something about you that was unkind. But you haven't always been the size that you are. You, if you set your mind to it, you can lose weight.

But the thing is, Dennis looked at you and he fell in love with you. I've never had that, Layla. I wanted it to be Deacon, but it wasn't meant to be. He already belonged to another woman. He never meant me any good. It was a hard pill to swallow, but I've finally swallowed it."

Kacie leaned on the chair in the kitchen like she was exhausted. "Layla, every man that's ever given me the time of day has turned out to be a user, pretending he loved me and wanted to be with me for me. I used to think that when I became a woman that I wouldn't have to listen to people whispering about the way I walked, or stopping to stare. But they do. So when a man jumps in my face and turns on the come-on line, I fall hook, line, and sinker. Until he uses me up and leaves me with a big belly and another baby."

"You don't have to live your life like this," Layla spoke. "That's what I'm trying to tell you. Your self-worth is not based on what a man or any person out there thinks of you. I'm learning that myself. I don't have it all together yet, but God is showing me how to love *me*. He's showing me through His word how to love me while I'm fat. That's what it's all about. No one is perfect. Don't you see that? Yes, I can lose weight, but you make it sound so simple. All I have to do is choose to eat healthy, exercise, and change my mindset. Well, that's easy for someone who's already got it together. But for me, being a big girl has been a cushion of comfort. It's kept me from having to face the world and say, look at me. Food has been my stronghold, gluttony is my sin. As for you, men, laying up with one and the other has been your stronghold. Fornication is your sin. You've been blessed to have beautiful babies, but I know you don't want the cycle of low self-esteem and low self-worth to become a generational curse for them. You don't want them growing up insecure and thinking that having baby

after baby and no husband is the right thing to do, or as
for your sons, making baby after baby with this girl and
that one; because you and I both know that it's not the
way God designed it to be. We're grown women, Kacie.
We go to church almost every Sunday but we're still
living off the breast milk of God, like Kyland lives off
your breast milk. We should be on solid food, which is
the full word of God. We look at our lives and we see our
ugliness. God looks at our hearts and He sees our
spiritual beauty."

"I know what you're saying. And God knows I hate
being the way I am. I've hated being different. I've hated
having this disability. I've hated it all of my life. I
wonder why it had to be me born this way?"

"Tell me, what makes you so special, Kacie? What
makes you exempt from the hurts and troubles of the
world? How can you say that having Cerebral Palsy
shouldn't have happened to you? God is no respecter of
persons. Maybe you have CP because you can handle it.
Don't you know you've been an inspiration to me ever
since I first met you? You never give up, Kacie. You
have seven children and you do your best to take care of
all of them. You may get down and depressed for a while,
but what inspires me about you is that you never stay
down. That says to me that you're special; that God has a
special purpose for your life."

The two of them embraced one another. The love in
the room was apparent. If only they could simply let the
past be the past and allow God to move them into the
realm of His grace and forgiving love and mercy. If only
they could exchange the ugliness of sin for the beauty of
God's mercy and grace.

23

"No object is so beautiful that, under certain conditions, it will not look ugly." Oscar Wilde

"Layla," Envy said over the phone. "I'm going to the hospital to see Mrs. Rawlings. Do you have plans for today?"

"It's funny you should ask." Layla sounded excited. "I'm going to dinner with Dennis at his parents' house. Sunday he's going to church with me again, and after church, we're going to my parents for dinner."

"You two are really serious. Meeting the parents and all. Go on with your bad self, girl." Both ladies laughed. "You go on and do your thing. If you get a chance, call and say a few encouraging words to Kacie tonight when you get in; or should I say, if you come in."

"No more of that for me."

"What do you mean?" Envy stopped at the red light and pushed her glasses up on the bridge of her nose, something that unknowingly had become a routine habit for her.

"I mean that I'm celibate again. I refuse to keep laying up with Dennis. It's wrong. It's just plain old wrong. I believe him when he tells me that he loves me. I believe that he wouldn't do anything to hurt me intentionally."

"Okay, so what's the problem?" Envy asked.

"The problem is my relationship with God. I've made plenty of mistakes and I don't want this added to the list, especially when it's not a mistake but a choice; an outright sin against this temple of God," Layla pointed at herself. "God specifically tells how he feels about fornication. You and I know that it's written in His word that it's a sin against our very own temples; our bodies. I'm going to talk to Dennis tonight and tell him how I feel about it. It's his call after that. Either he'll understand or he'll say he doesn't want a celibate relationship and he'll be out of my life," Layla said dryly.

"He's not about to let you go. Every time I've seen Dennis, he looks like he can eat a mess of your homemade cookies." Envy laughed until she swerved partially into the other lane. A blaring horn forced her back to her lane.

Layla laughed too. "You and I both know that your cookies will send the best of them to the bathroom for hours."

They kept laughing.

"Tonight will tell. Let me get off this phone before I split my sides. You are too crazy for me. I'll call Kacie when I get back home."

When Envy arrived at the hospital, she was met with a surprise of her own when she walked into Mrs. Rawlings' hospital room. She was sitting up in her recliner chair. Several of her church members were with her. Envy felt good because she saw radiance about Mrs. Rawlings that she hadn't seen since she'd been in the hospital.

"Hello, everyone," Kacie said.

"Hello, they said one by one."

Mrs. Rawlings' pastor stood and offered the last seat in the room to Envy. She didn't refuse. Her feet were barking like crazy.

"Mrs. Rawlings, there's someone else here to see you," the Pastor told her.

The old woman tried to turn her head. She managed to do so too.

Envy clapped her hands. "Good job, Mrs. Rawlings."

Mrs. Rawlings forced out the words, "Want to see you."

Pastor spoke up. "I think that's the cue for us to leave."

Envy held her hand up to stop him. "No, you don't have to leave on my account. She loves it when her church family visits. It's the only family she has you know."

"Yes, we know, but I believe she's saying that it's you she wants to see right now." The Pastor smiled and spoke in a magnetic voice. He turned back toward Mrs. Rawlings and gently laid his massive hand on top of her balding head of gray hair. "Will you all join hands so I can pray for our sister, Mrs. Rawlings?"

When he finished, Envy saw tiny teardrops cascading down Mrs. Rawlings' aged face.

One of the members grabbed a tissue and lightly wiped her tears, then kissed her on the side of her forehead.

"Bed," Mrs. Rawlings muttered.

"You're ready to get in bed?" Envy said to make sure that she understood her correctly.

"Yes...bed."

The pastor and one of the deacons helped transfer Mrs. Rawlings safely to her bed before leaving.

After they were gone, Mrs. Rawlings extended her trembling hand toward Envy. Envy held it and then laid her head on the side of the bed close to Mrs. Rawlings' shoulder.

"You are such a sweet girl. You don't understand how much God loves you."

Envy popped her head up. She looked around the room in a daze. Then she looked back at Mrs. Rawlings. "You're talking plainly. I mean just a second ago, you were struggling to get out one simple word, and now you're talking like nothing is wrong with you." Envy broke into a huge smile.

"Talk to me, child. What's on your mind and in your heart?" Her words were slow but clear.

Envy cried and touched the skin along Mrs. Rawlings' face. As if chains had been broken, Envy started talking.

"Mrs. Rawlings, all the time I thought I could hide my tormented heart and mind by having sex with one man after another. I controlled all the shots and not them. I looked at it as using them while steering clear of the word love and commitment. I feel so bad and have never been able to get over something I did a long time ago. Mrs. Rawlings...I."

"Knock, knock, time for your meds and supper," the nurse said as she and the dietician appeared.

"Hi, Mrs. Rawlings," each one of them said.

"God...good," Mrs. Rawlings spoke slowly.

"My, my, my. You are talking great. Your voice is much clearer. I am so proud of you. If you keep this up, you might be getting out of here soon," the nurse encouraged while the dietician sat the tray on the stand and turned to leave.

"Nurse," Envy asked curiously. "How can she go from not being able to talk just moments ago, and now she speaks almost clearly?"

"It happens. Stroke victims can show marked improvement over time. Now that her sugar level is stable, and her vital signs are returning to normal levels, it gives her more strength to fight."

The nurse switched her glance to Mrs. Rawlings and smiled. "The doctor should be making rounds soon. He's going to be glad to see how much you're improving, Mrs. Rawlings." She patted Mrs. Rawlings on her leg.

"Yea," Mrs. Rawlings said.

"I'm speechless. This is just fantastic," Envy told the nurse.

"God," Mrs. Rawlings said. "God."

Envy agreed. "You're right, Mrs. Rawlings. God."

"If you need anything, push the button, hon," the nurse said then turned to leave.

Envy was so thrilled that she called to tell Layla but there was no answer. She remembered Layla told her she was going out with Dennis. The only other person she could think of calling was Leonard. Leonard always asked about Mrs. Rawlings whenever Envy talked to him.

"Hi," Envy said when he answered the phone.

"Well, what have I done to deserve such a pleasant surprise?" Leonard sounded elated to hear Envy's voice on the phone.

"Quit it, will you? I had to tell somebody. I'm so excited. My neighbor, Mrs. Rawlings. Leonard, she's talking." Envy told him the story about the church members, the pastor praying, and how Mrs. Rawlings out of the blue started talking clear as spring water.

"That is good news. I am glad for her. And I'm glad for you too. You've been so attentive to her. You're just like a daughter to her and I bet that's how she feels about you. You are a remarkable woman, Envy. That's why I'm so crazy about you," Leonard flirted. "If you'll give me a chance, I'll show you. And no, I'm not talking about a romp in the sack. I mean I want to show you, spend time with you, take you places, and spend my life with you."

"What?" Envy laughed so hard she almost started to cry. "You will say anything to get your way, won't you?"

"You see what I'm talking about? Why do you always have to do this? I'm trying to be serious by telling you how I feel, but you keep taking what I say and turning it into a joke."

"All I wanted was to tell you the good news," Envy said and watched as Mrs. Rawlings began to drift off to sleep. "That's why I called you. Not to hear how crazy you are about me. Anyway, I've got to hang up. I'm going to spend some more time with Mrs. Rawlings. Then I'm going home to work on a project for a meeting I have tomorrow morning."

"Tomorrow's Saturday, Envy," Leonard told her.

"I know that, but I still have to work. This presentation is for a group of corporate executives flying in this weekend. They want to see the presentation first thing Monday morning, so I want to go over it and make sure everything is done. I don't have room for errors. Thanks for listening and for caring, Leonard, really, I'm sorry if I hurt your feelings. I'm flattered by everything you've told me. I really am. Bye now." Envy hung up the phone.

Mrs. Rawlings slightly opened her eyes.

"That was a friend of mine, Mrs. Rawlings. I'm always talking to him about you. He's glad that you're doing better."

Envy kept talking while she went to the sink and washed and sanitized her hands so she could help Mrs. Rawlings with her food.

Envy was encouraged even more when Mrs. Rawlings ate more food than she had in the two-plus weeks she'd been in the hospital. The doctor came in on his rounds.

"I heard you're feeling better, Mrs. Rawlings," the Indian doctor told her. "You should begin to get a little stronger every day." He examined her, asked her a few questions, and then gave his last assessment. "You still have limited use of the right side of your body. It may improve some over time and it may not. Your speech may do the same. You must keep going to physical and speech therapy."

"Home," Mrs. Rawlings said.

The doctor patted her hand. "Maybe in two days, or three if you keep improving. Goodnight."

"Thank you, doctor," Envy told him and turned to smile at Mrs. Rawlings. "Did you hear that, Mrs. Rawlings? You might be going home in a couple of days."

24

"Friendship without self-interest is one of the rare and beautiful things of life." James Burne

Sunday morning and the church was full of the spirit of God. The choir sang like they hadn't sung before. Dennis was in the congregation, sitting on the same pew as Envy and Kacie. His love for Layla seemed to beat against his heart when Layla sang, "Sometimes you have to encourage yourself... "

Envy listened to the lyrics too, and tears flooded from her eyes.

Kacie moved from side to side, holding baby Kyland in her arms as he slept. Her eyes brimmed with tears.

Envy had a long way to go before her heart would heal. The ugliness she saw each time she looked in the mirror made her cringe. Her physical beauty was just that - physical. She used it to get what she wanted, but thanks to her friends, and God, Envy started listening and internalizing the words of love and forgiveness being spoken over her life. The men she used like a secret government weapon for her temporary pleasure slowly stopped.

Leonard was the only man she continued to talk to. For some reason, she viewed him as more than a bedmate, he was a true friend. He seemed sincere when he told her that he had deep feelings for her. There were still tempting times, so tempting that she changed her cell and home phone numbers.

The day turned out to be one of the changing points for the three women. It was no special Sunday, no holiday, no special occasion. It was the power of God to heal wounded and broken hearts.

Pastor Betts ran up to the pulpit and took his place behind the podium. "Hallelujah," he cried out. "Encourage yourself in the Lord," he repeated the words of the song. "Sometimes you can't depend on your friends to encourage you. Sometimes you can't look for your mother, your father, your brother or sister to encourage you. You can't even depend on your pastor to encourage you all the time. Sometimes you have to do it yourself. You have to get up off that seat of self-condemnation. You have to stop speaking negative things over your life and speak words that will lift you up. Encourage yourself in the Lord," he said with power in his voice.

At the closing of his message, Pastor Betts extended an invitation for people to come forward for prayer, for salvation, or to join the church as a transferred member. Several people, young and old, moved forward from the pews.

Layla started shouting and screaming from her seat in the choir stand. Her arms stretched forward and her voice rang out again with the words of the powerful song when she saw Dennis move from where he stood and began his walk down toward the altar.

***

Sunday afternoon Envy sat in the chair next to Mrs. Rawlings' bed. The ladies chatted while Envy packed her things. Mrs. Rawlings was going home today. The nosy neighbor had become her confidante, her family. Envy had already made up a schedule that she planned to stick to every day to make sure Mrs. Rawlings would be well taken care of.

Every morning at six o'clock Envy got up, walked Fischer, and returned home to take her shower and dress for work. Next, she went to Mrs. Rawlings' and prepared a light breakfast for her. Lunch was delivered by a special food program for seniors through the aging commission. They also provided Mrs. Rawlings with an aide and a nursing assistant that came five days a week during the day while Envy worked. Envy loved having Mrs. Rawlings to take care of. Envy felt like she was finally part of a real family.

"Mrs. Rawlings, do you need anything before I leave for work?" asked Envy.

"No, honey. God is here with me and Fischer," she said and rubbed Fischer's head.

Since Mrs. Rawlings' discharge from the hospital, she and Envy spent most of their time together in the evenings when Envy made it home from work. So much was transforming in Envy's life and in a way, it frightened her.

Opening up and talking to Mrs. Rawlings, became easier for Envy with each passing day. She found Mrs. Rawlings to be a great listener. Mrs. Rawlings told her that there was nothing she hadn't seen, heard, or experienced during her eighty-plus years on God's earth. She didn't come off as shocked or surprised, no matter what Envy shared with her. Mrs. Rawlings gave Envy a feeling of acceptance for the first time in her life. Slowly, Envy imagined that she could break free from the bondage of her past.

Through conversations, Envy opened up to her about the hundred-plus men she'd laid with starting at the age of twelve. Mrs. Rawlings didn't blink an eye or act like she was appalled at all as Envy talked.

"Mrs. Rawlings, I don't know what's wrong with me. But when my daddy walked out on us I was devastated. I rarely heard from him when he married someone else. So I started doing whatever I wanted to do, hoping that if I was bad enough or wild enough he would come back home to me because I needed him."

"Baby," Mrs. Rawlings told her, her words still somewhat slow to get out. "I want you to understand something. No man on this earth can take the place of your father's love. I don't care how many you sleep with. It won't change the past and it will stalemate your future and all the things God has prepared for you. Only God can fill that empty spot." She laid her bony hand on top of Envy's while they sat on the couch.

"I know that now. For the first time since he left, I believe I understand that. Whatever happened between my father and mother wasn't my fault. It didn't mean that he stopped loving me. I think I can finally forgive him for leaving us, Mrs. Rawlings. But that's not what haunts me. I've done something that even God won't forgive me for. And I know I will never be able to forgive myself." Envy cried.

"Child," Mrs. Rawlings placed her frail hand underneath Envy's cheek, "you know you can tell me anything. No one will ever know because I promise I'll take it to my grave." Mrs. Rawlings began to look tired.

Envy had been around her enough that she could tell when Mrs. Rawlings needed to rest.

"We'll talk later. Right now, you need to get some rest." Envy stood, and like a child, she reached down and helped Mrs. Rawlings to stand and led her to her bedroom. Envy pulled out her favorite bed duster from the closet, and helped Mrs. Rawlings get undressed and into her duster.

"You're an angel from heaven, Envy."

"Not hardly," Envy responded.

Envy pulled the floral bed covers up around Mrs. Rawlings' shoulders and kissed her on the top of her head. "Get some rest. I'm going to go home for a while. I'll be back later on after I take Fischer for his walk."

"Take your time. I'll be here unless the good Lord says otherwise."

"You'll be here." Envy grinned.

Mrs. Rawlings smiled. "'Member to get the keys so you can get back in."

"Yes, ma'am." Envy picked up the extra door key from the table near the door. She did as she said, walked Fischer, and then went home and cleaned up the house. Next, she called and talked to Kacie and Layla on three-way. She wished she could find the release from the past like they seemed to have found.

"Guess what, y'all? I told Dennis that I love him," Layla admitted.

"What?" said Kacie.

"When?" asked Envy.

"Today. We were hanging out, walking at Tom Lee Park. He's always telling me how beautiful I am, and how much he loves to be with me. He told me again, but this time, I stopped and held onto his hand, right there on the walking trail. People walked all around us. I think I saw some lady give us a nasty look for standing in the middle of the walking trail. But I didn't care. I had something to say and I wanted to say it."

"Good for you," replied Kacie.

"Keep on," said Envy. "What happened next?"

"I said it," confessed Layla.

"Said it how? Come on, stop making us beg," Kacie told her.

"I know that's right." Envy added.

"I said, Dennis, I love you. I told him how I believed that God brought us together and that I wanted to be his girl forever."

"Oh, my, no you didn't." Excitement rang through Kacie's voice.

"Girl, you are so bold. How did he take it?" inquired Envy.

"He got down on one knee," Layla continued.

"Ahhh," both Envy and Kacie interrupted with their screams.

"Shut up, y'all, if you want to hear what he said," Layla insisted in the middle of her laughing on the phone with her friends. "He got on one knee and he said, 'I love you with all of my heart too, Layla.' By this time, I was feeling a little bit embarrassed because a few people were gathered around. I guess they knew something was going on, seeing a man kneeling on one knee. Anyway, he went on to tell me that he thanked God for bringing me into his life. Then he said, 'Layla, will you marry me?' Tears were streaming down my face by this time. But I managed to answer. I told him, 'Yes.' Then he got up and in front of the people who were standing around us, he grabbed me in his arms and kissed me like he was never going to see me again. People started clapping and everything."

Kacie spoke up first. "I am so happy for you. You deserve it, Layla."

"Yea, and Dennis is getting himself a real jewel," added Envy.

"What about a ring?" Kacie asked Layla.

"Oh, yeah, I forgot. Do you know he had the ring in his car? He said he was already going to propose at sunset. He said he didn't care if I admitted I loved him or not; he was going to take his chances. And that's exactly what he did. When the sun began to set over the Mississippi River, we sat on the bench. He proposed all over again."

"Wow, what a love story," cried Envy.

"I'm telling you," said Kacie. "Have y'all noticed how different our lives are becoming? I believe God is doing something new in all of us. Good things are going to open for us, and, Layla, He started with you."

"You think so?" Layla inquired.

"I do," Envy agreed. "Kacie, the blessing for you in all of this mess with Deacon is that he is a married man, and who knows, he may have gotten custody of little Kyland like he said he was going to do if he had been proven to be his father. You have the chance to make something more of your life without the added pressure and drama," Envy told her.

"She's right, Kacie," Layla said.

Kacie grinned and said, "I know. And that's why I have my own story to tell y'all."

"What is going on here tonight? Is it true confessions or what?" Envy asked.

"I guess so," Kacie said. "I decided to enroll back in school. I'm going to start classes in two weeks in Pharmacy Tech. I'll have to go to school for ten months. After I finish, I'm going to apply to work at one of the pharmacies. And, that's not all," she said.

"Eww, Kacie." Layla was crying hard over the phone. Her voice trembled and she sniffed and snorted. "God, thank you, Lord. Thank you, God."

"Don't start shouting on this phone," warned Envy in a playful voice. "What else do you have to tell us, Kacie?"

"I made an appointment at the Health Loop. I'm going to have my tubes tied. But, hold up before you get too happy. They can't do it until the first of next month."

"Now you can shout, 'cause I'm about to cut a step over here," she screamed. "Thank you, Lord."

"Y'all so crazy." Kacie laughed loudly into the phone.

After they laughed for a few minutes, Layla asked
Envy, "Okay, tell us what's going on with you. We rarely
see you since you've been taking care of your neighbor.
What's up with you?"

Envy hesitated then released a long sigh. "Well, my
news isn't as grand as what y'all said. But I want y'all to
know that I've turned over a new leaf in my life. I'm
going to stop living my secret life. And I'm also going to
make a move to get closer to my sister and her family.
Life is too short to hold grudges. After all, Nikkei is a
good sister. It's always been me who's pulled away from
her."

"Okay, I understand about family and I agree with
you, but what's this about a secret life?" Kacie asked like
she was really curious.

"Yeah, cough it up. Get it all out," commented Layla.

"Don't pretend like y'all don't know already, though
you didn't know the extent. But I've been around the
block more than a few times," Envy finally confessed.

"How many times?" asked Kacie and she started
snickering.

"You ought to be ashamed," Layla told Kacie.

Envy stopped them. "No, it's all right. I'll answer her
because I've always downed her about having all them
baby daddies. Had I not been dropping birth control pills
faithfully and making the man use protection every,
single time, I would probably be in Kacie's shoes too.
Especially since I've slept with," Envy paused. She didn't
know if she could admit it even to her best friends.

"You can do it," Layla told her. "Let it go. Don't let
the devil keep you caged. Tell it so he won't have a hold
on you anymore."

"Since I've slept with almost a hundred men since I
was 12 years old." Envy heard their gasps. "See, I knew
it. I knew you would react like this."

"React lie what?" Kacie said forcefully. "All we did was gasp. Who wouldn't have, hearing something like that, especially coming from you? Shoots, people gasp all the time when they hear how many kids I have and then on top of that see how I walk, but so what. They don't live my life."

"She's right, Envy," Layla chimed in. "I used to get so many oohs and aahs because of my weight. But I had to deal with it. Me and Kacie weren't gasping to make you feel ashamed. It's just that it's hard hearing you admit that you've got flaws too. That's what makes us special. I understand that now."

"There's one more thing. There is one man who I care about. I've been seeing him on and off for a few years. I never wanted to listen when he told me how he felt about me. I refused to allow myself to open up my heart to any of the men I slept with. But there's something different about Leonard. And the thing is, he's no fool. He knows I'm no angel. I'm not saying he knows everything about my sordid past, but he knows enough. But that's what's crazy because he *does* want me. He wants to be part of my life regardless of my past. And, I think I'm going to let him. It's time I open up my heart."

"Don't y'all feel better now?" Kacie said. "We need to be sitting around the table chomping on cheesecake and ice cream." They laughed into the phone.

The friends talked for another ten or fifteen minutes until Envy told them she had to hang up so she could go and check on Mrs. Rawlings. They each said goodbye and ended the call.

Envy walked to her bedroom walk-in closet. She used the step stool she kept inside the closet so she could reach the items on the top shelf. Envy went to her security box stacked with loads of documents and personal files and papers. She dialed the combination on the box until it opened. Envy shuffled through them until she found what she was looking for.

The articles were still neatly folded inside a plastic Ziploc bag where she'd placed them years ago. She removed the articles and sat on the bed and began to read each of them. With each clipping, her sobs became harder and louder. Her chest heaved in and out like she was hyperventilating. Fischer stood next to her, looking like he didn't know what to do. Envy fell to her knees and cried out to God.

"Save me, Lord. Forgive me, God," she repeated over and over again. She cried so hard that she started jerking. Fischer whined until Envy hugged him. "I'm all right, boy. Momma's fine," she said to Fischer. She removed her glasses and wiped her face of the tears.

Envy placed the security box back on the shelf, but left the articles and plastic bag on her bed. She took a hot shower, and after putting on a pair of shorts and shirt, she picked up the articles and with Fischer following her, she went to Mrs. Rawlings' house to prepare her something to eat.

The next morning, she pulled out the crinkled news clippings. Without a word to Mrs. Rawlings, she left them next to Mrs. Rawlings' breakfast tray.

"I'm leaving now. I'll call and check on you later and I'll see you after work. She kissed the old lady goodbye and left.

Mrs. Rawlings ate her oatmeal and her banana and drank her cup of decaf coffee. She saw the yellowed paper. Her eyes had been dimmed by age, but she managed to read it. The article was dated October 7, 1992.

Search Continues For Mother of Infant Left In School Lavatory

Memphis, TN (Memphis Appeal) The body of an infant, said to have been only hours old, has been found under shocking circumstances. The baby's lifeless body was discovered by a maintenance worker at Germantown High School. Police state the body appears to have been in the second-floor bathroom toilet for as long as five to ten hours. Homicide Detective Monica Bell said the newborn girl was well-developed and was more than likely full-term. A post-mortem examination of the newborn will be done to determine the cause of death and whether she was alive when she was left in the toilet.

"One of the major concerns now is to locate the mother of the infant," states Bell. "We are concerned about her health physically and psychologically." Detective Bell further states, "Everything is being done to locate the mother. We urge anyone who has information that will lead us to the mother to contact 333-TIPS. We are also pleading with the mother to contact the police right away...."

***

Envy, though uneasy, called Mrs. Rawlings during the day to check on her. The home health aide answered the phone and then gave it to Mrs. Rawlings."

"How are you feeling?" Envy asked.

"Honey, God is good to me. And if you'll open up your heart and your spiritual eyes, you'll see that He's good to you too. I guess you know we have to talk, right?" Mrs. Rawlings stammered.

"Yes, I know." I'll see you later this afternoon. We'll talk then," Envy replied nervously.

For the remainder of the day, Envy paced around anxiously. She went about her day's work, but her mind was on the conversation she was going to have with Mrs. Rawlings later. It was the first time she had revealed her horrible secret to anyone.

The day couldn't end soon enough for Envy. But as soon as it did, she jumped in the car. She stopped off at a restaurant and brought a dinner plate for Mrs. Rawlings.

When Envy arrived, she carried on with her usual routine. Afterward, she had the chance to finally sit down and be confronted by Mrs. Rawlings. She was prepared to hear her lashing out at her for what she'd done to her flesh and blood.

Mrs. Rawlings was sitting in her rocker in the den watching the news when Envy came over. She looked up and stretched forth her hand toward Envy. Envy walked to her and sat down on the rug next to her.

"My child. There is nothing that God won't forgive us for. There is nothing that, as His children, we can ever do to make Him leave or forsake us. That's what His word says. I told you that there is nothing under the sun that I haven't seen, heard, or experienced in my years of dwelling on this earth."

"I committed murder. God says that murderers won't go to heaven. I hear it all the time."

"Baby, you must know what the word of God says for yourself. The Bible also says in First Corinthians chapter six and verses nine through twelve—"

"Let me go get your Bible and I'll read it," Envy offered.

"No, I have God's word in my heart." Mrs. Rawlings began to say the words she knew all too well. "Know ye not that the unrighteous shall not inherit the kingdom of God? Be not deceived: neither fornicators, nor idolaters, nor adulterers, nor effeminate, nor abusers of themselves with mankind, Nor thieves, nor covetous, nor drunkards, nor revilers, nor extortioners, shall inherit the kingdom of God.' Now listen very carefully to what I am saying, girl. The word of God says, 'And such were some of you: but ye are washed, but ye are sanctified, but ye are justified in the name of the Lord Jesus, and by the Spirit of our God. This proves that God is a forgiving God. Ask Him to forgive you. He'll do it."

"I've tried to forgive myself, but I can't. I can't forget."

"That's because you were turning toward the wrong man. Laying up with man after man can never remove the stench of sin, Envy. Sin that is deeply rooted from that horrific day, when at the age of fifteen you gave birth to a baby."

Envy bellowed. "But I left the baby in the bathroom. I left it to die. I was so confused. My heart was crushed when I learned I was pregnant. And then the boy who said he loved me, who promised we would always be together, turned out not to love me at all. He only loved my body, Mrs. Rawlings."

"Go on, cry, baby. Let it all out. It's the beginning of your healing," Mrs. Rawlings told her.

"I didn't mean to leave my baby in the bathroom. I thought it was just a bad stomach ache and that I had to use the bathroom. I didn't know I was about to give birth. My stomach was cramping so bad. When I got up, I saw it. I saw my baby. I saw my baby girl. She was dead, Mrs. Rawlings. I remember washing myself off and then running out of the bathroom. I was just a child and here I was lost and all alone having a child in a bathroom stall. I had no one I could confess the horrible thing I did. No one could ever tell that I was even pregnant because I didn't show anything but a tiny bulge. I was too terrified. But there was no one to tell, I promise there wasn't. So I kept the secret hidden. I was going to pay back every boy or man I met, because of what my dead baby's daddy did to me. He ran scared and I couldn't forget it. I grew up with girls envying me when all I heard from men was how pretty I was. But they didn't know that I may have been pretty on the outside, but I was ugly on the inside." Envy sobbed.

"Listen to me." Mrs. Rawlings' voice was soothing and sounded so forgiving and loving. "Condemning yourself is not what God wants. He wants you to turn from the ways that are not pleasing to Him. You said you've pleaded with God to forgive you. He has already forgiven you, my child. Holding onto what happened then and even now is not the way. Once you ask God to forgive you, He immediately forgives and forgets. You can't keep doing this to yourself because it means you're not trusting in God, child. Only God has the right to judge, so how can you walk around like you have the right to judge yourself? I'm not saying that what you did back then, and what you've done since then, is right. But it's not for you to place judgment over your life because you were bought with a price and you are not your own. You belong to God, Envy."

Envy looked up at Mrs. Rawlings. She wiped the tears from her eyes and got up from the rug and walked over to the table where the articles laid. Picking them up, Envy stared at each of them. One by one, Envy tore the articles into tiny pieces.

"That's right, baby. Let go of your past," she heard Mrs. Rawlings' angelic voice tell her. "Let go and let God. He'll take care of you. He loves you, baby. You're beautiful. Because of what God did on the cross, you're no longer ugly with the mark of sin."

Envy felt joy, peace, calmness, and love filling up her once ugly, sinful past. She finally understood that she had carried around the weight of her sin when God had already taken the burden of it off of her back.

"Come, my child," she heard Mrs. Rawlings say to her.

Envy turned around and faced Mrs. Rawlings. Mrs. Rawlings' countenance was a radiant glow. Envy imagined an angel of God cleansing her life through the form of Mrs. Rawlings.

She walked to the sofa and sat back down next to Mrs. Rawlings' rocking chair. The radiant glow had disappeared, but Envy knew that she would never forget or question the power of God again.

Mrs. Rawlings gathered Envy into her arms. "Leave your hurts, your pain, all of your experiences, past, present, and future with God. You are His, Envy."

"Yes, I *am* His," Envy cried as a peace that surpasses all understanding saturated her soul.

Words from the Author

Layla Hobbs, Kacie Mayweather, and Envy Wilson equated beauty with the physical, outer trappings of a person's body. Through their life experiences, they discovered that their physical shell was not what needed a makeover. One by one, they start to understand from all that happened in their lives that they needed spiritual beauty makeovers to remove the ugliness of sin in their lives. A makeover that only God, Himself could give.

To arrange signings, book events, or speaking
engagements with the author,
Contact sheliawritesbooks@yahoo.com

To send your comments
to the author:
Website – www.sheliawritesbooks.com
Email – sheliawritesbooks@yahoo.com
Twitter: @sheliaebell
Instagram: sheliaebell
www.facebook.com/sheliaebell

****

Please join my mailing list
for literary updates and new book release information
www.sheliawritesbooks.com

#iwriteforfilmandtv
#iwritebestsellers
#iwritepageturners
#iwritenewyorktimesbestsellers
#iamgodsamazinggirl

More Perfect Stories About Imperfect People
Like You...and Me

<u>*Nonfiction*</u>
A Christian's Perspective: Journey Through Grief
How to Live Your Life Like It's Golden

<u>*Journals*</u>
Journal Your Way Through It
Sister Sister Book Log Journal

Contact information
www.sheliaebell.net
www.sheliawritesbooks.com
sheliawritesbooks@yahoo.com
www.facebook.com/sheliawritesbooks
@sheliaebell (Twitter & Instagram)

If you enjoyed this book or if you have enjoyed reading any books by Shelia E. Bell, please go to your favorite online site and leave a review. Reviews help determine the success of an author. It is the ultimate display of support readers can give. Whether this is your first time reading a book by me or whether you have followed my literary career from the beginning, I say THANK YOU!

There is no ME without YOU!

Shelia E. Bell

www.ingramcontent.com/pod-product-compliance
Lightning Source LLC
Chambersburg PA
CBHW020942260626
47169CB00006B/1781